Praise for *Lydia's Party*

"Captivating . . . There is much to enjoy in Hawkins's incisive obser-
vations. . . . You'll like these women . . . [and] the story keeps you
reading as it examines the gap between how we think we build our
destinies . . . and how we actually build them."
—*O, The Oprah Magazine*

"*Lydia's Party* is a brilliant story, so perfectly told, the characters
instantly recognizable and unforgettable, that they take up residence
in one's heart. It is destined to be a classic for this generation."
—Jo-Ann Mapson, author of *Solomon's Oak*,
Finding Casey, and *Owen's Daughter*

"With wit and insight Margaret Hawkins gives us a sharp, soulful
look at love and regret, women's friendship, art, aging, and ambition,
and what it means to live a life. At once funny and moving, *Lydia's
Party* is a pure delight." —Rilla Askew, author of *Fire in Beulah*

"A tender and clear-eyed look at the tangles in women's lives."
—*Good Housekeeping* (A New Book Pick)

"Like Carol Shields's *Larry's Party*, a completely winning book about
friendship, an elusive and almost never written about subject, which
makes this a rare achievement."
—Diane Johnson, author of *Le Divorce* and *Flyover Lives*

"This book feels like what lifelong friendships really are."
—*Minneapolis Star Tribune* ("A Fave of the Mome

"Impossible to put down. The characters are quirky, endearin
relatable. . . . Lydia's unrelenting examination of her own lif
the readers to reflect on their own choices and passions—a
what makes this book a must-read." —DolceI

"Hawkins's smart, crackling novel is a snowy, Midwestern *Mrs. Dalloway*, with Elizabeth Berg-ish charm and Hawkins's own edgy, artfully particularized humor. . . . As Lydia and her circle pull together in her time of need, Hawkins considers the profound gift of friendship and the ways art and life converge to forge meaning and preserve truth and memories."   —*Booklist*

"Hawkins's protagonists are well drawn and interesting."
                                                    —*Library Journal*

"Plot is one of the great strengths of the book, beyond the expert characterization of these women. The story takes several entirely unpredictable and yet satisfying turns. . . . [A] lovely life-affirming tale, making this meditation on mortality and friendship a pure delight for readers."   —Bookreporter.com

"With shades of *Mrs. Dalloway*, much of the novel takes place in a day, as Lydia prepares for her annual winter party. . . . Hawkins's novel is beautiful . . . and the plot takes a number of unexpected, hugely enjoyable turns. It is this kind of book: the kind one buys extra copies of to pass out to friends."
                                        —*Kirkus Reviews* (starred review)

"Sumptuous . . . a repast that's alternately uncomfortable and soothing, weepy and jubilant, evocative and realistic. Party host and art teacher Lydia is having her annual dinner for her women friends . . . a quirky, impossibly magical and sweetly charming twist, Lydia s guide them all to forgiveness."   —*Publishers Weekly*

ia's Party is a literary celebration of dark secrets, enduring hip, and the slow crawl of regret. A luminous reflection that er long after the last page, Margaret Hawkins's latest novel e you examine what and whom you hold most dear while you perfect sentence."
                                —Sally Koslow, author of *The Widow Waltz*

PENGUIN BOOKS

LYDIA'S PARTY

Margaret Hawkins is the author of two previous novels, *A Year of Cats and Dogs* and *How to Survive a Natural Disaster*, as well as a memoir about her sister, *After Schizophrenia: The Story of My Sister's Reawakening*. She wrote a weekly column about art for the *Chicago Sun-Times* and is a senior lecturer at the School of the Art Institute of Chicago.

To access Penguin Readers Guides online, visit our Web site at www.penguin.com.

LYDIA'S PARTY

MARGARET HAWKINS

PENGUIN BOOKS

PENGUIN BOOKS
Published by the Penguin Group
Penguin Group (USA) LLC
375 Hudson Street
New York, New York 10014

USA I Canada I UK I Ireland I Australia I New Zealand I India I South Africa I China
penguin.com
A Penguin Random House Company

First published in the United States of America by Viking Penguin,
a member of Penguin Group (USA) LLC, 2014
Published in Penguin Books 2015

THE LIBRARY OF CONGRESS HAS CATALOGED THE HARDCOVER EDITION AS FOLLOWS:
Hawkins, Margaret.
Lydia's party : a novel / Margaret Hawkins.
pages cm
ISBN 978-0-670-01576-4 (hc.)
ISBN 978-0-14-312611-9 (pbk.)
1. Middle-aged women—Fiction.   2. Parties—Fiction.   3. Female friendship—Fiction.
4. Life change events—Fiction.   5. Chicago (Ill.)—Fiction.
6. Psychological fiction.   I. Title.
PS3608.A89345L93 3024
813'.6—dc23   2013018398

Printed in the United States of America
3   5   7   9   10   8   6   4   2

For my friends

We cannot live the afternoon of life according to the program of life's morning; for what was great in the morning will be little at evening and what in the morning was true will at evening have become a lie.

CARL JUNG

PART ONE

Lydia: 9:00 A.M.

Lydia needed to prepare. In ten hours the women would begin to arrive for what they'd come to call the Bleak Midwinter Bash. Lydia gave the party every year, and every year she dreaded it, not the event itself but the possibility of failure. It hadn't happened yet but this might be the year.

Lydia had named the party after her favorite Christmas carol, a hymn in a minor key. Mostly she liked the beginning: *In the bleak midwinter frosty wind made moan / Earth stood hard as iron, water like a stone / Snow had fallen snow on snow, snow on snow.*

Beautiful, she thought, that ingenious repetition. Clearly written by someone who knew her snow, knew its hypnotic properties, its ability to bury and silence. The song sounded to Lydia like here and now, Chicago in January. Lydia remembered the year the temperature hit 27 below, when it hurt to breathe.

The tradition, if you could call it that, had started nineteen years before, as the Christmas party Lydia didn't get around to organizing until the last week of January. The date stuck, long enough after the holidays to offer fresh appeal. By then everyone was ready for something again, minus all that red and shininess and expectation, when the seasonal imperative to be cheerful had passed. Being warm and having enough to eat and, particularly, to drink, was party enough, in January.

As often as not the night of the party turned out to be the coldest night of the year. Some years the thermometer read well below zero when guests arrived; those years she'd handed them blankets and shawls at the door in exchange for their coats. One year half the guests stayed overnight. Cars wouldn't start. Just as well, they'd agreed the next day. None of them was fit to drive.

When her friends asked, Lydia said she didn't know how many times she'd given the party—didn't want to appear compulsive—but she did know. She remembered every one and what she'd served and who was there. It was an unlucky thirteen, counting tonight.

The first year had been spontaneous, a whim planned at the last minute for a few colleagues. She hadn't expected most of them to show up but everyone did, and the next year someone said, *Are you going to have that party again?*, so she did and again everyone came, and after that it was expected. She'd missed a few years early on for various deaths and rough spots, though not lately. Not that there hadn't been more of those, just that she'd come to realize she had to give it no matter what, that death and disappointment were no reason not to have a party, that in fact they were the best reason of all.

They, the women, Lydia's friends, would start to arrive

around seven. Lydia checked the temperature—two below now, though it was supposed to go up to a high of twelve. She hoped their cars would start, but she no longer worried, as she had in the early years, that they wouldn't show up. If someone were stranded—Celia, probably, in that old beater of theirs—someone else would collect her. It had gotten to be that important, a kind of summit meeting. Norris was the only one who was iffy but even she had said she'd come this year. Now Lydia just worried they'd show up early, before she was ready.

She had much to prepare—the house, the food, herself. The letters. Maxine needed a walk. Somewhere Lydia would need to fit in a nap so she'd seem bright, unfazed by the effort this was going to take.

Now Lydia stood in front of her open closet, trying to decide what she'd wear. She'd narrowed it down to two possible outfits, both black, for two of her various selves. She didn't know yet which one she'd be tonight, though the range of choices had narrowed considerably. Formerly it had included carefree, seductive, demure, bookish, sporty, sexily sporty, sexily bookish, sexily oblivious to how sexy she really looked, recently broken-hearted and sexier than ever. *You get my drift*, she imagined saying, to Celia, if she'd felt comfortable broaching this delicate subject with her, which, lately, she hadn't. What she would have meant was it had mostly been about men.

The theme around which she organized her closet these days was damage control. Should she be *the woman who has embraced aging*, a look that was sliding dangerously close to *who cares*, or *the woman who seems ageless*? For years she'd coasted on *the woman who looks incredibly young for her age*, but lately things had taken a turn. And it wasn't just her wardrobe that had to be recalibrated. What about makeup—how to handle this strange color she'd turned? How much effort she put into that depended partly on whether she could risk wearing mascara, which mostly these days she could not, never knowing when she'd dribble sentimental tears.

At least she didn't have to worry about looking good for men tonight. Men weren't invited to this party, though someone's husband or ex or boyfriend or, in the old days, "secret" lover—Lydia's, usually—posing as a helpful friend or delivery person or unknowing drop-in visitor always sneaked in, determined to defy the no-men ban, pretending to be there to pick up or drop off an invited guest but really wanting to linger and spy, to listen and graze, to suss out the thrilling essential femaleness of it all. Or at least that used to be the case. Not so much these days, Lydia thought.

Spence didn't count; he lived here.

This aging thing had taken her by surprise. She'd heard tell, of course. She knew it would happen, just not yet, and not all at once. Of course she'd known in the abstract, she just didn't *know*. She hadn't understood how bad it would get, didn't expect these ongoing losses, this sense of parts falling off the wagon as it rolled downhill. When she was younger she hadn't fully comprehended that she was part of this cycle, too, that she too would grow older, then old, and only then if she was lucky.

8

Somehow, a[
while, in her t[
stay the way it[
the future wh[
this, this pr[
downward s[

Her par[
and gracef[
always to[
age. Thei[
choice, a[
could no long[

uninvited guests and then ate it [
And her parents hadn't compla[
now that they'd hidden thes[
as ashamed as she was n[

Lydia stood in fro[
brush, wonderi[
night. Wint[
miniblind[
so long[
with[

squeeze happily into the passeng[er] she'd felt sad, but still, it wasn't her. And here was the [...] and shameful part she hated to admit: she'd thought they'd brought it on themselves. They hadn't taken care of themselves is what she'd thought. Sometimes she even thought they were that way by choice.

They *liked* those shoes is what she'd thought. They moved that way because they *wanted* to. She'd thought they'd done everything slowly on purpose, to annoy her, that they didn't care about swiftness or grace. They chose not to square their shoulders when they walked, not to lead with their sternums or tuck their tailbones or hold their stomachs in.

Lydia felt ashamed now, and wildly regretful, thinking of her cluelessness, callousness, even. But what had she known about collapsing spines, collapsing arches, surgical mistakes, insidious diseases that took possession of the body like

live from within? Nothing.
ned, at least not to her. She saw
things from her, that they'd been
w.

t of the bathroom mirror, holding a tooth-
g if she had enough white candles to last the
r light raked unkindly through the slats of the
. She stepped out of its glare, recalling a time—not
ago—when she'd enjoyed the sight of herself this way,
out clothes or makeup. It wasn't that long ago, she thought,
hen she'd looked better out of her clothes than in them.

She heard Spence's voice, drifting up from the kitchen. He was talking to Malcolm, the cat, in an intimate falsetto. "Who is the alchemist of Malcolmness?" he was saying. "Is it you, my cuddlesome one? Is it you, my darling? Yes, you is."

Maybe he would have liked having children after all, Lydia thought, filled with regret this winter morning. This delay in her awareness of passing time, Lydia knew, had everything to do with the fact that they hadn't. Her friends who had—Cel, Betsy, her sister-in-law Liv, Jayne if being a stepmother counted, even Norris, unmotherly as she was—had acquired a sense of slippage sooner. They'd been forced to see a timeline. They recounted matter-of-factly how they compared their own declining energy with the increasing vigor of those smooth, plump, voracious, ever-expanding bodies at their kitchen tables. Lydia knew, even loved, those monstrously healthy, fresh-scented children—the ones who appeared to feed off their own mothers' flesh—but she saw now that the rate of their alarming growth had been linked all along to her own diminishment.

She'd had dogs, of course. Lydia knew well the doom *that* love always led to. She'd seen them go from the sweet energy of puppyhood to robust maturity to long naps and then cruel putrid decrepitude and finally bitter nothingness. But that was different. You expected it. Animals were a parallel universe of collapsed time, and when they went you were so blinded by grief you didn't stop to think it would happen also to you.

What to do? She knew what her brother would say. *Pray.* He'd tell her to go back to church, to the God they'd been raised to believe in. Sometimes she almost wanted to. *Yea though I walk through the valley of the shadow of death I will fear no evil.* What a comfort, to believe in that, eternal life.

Lydia splashed cold water on her face.

She felt alone, left without a strategy. In better days, she would have figured something out. She'd been working on it, even, weighing two possible approaches to what she'd expected to be the third third of her life. She'd figured it was a little like the two approaches to money—saving and spending. According to one way of thinking, the way she'd been raised, if you had something, looks or cash, say, you saved it. You put it away and pretended to yourself it wasn't there while in some secret part of your mind you husbanded it, you stewarded it, you watched it like a hawk. Kept it fit and firm and fungible, slathered on cream and did sit-ups, bought treasury bills and blue chip stocks, and when you were old you pulled it out—ta da—and there it was when you needed it most.

It was stingy though, Lydia saw now, and it didn't even always work. It assumed health and longevity, of the market and the body both. It assumed the market wouldn't be hijacked by some diabolical pied piper of a Ponzi schemer or that you wouldn't be struck by a drunk driver on the way to the party or the way to the bank, that you in fact would not be the drunk driver, who plows into the lamppost or the oncoming van full of Sunday school teachers on your way home from a boozy dinner with your college roommate on the eve of your fifty-fifth birthday.

It assumed you wouldn't get cancer and die at fifty-four.

Ah there's the rub, as Lydia's Shakespeare-loving father would have said, though it had been his idea to be so tight. *Neither a borrower nor a lender be*, she could hear him intone, refusing to give her a loan. The rub was, the body wouldn't keep. Money sometimes either, but the body, never, no. Try your best to preserve it—go ahead, try—when you went to cash it in, you'd find it gone.

All of which led her by logical necessity to the other approach. Use it up, spend it down. Carpe diem, as an old boyfriend of Lydia's used to say, writing it in the steam on the bathroom mirror, in the dust on the trunk of her car. He'd meant that Lydia should hurry and take off her clothes, but she saw now the expression had other applications as well.

Lydia's thrifty father would have disapproved, of course. Even now, so many years after his death, she felt him sensing her thoughts, spitting out his own ashes to reclaim his voice, to disown her from his grave, for turning profligate in middle age. But, though she was raised to be a saver and meant no disrespect, she'd decided to switch camps.

It was harder than she'd expected, making a change like that. She wasn't in the habit of spending, didn't know what to buy. She'd splurged on two dozen pink tulips for the party, but they hadn't opened, and she could see it had probably been a mistake, in this cold. They were turning more wrinkled and gray by the hour, like a dead man's testicles.

She'd begun to shop online, trying to find the pleasure in it that other people seemed to. So far she'd bought two bathrobes she didn't wear, an indigo lace bra that didn't fit, curtains she hadn't hung, books she'd never read, an upholstered chair she had no place to put, and a raincoat that cost more than she'd spent on her first car.

Sometimes Lydia didn't even open the packages. The pleasure—what little there was—was in the ordering, not the thing itself. At least she'd opened the fleece blankets she'd bought for tonight, in different colors, to give as warming gifts when each guest arrived, in exchange for her coat, the last to keep for herself. She'd bought them as much for the names of the colors as the warmth they were purported to give—Spruce, A-maize, Pumpkin Dream, Thrush, for herself, which the picture had made seem blue but was closer to olive drab.

Two days before, Lydia had ordered the largest available version of a fancy French enameled iron casserole, for tonight's chicken stew. She'd bought it for the color, an orangey flame red she'd never wear but thought she'd like to have around. She felt a little guilty. The cost, including overnight shipping, could have fed a family of four for a week. Every other year, Lydia had made the stew in her grandmother's grease-stained cast-iron pot, the one she'd brought to Chicago from Massachusetts in 1908, and it had worked perfectly well. Lydia hadn't needed a new pot. She'd just wanted one. Or not even. She just liked the color. But if this was what people did to enjoy their lives, Lydia thought, clanging the thing down on the stove when it arrived, then so be it.

Lydia was doing some of the cooking tonight. She always did, though officially the party was potluck. Lydia did like a nice potluck supper. People liked to bring things, and she liked surprises, to a point. Though this precipitous decline of hers was one surprise she could have done without.

Lydia had already begun shifting to the use-it-up approach to aging even before these other, darker developments got under way, about a year before, when it occurred to her that even if she started counting from age twenty and lived to the full extent of what actuaries predicted was her probable life span, she was already halfway through her productive life. She could see that things had tilted out of proportion. She'd saved. She'd waited. She'd been patient, and all of a sudden she felt overdue for something good to happen. She began to feel afraid she'd die—just a theoretical possibility at that point—with too much of everything left. She'd lived her life under the assumption that if she waited her turn, her turn would come, though for what, she no longer knew.

She saw now, she'd been too patient. That too-expensive

hiking trip to Nepal she'd wanted to take, that she'd let Barry, who was her boyfriend then, talk her out of—she should have done it, she thought. It was too late now. Even a year ago it would have been. Not absolutely, but enjoyably—something to do with her feet, a result of cramming her toes into those fuck-me pumps all those years ago, the red ones. She'd worn them to work, of all places. Maybe she had lived a little, she thought. But she could have lived more. She saw now that the impatient ones were the ones that did it right. Now, at this late date, she was trying to change her ways.

Ice cubes, she thought, noticing, out the bathroom window, icicles hanging from the gutter. That's what she'd forgotten. She'd e-mail Jayne to pick up a bag on the way over. So many details. She remembered when the idea of giving a party was simply a terror, an impossibility, one of the things on her List of Fears.

Don't tell me you don't have one, she imagined saying to someone, Celia probably. At least she supposed everyone had some version of one, a chute of impossibilities that bumpered their lives. How could you not? Fear ruled the world, didn't it? It had ruled hers.

Lydia had made her first list of fears when she was fifteen, in curly cursive handwriting, on lined notebook paper in romantic blue ink. The school psychologist she'd been sent to for turning in a particularly gruesome art project had told her to make a list of everything she was afraid of, and she'd taken to the task with alacrity, discovering she had a talent for fear.

She'd lost track of the many-times-folded sheet of notebook paper, which she'd moved from hiding place to hiding place, but that hardly mattered now—she could recite the list from memory.

Lydia's List of Fears—her own private catechism. Her fears then had numbered twenty-nine, the same as the number of lines on the page. She'd wondered sometimes, over the years, if her life would have turned out differently if she'd had a smaller notebook that day. But too late now. The count came to twenty-nine. She'd liked, at least, that the number was prime.

Lydia would have liked to be able to say she'd mastered all the fears on her list before she died, or at least that she planned to die trying, but it wouldn't be true. The fact was she'd mastered a few, and some went away. As for the rest, she'd built her life around them.

Not that she would admit it, or even what was on the list. Or not anymore. She had, once. She'd recited the entire list to an old boyfriend, not Barry, a different one, the carpe diem guy, on a road trip, for something to talk about in the forced intimacy of a car plummeting unobstructed through the Badlands and across the hot brown prairie on the way back from Rapid City, South Dakota. They'd gone so he could photograph the big carved faces in the mountain. It was supposed to be funny, an ironic adventure, though the land was unexpectedly beautiful and the people open and kind. He'd made her list into a song, sung to the tune of "My Favorite Things"—he'd called it "These Are a Few of My Terrible Things"—and sang it all the way back to Chicago.

Even now she could hear it, in his voice:

> big black dogs
> singing in public
> going to parties
> giving parties
> driving
> diving (especially scuba)
> marriage
> dentists and doctors and

Mean as it was, Lydia had to admit it was funny, how well he'd made it fit with that lovely old Rodgers and Hammerstein tune, with the addition of a few *and*s and a little bounce and by throwing in a line ending in *Cuba*, though that part was purely made up. Lydia couldn't have cared less about Cuba as a girl.

She'd come a long way since then, she thought, glancing at dear Maxine, an aging Rottweiler shepherd mix of exceptional beauty who gazed knowingly at her from her shearling-lined bed. Maxine sighed, her orange eyebrow-like markings furrowing with concern.

Lydia was moisturizing her face now with the antiaging upward strokes recommended by beauty experts and wondering who among her circle of friends had had plastic surgery. She regretted not getting that eye tuck she'd considered a few years before. She'd planned to pay for it with the unexpected tax refund she got that year but felt guilty and ended up donating the money to an animal shelter instead. Elaine had breast reconstruction after her mastectomy—she'd had both of them done so they'd match—but that didn't count. Maybe Jayne? She had that perfect little nose, but some people just did. Lydia would never ask.

Lydia: The Guest List

Lydia made a mental list of who was coming tonight: Elaine, Celia, Maura, Jayne, and Betsy. Them, plus her, made the usual six. Seven, if Norris showed up.

Usually she didn't. Though every year Lydia invited her, and suggested that Norris stay at the house, to make it clear it was a sincere invitation. Norris had never taken her up on it. Chicago bungalows were not her style, not anymore. Lydia knew for a fact that when Norris did come into town she stayed at a hotel.

Lydia no longer expected Norris to come to the party. Lydia's friends weren't really Norris's friends and Norris spent most of her time in Michigan now. The years she'd shown up, she'd only stayed for an hour or two, on her way to somewhere else. So Lydia was surprised this year when Norris e-mailed to say she had business in the city and planned to stop by.

They'd all met twenty years before, at the godforsaken suburban community college that still employed Lydia, an association that Lydia supposed Norris wanted to shed.

The first year she'd given the party, Lydia had just been

hired, adding the school to the roster of small colleges where she already taught part-time—a course here, a course there. They'd given her three classes the first semester and implied there might be a real job in the offing. The possibility had made her feel hopeful and expansive, more open to making friends than usual, in these often transient posts.

She taught a little of everything in those days—drawing, painting, art appreciation. The art department had shared office space with English and Humanities then, and that's how most of them met. They'd hung out together in the faculty lounge, a smelly, windowless room outfitted with a mini-fridge, a filthy microwave oven, and two leatherette sofas. They'd brought their lunches to save money and gathered there to gripe. They graded papers and shared food. Bonds were forged.

Elaine had been Lydia's first friend there. Elaine was older than Lydia. She'd worn boxy suits in an era of blue jeans and had taught English composition; she was the only one of them with tenure. Lydia got it later, but back then the place was a boys' club. Most of them weren't even full-time. They were paid per course, a fraction of what the full-time faculty got, and worked multiple jobs, hoping something would happen to change their lives. They'd felt abused and scared, buried alive, commuting into the arid and airy suburbs from their dark city apartments in broken-down cars, their trunks crammed with books and papers. It had been an uneasy time, though looking back, Lydia could see that being an outsider had had its advantages. She'd had impetus to paint, then. Teaching was a side-line, she'd thought, a way to pay the bills.

Of course, it hadn't worked out that way. Teaching, not art, became her career. Eventually she found she was good at it, and when they offered her a real job she'd grabbed it, for dental insurance and a retirement package that now she might never use.

Mental note, she thought—reread the packet on short-term disability insurance.

Much later, Lydia found out they'd offered the job to Norris first, for better pay, and that Norris, two years out of grad school and twelve years younger, had turned it down. Norris had gotten a better offer, at a real college, the same week, from someone she'd met at the residency she'd gotten Lydia bumped from. Now Norris didn't have to teach. She was that rarest of all creatures, an artist who lived—and well—off her art.

More water under the bridge, Lydia told herself, counting out cloth napkins. Her policy was to have plenty of extras. After the first few bottles of wine they tended to slip off laps and onto the floor.

Still, it had stung, she thought, Norris getting that good job so easily and so young, all those years ago. It had hurt to be surpassed that way, by a friend. Briefly, they'd been colleagues, fellow artists. Lydia had wanted to mentor Norris, show her the ropes, bring her along. But Norris had flashed past while Lydia stood still. Lydia had kept in touch, to prove there were no hard feelings, but of course there were. Norris reminded Lydia of what she'd had and lost. Promise.

Though Lydia had to admit that Norris had something else, too. Not more talent exactly, but more certainty. More belief, less doubt. She'd expected to succeed. Now it was hard to believe she was ever one of them. Lydia had looked up her website. She didn't even put their little school on her CV.

Lydia banged the iron down hard on the linen napkin she was ironing. Steam sizzled. She tried to let all that go. That's what they'd said to do in the one session of disease management counseling she'd attended, free of charge. They'd been given bumper stickers that said *Holding on to hurts, hurts!* Letting things go was good for your health, they said. And she had tried. But the things she let go of came back, and she'd have to let them go again. It got tiring, Lydia thought.

She hadn't known the whole story until much later, years later, recently in fact, when she'd found out at some faculty party. Someone brought it up as if it were old news, a joke by now since Lydia appeared to be way past it, and she'd pretended not to be surprised.

Cruelty is as common as the common cold, Lydia remembered her tough old grandma saying, brushing off her apron with excessive force. *Get a hankie and get used to it*, she'd say. She didn't put up with crying over playground slights.

Lucky she hadn't found out sooner, Lydia thought. Too late now to take up a grudge. She'd have to let go not only of Norris but also of this idea, that they'd been friends all these years. It was too much to give up. She'd have to stop inviting Norris to the party, and at this late date, she'd be embarrassed to explain why. Everyone thought she'd already forgiven her.

. . .

Lydia went back to her mental guest list: Elaine, Celia, Maura, Jayne, and Betsy. Maybe Norris. Lydia was the only one of them still teaching. Or she had been, until this happened. Now she was on medical leave and probably wouldn't go back, if her doctor was to be believed. Elaine, that cagey devil, had gotten out fifteen years earlier, saved up to pay off her mortgage and gave notice the day she wrote the last check. She said she couldn't stand teaching anymore, couldn't stand the tedium of hearing her own voice repeating itself semester after semester, telling the same jokes and the same stories, acting out the same rehearsed epiphanies, year after year, and Lydia knew what she meant, felt the same way about her own tired performances. Though Lydia thought that in Elaine's case it was grading papers that finally did her in. Four sections of English composition every semester—she'd felt she had to correct every superfluous comma.

Elaine had invited a few of them over on a Saturday morning, after her last exam, for what she called an office cleaning brunch. She'd set out a box of doughnuts and a carton of orange juice and someone had dug out a bottle of single malt Scotch and they'd spent the morning dragging bins mounded with old blue books into the parking lot, heaving armloads of term papers into a Dumpster. As the day, and the effects of spiked orange juice, wore on, their aim worsened and by mid-afternoon student papers, blurred by May drizzle, littered the pavement. Two months later, Elaine took a part-time job as a fact checker at an in-flight magazine and quit the day she qualified for social security.

Lydia had wondered at the time if Elaine had been hasty. What about her career? Now Lydia understood and wished she'd done the same. Elaine had been the bellwether, the one who went first through this difficult terrain—the shucking off of (what little remained of) status, the scaling back of expenses, the sexless clothes, the lopping off of body parts, the living will, the going gray. She had a snow-white buzz cut now, cute and efficient.

Then there was Celia. Celia had started teaching at the community college one year after Lydia and they'd instantly become friends, but she'd quit as soon as she married Peter. Her plan—Peter agreed to it, Celia claimed—was to become a full-time, subsidized artist. Later, quietly, she'd gone back to school and started taking courses toward a degree in library science. A few years after that, Griffin was born. He was a somber, wrinkled infant who seemed to know he was Plan B. Lydia thought he resembled a baked apple.

For a while after Griffin was born, Celia worked part-time at a suburban weekly, as its arts critic. *They have an art critic?* Lydia had said, meaning to be supportive. *Arts*, Celia had corrected her. She covered community theater, craft shows. *It's fun!* Celia had said. After a year they cut her hours and six months after that they let her go, then gave her what they called a column. For a few years after that she wrote a bullet-point list—"Shows to See"—every other week and was paid slightly less than it would have cost them to reimburse her for gas. Celia claimed not to mind—it gave her more time for her business, she said, building birdhouses in their spare bedroom. Lydia couldn't remember what she was doing now.

Maura had been Lydia's student, though they were around the same age. She worked near the college in an industrial park, as an administrative assistant at an insurance company, and had turned up in Lydia's evening art appreciation class. She was by far Lydia's brightest student that semester and Lydia had encouraged her to take more classes. Go on to a four-year college, she'd told her, part-time, if you need to, but finish your degree. Though Lydia came to know, because Maura eventually told her, that school had been a way to distract herself, occupy her evenings when Roy wasn't free. Roy in fact wasn't free most evenings, occupied as he was with dinner, with his wife and children.

Roy was Maura's boss.

The first year Maura came to the party, everyone acted strange around her, in her shiny hose and big hair and nervous eagerness to not seem different that made her seem so different. But the next year she'd toned down her look and eventually Lydia's friends got used to her. When Maura and Elaine got close, Lydia was surprised but mostly just relieved. Let Elaine take on the problem of Roy, Lydia thought, and Elaine had, with a vengeance that continued even after he died.

Jayne had taught art history, until she finished law school and got a better job. They all said *go, girl* to that.

And Betsy—they'd met her through Ted. He'd been thin then, cute, really, with that big head of wavy orange hair. Ted had taught music theory in those days and hung out with them in the lounge, one of the girls, almost. He'd begged an invitation to the party the second year and brought along Betsy—this was before they were married—and they'd all become friends. Later, he'd sulked when Lydia told him she'd decided the party should just be for women. Now Betsy was Lydia's friend. It was good to have someone in the group who was so different from the rest of them, a former social worker with a successful private psychotherapy practice. When they got down to gossip, Betsy took a harder line than anyone.

There'd been others Lydia had invited the first few years. June, an oboist, came once but she moved to Maine and later they heard she died in a car wreck. And there was Marcie, the performance artist who'd been hired to teach one section of art appreciation, who got fired when she used her guest speaker stipend to bring in a friend to talk about body art and he'd taken the opportunity to show the class his tattooed penis. Lydia had always liked her. She was fearless. She'd brought her partner Kate to the party one year and they showed up in tuxedos and top hats and did magic tricks. But they broke up, and Marcie's new girlfriend didn't like her friends and that was the last Lydia saw of either of them.

In the beginning Lydia had invited everyone—husbands, partners, dates, visiting houseguests, even children, but that didn't last. The women hadn't felt free to talk.

Now it was just the six of them, and Norris if she showed. A slightly unstable group, Lydia thought, more volatile than couples. She'd been part of a group like that, back when she and Spence were still married. Four couples had met four times a year for dinner, like clockwork. They'd each taken a season—theirs had been fall. One October, Lydia had made lamb stew she served from a hollowed-out, roasted pumpkin, before Spence went vegan. Instead of a tablecloth that year, Lydia had covered the table with rubbery yellow leaves from their oak tree. For dessert she'd served pumpkin pie with marshmallows they'd roasted on sticks over a fire pit in the backyard.

It had gone on like that for three or four years, every dinner party more imaginative and ambitious than the last. She missed it sometimes. If the privacy of marriage had tended to blunt whatever female friendships the women might otherwise have formed, the arrangement had a certain stately symmetry to it, too, like dancing the Virginia reel. At the very least, it had made for some lovely evenings. She'd tried to stay in touch with the women after her divorce as the group dispersed—she and Spence weren't the only ones—but without their spouses they were like crabs without shells and they lost touch.

These friendships were messier, Lydia thought. Without cover of men they had fewer secrets, weaker boundaries.

Celia

Celia had been looking forward to Lydia's party for a month, or longer, to be honest. Now she just hoped she could stay awake. She was working the early-morning shift, at the hospital library, and it would be hard if the party went late, which it usually did.

Mostly Celia didn't mind her job, except when it collided with something like this. Or when people she knew came into the hospital. Neighbors, that was awkward. She tried to avoid them, kept her head down or went in the other direction. She'd seen Lydia the other day—that was a surprise—but Celia had managed to duck into the ladies' room just in time. Luckily the cart was still there when she came out. Celia didn't think Lydia had seen her. Even people like Lydia didn't usually notice the faces of people who pushed carts.

Celia knew she should tell her about the job, put a positive spin on it. *It's interesting!* she'd say. It was interesting, Celia thought. Maybe tonight she would. It was nothing to be ashamed of. Lydia would be supportive. *Sounds like fun*, she'd say, or something like that. Some parts were fun, sort of, in a mindless way. Celia didn't mind walking around, delivering things. It left her free to think. And she loved libraries. So what if she had to ask permission to go to lunch?

Celia had been looking for a real job for years. Just this past fall, she'd written to sixty-two libraries within a seventy-five-mile radius of her house—she figured a ninety-minute commute each way was her limit—including school and corporate libraries, but there were no openings for art librarians. When this came up, library assistant at the local teaching hospital, she'd grabbed it.

Though she'd thought she'd be working more with actual books. Mostly she photocopied journal articles for medical students and—her specialty—walked up and down hallways delivering books and what she thought of as AV equipment, though that's not what they called it. Occasionally she had to wheel around an old cart with an ancient film projector on it, but mostly Celia delivered laptops to meetings or DVD players to birthing classes.

She'd show up at some room full of shiny-faced, big-bellied, giddy girls, almost every one young enough to be her daughter, pop the DVD in, and stay just long enough to make sure everything was working properly. She tried to get out as soon as she could after that, before it got gory. It was easy enough. The truth was they didn't even see her.

Lydia: The Food

Lydia was serving her spicy chicken stew tonight, the one she made every year. This year she'd added cannellini beans along with the usual mashed potatoes, to thicken it. Also vegetables, stewed tomatoes, hot sauce, rice. A can of corn, a glass or two of sherry. She used to add andouille, which she'd ordered online from a little boudin place outside Jeanerette, Louisiana, but she'd given up red meat this year and put in turkey sausage instead. She wasn't convinced it quite did the job. She'd made the stew the day before and when she'd tasted it, then, it wasn't bad, but she hoped a night in the fridge had improved it. She planned to make Parmesan cheese dumplings, too, which she'd drop in the stew at the last minute.

Lydia did the inventory in her head.

Wine—she'd gotten a case, mixed red and white. That should more than cover it, since most of them would bring a bottle, too. Jayne always brought champagne.

Appetizers—Celia and Jayne were handling that. And Betsy, who didn't cook, would bring Ted's Famous Meatballs, which is what he called them, and a jar of his special soy sauce and sambal barbeque concoction, which he made every year especially for the party and which was his way of letting Lydia know he wanted to be invited back. The thought of the meat-balls reminded Lydia to put out toothpicks.

Bread—Peter would send some with Celia, as he did every year. He claimed it was no trouble, since he baked every Satur-day. Lydia knew he'd like to be invited, too. She loved Peter, everybody did, and after all these years of enjoying his dona-tions, wonderful coarse, crusty, fragrant loaves of bread and sometimes also a pie or tarte tatin, she would have liked to invite him, but if she did that she'd have to invite Ted, and that was out of the question.

Salad—Elaine.

Side dishes—Jayne and Maura, though Lydia knew from past experience that Maura considered baked ham a side dish. Lydia was counting on Jayne for vegetables.

Dessert—Lydia had bought it this year. Usually she baked, but this year she hadn't had the energy, though either way, it was superfluous, really. Everyone brought dessert—she couldn't have stopped them if she'd tried. Still, Lydia had made a special trip and picked up two dozen cannoli at D'Amato's.

That should be plenty, she thought. She liked to send them home with leftovers. She'd even bought expensive little baskets this year, with hinged lids, woven in the shape of animals, to pack the leftovers in. Lydia knew no one needed baskets. This was part of her spending campaign. Lydia knew that Norris, if she even came, would pitch hers out the car window the minute she hit the highway—food and basket both. With any luck some homeless person would find it, or at least a raccoon. Lydia reminded herself to wrap Norris's portion loosely. At least then, if an animal found it, he could get at it easily, without having to chew through wax paper and foil.

Elaine

Elaine had been looking forward to the party all week but now the day had arrived and she didn't want to go. She would, of course—if she didn't show up they'd probably send the police—but she dreaded it. She didn't feel like talking to people tonight. And not just tonight. Lately. She'd considered calling to say she'd be late, to skip all the preprandial chitchat, maybe show up in the middle of dinner, except that she was supposed to bring the salad and didn't want to mess things up for Lydia. Or she could get there early, she supposed, drop off the food, and leave. She still had a sick person's prerogative, though it had been two years.

At least she'd already made the apple crumble. It was good, too, her mother's recipe. She was nothing if not reliable in that department, though what was the point, she thought. By the time they got to dessert everyone was too drunk to taste it. She'd even, in a dark moment, considered taking a store-bought pie this year. She knew if she put it in her pie carrier, no one would even notice. She'd already compromised by buying canned whipped cream this year. She'd tasted it—not bad, maybe a little too sweet. Usually she whipped the cream herself, there at the party, with a whisk, after dinner while everyone marveled at what a perfectionist she was, but she didn't feel like it tonight.

Ever since her mother died, Elaine had felt listless. Then Boswell—it was too much, one after the other like that, on top of her surgery. People said it's only a dog, buck up, but they had no idea. In six months her hair had turned white. Then she'd gotten fat, from shock, she supposed, although the death of the old was hardly a shock. Her mother had been ninety-two. Grief, then.

Now she had to figure out what to wear tonight, another small agony. Nothing fit. Grief was supposed to make you waste away, she thought, but no such luck. It didn't help that all her friends were younger. She'd been waiting for Lydia to stop being so svelte, but every time Elaine saw her she was thinner, not fatter. Norris, too, but she was young. She could be expected to hold up another ten years. But Lydia, enough.

Here was a question: When could they all give up and wear elastic-waist jeans? Thank God at least for stretch denim, Elaine thought. That's what she'd be wearing tonight—flannel-lined, elastic-waist stretch jeans that made her look like a two-car garage. Though she'd prefer pajamas.

Lydia: The Dogs

Lydia wove a red ribbon around Maxine's collar and brushed her coat so she'd be shiny and soft for later. Standing upright, too fast, Lydia felt her head swim, and she almost fell. She leaned on the big dog for support.

Maxine's presence at the party—under the table, lying sideways across at least two pairs of feet during dinner, confident that food would be passed her way at regular intervals—had become part of the tradition, and one year Lydia invited everyone to bring their dogs. Betsy had taken Lydia up on the offer and brought Pudding, her and Ted's eight-pound Yorkie. He and Maxine got along so well that she continued to bring him, every year.

Betsy called him Pud. *Rhymes with hood*, she told people. Out of Betsy's earshot, Celia and Elaine called him Pudenda. Jayne always reminded them the word was Latin for shame, which always inspired someone else to say *Can you believe the word for female genitalia means shame*, which in turn inspired someone else, usually Elaine, to say *Yes*. Then everyone laughed. The party had taken on a ritual quality, like some scripted high church pageant that played out every year. Lydia found this both comforting and maddeningly repetitive, often at the same time.

Ted usually dressed Pud in some version of a coat—the year before it was a red plaid fleece wrapper with a Velcro closure—and carried him from the car to the house in his pocket when he dropped Betsy off. He insisted on it, and on picking them up at midnight. Lydia knew exactly how it would go. Ted would carry his meatballs into the house in a chafing dish, with his special sauce in a quart Ball jar in one overcoat pocket and Pud in the other. He would set the chafing dish in the dining room and the Ball jar on the kitchen counter and Pud on a kitchen chair, then lean down to kiss Lydia on the cheek and proceed to snoop around the kitchen and comment on her cooking.

Do I detect a tad of cumin in the stew this year? he'd say—or oregano or sumac—squinting like Columbo. Finally, after enough of the women had reminded him to drive safely, he'd leave. They'd hear him as he made his way out the door, onto the front porch, singing something Broadway in his velvety tenor. *Don't throw bouquets at me.* Anyone who bothered to watch him recede in the dark would see him shuffle off a few dance steps in the snow and be newly surprised at how graceful he was, for such a big man.

He does have a nice voice, someone always said, after shouldering the front door closed behind him, against a gust of wind. Sometimes Lydia felt tempted to let bygones be bygones and invite him to stay for dinner, but there were too many reasons not to and she knew if she did no one else would get a word in edgewise. Besides, the rule they'd decided on was no men, a rule they'd made largely to keep Ted out. Not that there was any keeping him out for long. He was always back by midnight to collect Betsy and Pud and his grandmother's chafing dish. There were lots of pumpkin and Cinderella jokes then.

"It's creepy," Celia always said, to Lydia, after they left. "It's like he's her father." She said it every year. "More like her mother," Lydia had said once. Celia didn't know the half of it, Lydia thought but couldn't say; she was bound to silence.

The truth was, Lydia would have liked him to stay, if he could have just behaved. She would have liked to know how he was. He seemed better now, Lydia thought, after he and Betsy decided to get back together, though she wasn't so sure about Betsy. Ted was all promises and recipe cards now, proving how devoted he was, though Lydia was sure he still saw Raymond. Or someone like him. Who knew if Betsy knew. Probably she did, and kept it to herself.

Lydia had not asked to know any of this. Ted had told her. He'd called her six months ago to tell her that he and Raymond had lunch, after he saw Lydia walk by the restaurant. "And that's all we had," he said.

She'd told him for the hundredth time she didn't want to hear about it.

"You have to hear about it," he'd said. "You're my best friend."

"Come on."

"You are," he'd said. "Talk to me. I'm struggling with this."

Lydia had kept quiet, resisting the urge to tell him to cut the crap.

"I do," he'd said, reading her mind. "I struggle. I struggle with these . . ." Here he'd paused, sighed. Lydia heard rattling and wondered if he'd had an EKG lately. He just kept getting bigger. "These unnatural impulses. I need someone to talk to."

Lydia cringed when Ted talked this way. He didn't used to. He used to count all his impulses—toward food, men, women, in approximately that order—as natural. Or he'd at least conveyed that impression. Now that he'd gone back to church, Ted had started to talk about sin.

Ted rediscovered religion shortly after he was fired from his job as a junior high school music teacher, details of which dismissal he would not divulge, even to Lydia. His return to faith had been precipitated by what he called a "particularly dark night of the soul." Despair had beset him, he said, late one Thursday when the mashed potato machine broke down during the 3–11 shift, in his first week at his new job as an assistant manager at a fried chicken franchise, a job Betsy had insisted he take. He realized then, he needed to go back to church.

Or rather to the Church, as Ted put it, the church of his youth. He'd told Lydia then that he considered himself a prodigal son, a man returned to his god. She'd told him she thought the real reason he'd gone back to church was for the choir. Maybe he just missed singing, she said.

"Liberal churches have choirs, too," she'd pointed out, meaning to be helpful. He'd laughed, but she'd meant it.

Really, though, who cared where he went to church. Her problem was Betsy. Ted thought he was being virtuous, that he'd done her a good deed, going back. He saw it as a cleansing sacrifice. "What about her?" Lydia had said.

"She's fine!" Ted said.

Lydia told him to find a new church. "Become a Unitarian," she'd said. "Give yourself a happy ending."

But Ted said she didn't understand. Lydia told him she thought she did, that she thought he loved his guilt more than he loved his mean old god. Then she'd told him she thought he was a phony and that Betsy would be happier without him.

"Don't say that," he said. "We have kids."

"They're almost grown," Lydia said.

This time Ted went silent, and when Lydia said she thought he was being selfish he started to make sounds like he was going to cry. She held the phone, listening to him sniff. She heard a sob, then more sniffling, and after a while the sound of a fat man breathing raggedly and hard. Just when Lydia couldn't stand it anymore and was about to apologize, he burst into song.

"*Call me irresponsible . . .*"

"Jerk," she said. "Faker."

"*Call me unreliable . . .*"

"Stop it, or I'm hanging up."

"Gotcha!" he said, back to his jolly old self.

"And stop telling me these things," Lydia said. "You don't follow my advice."

"I like to tell you things," he said. "You're the only person I can talk to."

"It's compromising," she said. "I'm supposed to be Betsy's friend."

"No," he said. "Mine. You were my friend first."

"Ted, one of these days I'm going to wring your neck" is how Lydia usually ended their conversations.

Lydia went back to thinking about dogs. It would be the first year without Boswell, Elaine's fat yellow Lab, who, with his soulful brown eyes, was more of a person than a dog. Elaine had brought him every year since the first dog year and every year he'd lie on the couch with his head in someone's lap. He'd died last August, at fourteen.

That had been hard. They all still felt bad about it. Not Norris, but everyone else. Elaine was talking about getting another one, something smaller this time—a min pin, maybe, easier to walk, she said—but Lydia could tell her heart wasn't in it.

Elaine

At the last party, Celia—who'd had too much to drink and was making a show of sticking up for Maura after Elaine had just made that one little joke about Roy, who was dead by then anyway—had called Elaine a sexually confused crabby old grouch.

"So?" Elaine had said. "It doesn't mean I'm not right."

Elaine had expected Celia to agree, that Roy had been a disaster.

Romantics thought she was bitter, but Elaine thought of herself as a realist. She didn't expect love to save her. She didn't expect anything to save her. She'd learned a long time ago not to rely on that kind of thinking. It was a drug, a palliative for the powerless, entertainment for the ignorant, and if you insisted on poisoning your brain you were better off taking drugs, in Elaine's opinion. Consider Maura and her darling dead married Roy, she thought. Or even Lydia.

Where had all that drama, that overvaluation of the male member, gotten her, really? Exactly nowhere, as far as Elaine could tell.

God save us, Elaine thought, from Lydia's pink-lit fantasies, even of Norris.

Lydia: The Questions

Lydia set out the shoes she planned to wear tonight—boots, really, warm and low-heeled (*so there's no falling down after a few drinks* was her usual joke, though now she couldn't drink). Out of habit, she composed her annual mental list of questions.

Every year, from almost the beginning, there'd been a theme to the party, some project that made it feel useful, or some order of business that needed to be conducted. One year it was to adopt out a cat that had been left with Lydia by a neighbor. She'd meant to keep him but he and Malcolm didn't get along, so the women had spent the night compiling lists of cat lovers and making increasingly drunken phone calls to likely owners. Other years it was a book exchange. Once, Maura got everyone to bring warm clothes to donate to the homeless shelter where she volunteered. Elaine had brought her grandmother's mink, a tiny coat for a tiny woman, with a tattered red satin lining, and when Betsy tried it on and it fit perfectly she decided to keep it and wrote a nice check to the shelter. They'd ended up trading all the clothes, donating money instead. This year it was Lydia's little agenda item, although no one knew about that yet.

For a while they'd done the Questions, too. It had started with a truth-telling session where everyone was supposed to sit in a circle and tell something personal they didn't think anyone knew about them. It had been Betsy's idea—she'd just opened her family therapy practice and had gotten very bossy and said it would be good for them to share—but no one cooperated, so the next year she came up with an amended version, a game she called the Questions. They were supposed to bring one anonymous question, typed so no one could guess the handwriting and sealed in a blank white envelope, and put it in a bowl. Then everyone picked one and read it out loud.

The rule was you had to tell the truth or pass.

The questions had ranged from easy to impossible. *What's your favorite book? Do you love one of your parents more? Would you rather be happily married or rich? How will you die?* After the first year, Lydia added extra questions, to make it harder to guess who'd asked what.

They'd done it only a few times—the year Elaine refused to play, they dropped it. But Lydia still thought of the party in terms of questions she wanted answered. She had two this year. Her first was: *Do you know anyone who is truly happy and if so who?* It was a trick question, a skill she'd perfected over years of exam writing. It was a sneaky way of asking if they were happy. Her second was even better: *What do you regret?*

She supposed—if they were still playing the game—that she could throw in *Have you ever had plastic surgery and if so for what?* but she wouldn't want to put anyone on the spot. They'd backed away from the ultrapersonal. They were past confession and mean-spirited truth telling, had moved on to acceptance, kindness, letting go. Or most of them had. The rest of them should, Lydia thought. Though sometimes she missed the drama of the old days. There used to be sex questions. She remembered one about removing stains from a silk scarf.

What a tedious party, Lydia imagined someone saying, Spence probably. Parties shouldn't have agendas, he'd say, already had said, in fact. Who had time to even eat?

Lydia had to admit, it was a lot to cover in one night. For years they'd talked about going away, meeting someplace, but they couldn't agree on where. An island someplace warm was one idea, a cruise was another. *But the cold is part of it*, someone always said. *It wouldn't be the same without a fire.*

It has to be a place that welcomes dogs. Lydia remembered she'd been the one who said that. Someone knew someone who had a derelict cottage on Washington Island they could probably rent for next to nothing.

Norris's suggestion—her recently built house in the Michigan woods, with its art and its guesthouse, its hot tub and heated floors, glossy pictures of which they'd all seen in *Chicago* magazine—was out of the question. As Elaine said later, after Norris left, it didn't look like them.

Maura

I hope this doesn't turn into another one of Lydia's man bashing parties, Maura thought, on her way to pick up the ham. Elaine was the worst. Maura loved her but sometimes she could be so unattractively bitter. And why? Elaine had had a real career. She'd traveled! But she said the meanest things sometimes. And she got so angry. She said things to Maura like *Maybe if you were more pissed off I wouldn't have to be*. Maura usually just said *Let it go*. Or *Who do you think you are, my mother?*

They argued about Roy. Elaine had even met him once—Maura had introduced them. What a mistake. Elaine had called him Uncle Roy to his face. Elaine was her best friend but some things were hard to forgive. Like that crack she'd made about sitting next to his wife at the funeral. Elaine knew Maura hadn't gone.

Still, Maura looked forward to seeing everyone tonight, some more than others. She always looked forward to seeing Lydia. Though Lydia was usually too busy to talk much at these things. The last time Maura had seen her at school, where she still took the occasional class, Lydia hadn't looked well. Maura almost said *Are you OK?* But then she didn't. Cafeteria lighting could make anyone look terrible, even Lydia.

Maura had offered to bring the main dish this year, so Lydia wouldn't have to cook. She'd told her she had a new chili recipe she wanted to try out at the shelter and said she could double it and bring half to the party, but Lydia had said no. She'd bought some expensive pot online, she'd said, and wanted to use that. Maura had even offered to come early and dump her chili into the pot—no one would know—but Lydia said no, people would wonder why she'd changed the menu. Besides, she wanted to cook.

Lydia: 10:30 A.M.

Lydia could hear Spence downstairs, whirring something healthy in the blender. She hoped he'd clean up the inevitable green mess before he left. At least there was no danger he'd snack on party food. He was single-mindedly devoted to nutrition these days.

Lydia was back upstairs, rooting through her closet, looking for the tablecloth she hadn't been able to find in the pantry, where she thought she'd last stashed it. Already she was tired. Maybe a quick rest, she thought, check her e-mail.

She shuffled the few steps to the tiny room under the eaves that she called her office, formerly her studio. There, among quarter-hourly news updates from Ted about the progress of his meatballs and a lengthy correspondence between Jayne and Maura about who was bringing which side dishes, was a message from Norris. Lydia supposed it meant she wasn't coming after all but when she clicked it open she saw that Norris had forwarded her a gallery announcement for some show she was in, with a note that said, *thought you'd find this amusing don't bother to go I don't plan to. see u tonight.*

Norris was the most successful artist Lydia knew, and Lydia wasn't sure why she felt the need to keep her informed of her increasingly eventful career. Not that Lydia wasn't happy for Norris—she was! It was just that the arrival of these announcements could still, on a bad day, arouse in Lydia an uncomfortable mix of gratitude, for being remembered at all, and its bitter aftertaste, envy.

It was a lot to accept—the rave reviews, the awards, the *museum* shows, and in all the right places. The way she'd just waltzed away from that job offer that had meant so much to Lydia the way you'd leave a restaurant you didn't like the looks of, assuming there'd be something better down the street. Of course, for Norris, there always was. She'd stayed at their little school three semesters. Lydia saw now that even then, she'd felt it was beneath her.

Lydia reread the message, trying to be glad rather than just flattered that Norris was coming tonight. It would take some diplomacy, though—she knew her other guests would prefer that Norris didn't.

The emerging artist residency that Lydia had recommended Norris for had launched her, really. Though anything would have, Lydia recognized now. Norris had been poised to be launched. You could even say she launched herself, Lydia supposed, though the contacts she'd made there, which Lydia had made possible, couldn't have hurt.

Lydia had been honored when Norris asked her to write the recommendation, and she'd had to pretend not to be disappointed, later, when she wasn't invited to speak on the mentors' panel. That was how it usually worked. You sponsored someone and if she got in they invited you to come speak, at the end. There was a cocktail party, dinner at the lodge. The artists and their so-called mentors—usually a bunch of old careerists, but still—hobnobbed. Drinks were swilled, connections made. Sometimes you got invited back for a residency of your own.

Or so Lydia had heard. She'd never been invited. People who had, said it was dreary, another petty honor in the petty land of academe, though Lydia had looked forward to it.

Looking back, it was obvious what had happened. She could see that Norris had been ashamed of their friendship, the community college connection. She'd already erased it from her official past. And of course Norris never asked Lydia for another recommendation, hadn't needed to. If anything, Lydia thought, she should ask Norris for a recommendation, if she'd felt comfortable applying for that sort of thing, which she didn't.

The thing about Norris, Lydia thought, almost deleting the gallery announcement without reading it, because she knew she was too tired to reply with the right mix of nonchalance and enthusiasm, but then deciding not to because she was curious, was that she always knew exactly what to do. She never questioned that rolling over other people was the right thing. And maybe it was, Lydia thought. After all, Norris should know. She was a nature painter. She believed in natural selection, survival of the fittest.

Her paintings were glorious, no doubt about that. Someone had described them as "acts of inspired realism, what God

would have done if he'd used a paintbrush." Certainly they
were technically excellent, no one would dispute that—dense
views into forests, prairies, ponds. Not landscapes—no sky, no
foreground. Some waggish critic had once said she'd made a
career out of seeing the trees for the forest. Mostly, though,
they loved her.

Norris was famous for this larger-than-life realism. Someone had called it her "masculine sense of pageantry," probably
because her paintings were so big, although privately, Lydia
wondered. She associated pageantry with a human presence
and Norris was not big on that. One reviewer cited her "almost
intolerably penetrating insights"—Lydia wasn't sure she'd go
that far—and her gift for "hauntingly expressive light effects,"
which, he'd said, "invite spiraling meditations on the sacred-
ness of all life."

Lydia would never have said it out loud, but sometimes she
wondered if Norris's work wasn't getting a bit . . . automatic.
Weren't the paintings starting to look a little rote, like copies
of photographs? Lydia wondered if anyone would ever call
Norris on it. Lydia wondered, also, if Norris noticed.

Lydia scrolled down to the text of the gallery announcement. It was hard to tell from the purple prose just what the
show was. She'd tried to keep up to date on her reading but this
didn't seem to make sense. The show appeared to have something to do with animals, or their parts—midway through the
e-mail there appeared a fuzzy picture of something identified
as a candied guinea pig heart—but the image of Norris's work
was the same as everything she'd done for the past ten years.

Lydia scanned the announcement. It seemed that Norris had been included in the show because she painted animals' *habitats*. I get it, Lydia thought, a force fit, anything to include her eminence. Still, why would Norris agree? Especially to a group show at an upstart gallery like this? For explanation there was only a picture of the gallerist, a starved-looking girl with a smudgy tattoo, staring combatively into the camera in front of a wall covered with thousands of pushpins arranged in the shape of what appeared to be a lemur.

String of Pearls Gallery in collaboration with Molotovia Cottontail presents Animus Animalia, with works by twelve selected artists including internationally acclaimed painter M. Norris Heaney and String of Pearls director Tiny Fabulous.

This groundbreaking exhibition of meta-narrative features utopian and dystopian projects that balance militant discipline with casual eroticism and always honor animals and their habitats by not overtly depicting them. Ectoplasmic projections of research society will include applied incubation environments conducive to agricultural science and sex rites.

Wine and light snacks will be served.

On closing night, Miss Fabulous will perform a ritual burial of her late pet rabbit, Petaluma.

For more information contact: Tiny Fabulous, Director

Norris was represented in galleries on four continents—why would she involve herself in this?

Then Lydia felt a tiny prick of recognition. Of course—the girl. Lydia remembered now. She was the daughter of a famous art dealer, slumming incognito in Chicago. Tiny Fabulous was her witty nom de pushpin, her arch alias. Norris, as usual, was politicking.

Well, good for her, Lydia thought, for knowing how. Though why send it to her? Unless she was trying to prove something, show Lydia she'd changed, make it seem like she was helping people now.

Determined to get this over with, Lydia clicked on reply and typed *ha!* Then she deleted it. It didn't offer the supportive tone she usually strove for. She hesitated, unable to think of anything else and then, giving up, typed *way to go*. She knew it was exactly the wrong response, laughably, painfully earnest, and that it would confirm Norris's opinion of her as a provincial and a weakling and make her snort, but, unable to think of anything better, Lydia sent it off into the ether.

Norris

Norris was taking a break from the painting she'd been working on all morning, zipping through her e-mail, looking for messages from her dealer and deleting everything else. Probably she shouldn't have forwarded that announcement to Lydia, Norris thought. Lydia would misconstrue. Norris hadn't meant to make fun of the girl, exactly, though she deserved it. She'd just thought it was funny. It *was* funny. Petaluma indeed. It was something they would have laughed about fifteen years ago. Besides, Norris thought, she wanted Lydia to see that she helped young people, too, that she also gave back.

Norris knew that Lydia's friends all thought she was a witch. What they didn't know, Norris thought, was that she was nicer to them, or at least to Lydia, than she was to almost anyone else. She was going to this party, wasn't she? Although, Norris thought, this might have to be the last time.

Lydia: Noon

Lydia was mixing Parmesan cheese into the dumpling batter now. She liked the gummy elastic pull of the dough on the spoon, the way the grit of the cornmeal roughed it up, added resistance. She was adding cheese a little at a time, the way the recipe said you were supposed to, but her mind was elsewhere and she'd lost track of how much she'd added. Perhaps a lot already—cheese was spilling over the edge of the bowl and onto the floor.

Maxine licked it up, which caused Lydia to feel guilty about the house, not cleaning it more thoroughly for the party, and this in turn made her wonder if her inability to thoroughly and energetically clean her house was medically excusable or just a failure of will. Or if—here was her new thought—maybe it really was all in her DNA, as new research suggested. She supposed that's what Norris thought. Maybe she'd been born to be this way, to be someone who didn't mind dog spit and cobwebs and teaching at a community college.

That's what they said now, that character was an outdated notion. Everything was genetically predetermined, they said, right down to what kind of beer you preferred. There was a pair of identical twins, somewhere in Oklahoma, Lydia remembered reading, named Dottie and Lottie, who'd been separated at birth. When they were reunited, at age fifty-eight, they found out they drank the same brand of beer. They'd quit smoking the same brand of cigarettes on exactly the same day. They were both divorced from pharmaceutical salesmen named Russ.

In a way it was comforting, Lydia thought, not to be responsible for these things, for one's bad choices and shortcomings. (She thought again of her question: What do you regret? What if your answer were "*Nothing*"!) But it was a disappointment, too, to think that everything, even the good, was the result of chromosomes, not character or taste. At the very least, she thought, it changed the game. Lydia had grown up thinking everything was a moral choice. *For the wages of sin is death.* That's what she'd been taught—hadn't everyone? *Make your own luck* is what she'd been told. *You've made your own bed, now lie in it.* The idea that faults or even talents were inborn seemed like lazy thinking, or worse. Girls played with dolls because they'd learned to, Lydia had wanted to believe. Now people of science were saying otherwise and it made her nervous. It opened the door for every venal gender, not to mention ethnic, stereotype to rush back in.

However. She had to admit it was freeing, at this stage of life, to consider the possibility that she couldn't have helped any of it, what she'd turned out to be, and to think that Norris couldn't have either, that her success had been predetermined, hardwired. Too freeing, maybe. Her father would have scowled and shook his finger in her face and said, *It lets you off the hook*.

This train was getting her nowhere, Lydia thought, tilting a metal measuring cup full of grated Parmesan cheese over the dough, which was by now too stiff to stir. And what was she doing? Wasn't there already too much food? Who cared if she made Parmesan dumplings? And how much cheese had she already put in? Two cups? Three? Four? She had no idea. She dumped the rest on the floor, for Maxine, who had been standing by, waiting for spillage.

Lydia began to form the dough into little oblongs and set them on a plate. She felt hot breath on her leg and looked down. Maxine was sitting next to her, still as a statue, her intelligent eyes following the movement of Lydia's hands from the bowl to the plate, watching the dough in its progress away from her. She had already forgotten the gift of cheese and now she wanted dough. She was patient, strategic. She knew the formed dumplings on the plate were not for her but she also knew that Lydia was genetically predestined to be a patsy and that her best chance lay in what was left in the bowl, an amount that was steadily decreasing.

Lydia knew that Maxine knew this because Lydia could read her mind, her eyes, her body, the anxious tilt of her shoulders, her tense ears as she calculated what she might get of what was left. Lydia sensed the dog's increasing anxiety as the bowl emptied. Spence called it the torture of the diminishing treat, laughing, as if there were anything funny about torturing Maxine. Lydia would never laugh at her, but she knew Spence was right. The thought of it made her toss the dog a little pinch of dough, as an apology for having even thought of laughing. Maxine caught the dough in her mouth like a first baseman fielding an easy out, then returned to her watchful pose.

When Lydia finished putting all the dumplings on the plate she selected a particularly choice one off the top and fed it to Maxine whole, from her hand. Maxine accepted it softly, gently absorbing it into her mouth in two precise bites, then swallowed neatly and looked back into Lydia's eyes as if she hadn't eaten a thing. *More*, she said, with her eyes. A dusting of cornmeal decorated her graying muzzle.

Lydia set the bowl on the kitchen floor and when Maxine stuck her big blunt nose into it and began to lick, Lydia bent to rest her face in the bristly, oily fur on the top of the dog's head. *We'll get through this, Maxine*, she told her.

~~ellee~~

Celia

Celia was shopping for Lydia's party on her way home from work—wine, goat's cheese, vegetables for crudités, dip. Maybe she'd stop at the bakery, too. A polite argument had erupted online yesterday about who would bring dessert and she'd lost, but who could object to a few cupcakes?

She didn't have to shop now. She could go home and try to nap, shop later, on the way, except that she wouldn't be able to nap, in her house, in the middle of a Saturday, and she didn't want to go home yet. Griffin would have some pregame crisis he'd expect her to sort out for him. And Peter would have some project going that she'd feel obliged to help with. She and Peter spent so much time together now, now that he was working at home. Too much time. Between her job and Peter and Griffin, Celia was never alone. Weekends, especially, were claustrophobic.

She never could have guessed that being happily married would be so stressful, she thought, almost sideswiping the car in the next lane as she made a wide left turn into the liquor store parking lot. She'd had no idea all this togetherness would come to feel so grating. Not that she had any right to complain, she knew. After all, this was what she'd wanted. She couldn't wait to marry Peter. She'd been desperate for a baby, eventually at least, when she'd seen it was almost too late. But as much as she loved her family—she did! she knew she was lucky— spending actual time with them was not as enjoyable as she'd expected.

For one thing, she hadn't expected family life to be so noisy. It hadn't been that way when she and her sister were children. Everything had been quiet then—house rules. Now children were encouraged to speak up, to weigh in on every blessed thing, but not then. She didn't remember her opinion being tolerated, let alone solicited. They'd been told to pipe down. Even when they were good, they'd been sent to bed early, made to take naps. It was hard to imagine now, trying to make a child nap. *You'd be reported to the authorities*, Celia imagined saying, to Lydia. Now, whenever Griffin was home, there was an ongoing soundtrack—complaint, commentary, cell phone conversation, doorbells, television, video games, the staccato of Griffin's basketball being dribbled up and down the hardwood floors.

And always, always some urgent request—a different kind of breakfast cereal, an article of clothing that needed immediate laundering, a ride. Celia looked forward to going to work, just to get some quiet.

Celia walked up and down the aisles of the liquor store, cruising the wines, wondering for the thousandth time if it would have been easier if Griffin had been a girl. *Oh, you wouldn't want that*, people told her. Girls were argumentative, emotional, complicated. They triangulated the marriage, then broke their mothers' hearts. Maybe, Celia thought. But it would have been someone to talk to, at least, and a girl might have taken charge of herself by now. Griffin, at fourteen, still seemed incapable of making a sandwich. Or not incapable, just disinclined. He preferred that Celia do it, and his standards weren't low. He seemed to relish mealtime as much for the opportunity for judgment as for the chance to eat, appearing at the table three times a day looking mournful, expecting to be disappointed. He almost seemed to want the food to be the wrong temperature or too spicy or too bland, Celia thought, so he'd have an excuse to complain, to her, his slightly dimwitted valet.

Celia tossed a bag of chips in her cart. Not that she begrudged him. She didn't! She understood, teenagers were moody. Taking care of him was a pleasure, she reminded herself daily. And on the days she wanted to smack him across the face with the vacuum-packed bag of special deli ham he had to have, she reminded herself that when he was a baby she couldn't get enough of him. Handling his smooth, sweet-smelling, surprisingly springy little body had been a drug, then. The talcum way he smelled, the feel of his velvety skin, those pink creased knees, the orange fuzz on top of his spongy skull—it was easy to forget that taking care of him, then, had drenched her with pleasure that was almost sexual.

One day she'd look back on this and miss it, too, she told herself, steering her cart toward the cashier, bottles clinking.

Still, she'd thought motherhood would be more *fun*,

somehow, more tender. Not so much like being a waitress. Sometimes, on weekends, she had to invent an errand and leave the house, if only for an hour, just to think, to get herself back. Simply driving, alone, was a vacation.

Privacy is a vacation. This insight came to her in the liquor store parking lot, where she sat eating potato chips, with the engine running and the heater on high. She was collecting her thoughts, pretending to be waiting for someone in the store.

She'd bought three bottles of reasonably priced Shiraz but she shouldn't even have spent that much, she knew. Lydia would have plenty, and they were on a budget, and politeness demanded that she bring only one. Still, her little crime felt good. Now she was taking her time before the next stop, enjoying the privacy of the mobile peace chamber that was the interior of her car. She'd been gone from work for only twenty minutes but her mind already had begun to clear and the four words seemed like a revelation that she wanted to hold on to.

Celia reached for one of the index cards she kept in the glove compartment and wrote it down—*privacy is a vacation*—then felt embarrassed and stuffed the card back, between the owner's manual and a badly refolded map of Michigan. She wondered if she should consider how Peter would feel if he found it, if he'd feel hurt or insulted by this apparently hostile sentiment, if he came across it, say, while fumbling for a screwdriver to fix something that probably she had broken.

She began to wonder if maybe she'd written it because she *wanted* him to find it. It might be good for a change for him to

encounter an idea like this, Celia thought. Then she wondered
if that was passive-aggressive, although it was a moot point.
Even if Peter did read the card, which was doubtful, it would
never occur to him that this idea had anything to do with him.
If he thought of it at all he would think of it as an abstract and
arguable premise, one that had appeared there only coinciden-
tally, in her car, in her handwriting, mildly interesting but un-
related to him or his life. Probably, he'd put the card back,
neatly, where he'd found it, and then, noticing the mess she'd
made, refold the map.

Celia stuffed another handful of chips in her mouth. It was
disappointing somehow. How could men be so incurious? Celia wondered. Griffin was the same. Sometimes Celia thought
she should combat it, this lack of interest they had in her inner
life, be more assertive in her communications with them, but
the thought always passed. Besides, she thought, in another
burst of clarity, it was this very lack of curiosity that afforded
her the little privacy she had.

Celia was driving from the strip mall where the liquor store
was to the strip mall where the inexpensive grocery store was.
She loved to drive. She turned on the radio, then turned it up,
loud, to listen to music Peter hated.

She played the oldies station now when she was alone in the
car and didn't care who saw her singing, or crying, even. She
used to be too ashamed. She hadn't allowed herself to listen to
any music in the car, not even classical, which was where Peter
always left the dial, when he even listened to the radio. Usually

he just played CDs he'd checked out of the library. He was deep into Mahler these days. For years Celia had viewed the radio as one more opportunity for self-improvement, studiously following every public radio story as if there'd be a test at the end of the month. She'd listened to oldies stations only when she rented a car, when she went to visit her sister in Cincinnati, and then only when she was alone. If someone had noticed and asked why, she would have said it was only because she couldn't find the local NPR station on the dial.

Now she didn't care. What good had all that self-improvement done, anyway? Now she had the button programmed—Peter must notice, she thought, but they'd never discussed it—and when she was in the mood to sing along, she went right there. "A Groovy Kind of Love." "Big Girls Don't Cry." "Dancing in the Street." "Do You Wanna Dance?" Yes, Celia did want to dance. She couldn't think of the last time she'd danced.

The songs they played weren't even old, at least Celia didn't think so. Last week they'd played Elvis Costello, "(What's So Funny 'Bout) Peace, Love and Understanding?" What indeed? And how could that be? It seemed like only yesterday that Elvis Costello was new. New Wave. Back then, only hip people had heard of him, let alone knew his real name was Declan Mac-Manus. Now he was a sing-along act for drunken businessmen at karaoke pickup bars. How did that happen?

Life is so short, Celia thought. Or rather the part you enjoy is. If she'd had any idea it was going to be over so soon she would have stayed up later.

Snap out of it, she told herself, out loud, almost rolling through a stop sign. She sounded to herself like her eighty-one-year-old mother. But she couldn't snap out of it. Ever since she'd turned fifty, everything made her sad.

Celia made herself do the gratitude litany: She was alive. She had all her body parts. Her car still ran. She had a beautiful healthy child, a more or less loving husband, wonderful friends, health insurance, a partially—at least—restored nineteenth-century farmhouse, even if it was mouse-ridden and cramped and mortgaged to the hilt. And she got to sing along with the Ramones. Celia turned up the volume. *Lo-bot-o-my!* It was all you could hope for, really, and more than most people got. People get old, was all. It was just a fact, and that's if they were lucky. I'm not even old, Celia thought, just pale. Pale people only seemed to age faster.

She was sitting at a stoplight now, looking at herself in the rearview mirror, wondering if she should dye her eyebrows. Someone behind her was honking. Apparently the light had changed to green. She looked past her reflection to see who it was—some dark, handsome young jerk with a shaved head, enthroned in an enormous vehicle better suited for the Australian outback. *Hold your horses*, she said.

Everyone young was so impatient now. And they were all so dark and good-looking, of no discernible ethnicity, with such beautiful, slow-aging skin. Asian Spanish African Semitic, who knew what was in the mix, maybe even some Northern European, though not enough to blunt the beauty. Celia had just read that Jackie Kennedy of all people was descended from a Moor. It just goes to show, she thought. Hybrid vigor was improving the face of the nation.

The brat in the tank was honking again. He was twenty, at most, barely old enough to think, let alone drive. It was a scientific fact that his brain wouldn't gel for another four years. She crept into the intersection and he zoomed past, giving her the finger.

Celia pretended not to notice. She remembered a time when a guy like that would be slowing down, not speeding up. Hanging out the window, flicking his tongue, following her home and parking outside her building to do God knows what out there under his coat in full view of her back window while she hid inside and called Lydia. Celia was not making this up, it had happened. They'd screamed with laughter. Choked. *Gross!* Lydia had said, laughing until she snorted. *Call the cops*, she'd said. But Celia didn't. They both knew it was more complicated than that. She'd liked it, too. Not him, exactly, just the thrill of it, the desire she'd inspired.

Celia had read recently that some researcher—a woman—did an intensive study over many years that involved hooking people's private parts up to sensors and determined, after all that, that women's sexual desire was sparked by men's—and other women's!—desire for them. The much-pondered secret behind what women wanted, the doctor had concluded, was *narcissism*. Women wanted to be adored.

Celia could have told her that. What a disappointment, though, to see it in black and white, in *The New York Times*. To hear it quantified like that by a woman of science. Women had been demystified at last and by one of their own. Celia had felt a little ashamed, reading it, knowing it was true. What a bunch of low-minded, self-absorbed characters we turned out to be, she thought. She'd wanted to talk to someone about it, and not Peter. In the old days she would have called Lydia. Maybe she'd bring it up tonight.

Celia pulled into the strip mall parking lot and waited for a crowd of teenagers to pass in front of her car. All these tightly swathed, sure-footed young people—in high-heeled boots, on this ice!—demoralized her. It wasn't her fault she wasn't still nineteen. Aging is *natural*, she told herself. She didn't even look that bad—did she? Though sometimes she thought if only she'd managed her life differently things wouldn't have turned out this way. She'd be a different kind of middle-aged person, she thought, pale maybe, but one of those *fulfilled* pale people.

She saw them everywhere around town. She saw them at the pharmacy, stocking up on midwinter sunscreen for jaunts to exotic locales or, in the summer, extended stays with their large happy families at handed-down-through-generations lake houses, where they probably worked jigsaw puzzles and played board games while sipping drinks, but not too many. Not a mean drunk among them, or so you'd think, they were so avid to go back and do it again.

Celia was personally acquainted with people like this. She knew for a fact that they cooked together. *Can you imagine?* Celia wanted to say, to Lydia. And they enjoyed it, or claimed to. Everyone had families, everyone cooked, but the Fulfilled People got along. Or so Celia imagined. She imagined if you shook out the maps in *their* glove compartments no index cards that said *privacy is a vacation* would come slipping out to spoil the day.

Celia saw them all over the place, out here in the suburbs, where she was marooned. She couldn't remember seeing them in the city, though she'd been younger then, and single, not so sensitive to this sort of thing. It had been a mistake to move out here, she saw that now. Peter had wanted trees, and she'd liked the idea, too, but these people were all around them here. Celia saw—heard!—them at the library, certain the *Quiet, please* signs didn't apply to them. She saw them at the hardware store buying fancy replacement knobs for their kitchen cabinets, in the specialty aisles at the grocery store, shopping for obscure condiments. *But do we have nori on the boat?* she'd overheard a khaki-clad woman say recently. *Nori!*

Celia, who'd been cruising up and down the parking lot lanes looking for a space, had stopped to wait for another troop of teenagers to pass when she felt the idling car shudder, then shut off. A little red light in the shape of a battery flashed on her dashboard. Now the teenagers were past and cars were backing up behind her. Someone honked. She turned the key, attempting to rev the engine. There was a trick to it, Peter had shown her. Finally the engine turned over.

What relief. The last thing she wanted was to have to call him, and if the car died completely she'd have no way to get to the party. Never mind what it would cost to get the thing towed, then fixed.

Celia wondered if it was only money that made the fulfilled-looking people so smooth-skinned and sure of themselves or if it was more than that, if they were intrinsically different, a different species, maybe, that could mate only with its own kind, and if you or I mated with them (she imagined saying to Lydia) the spawn would be sterile, like the spawn of a horse and a donkey. Maybe it wasn't the result of money at all, Celia thought. Maybe it was the opposite, money was the result of it, whatever it was—self-satisfaction, the belief you looked good in your khakis.

Her car shuddered when she turned it off. Please make it to Lydia's safely tonight, she prayed, to the car. After that, if it didn't start, it wouldn't be the worst thing.

Celia pushed a shopping cart up and down the produce aisle in the big discount grocery store. Even with her coat on, it was cold. And the store was too brightly lit, and the floor was wet and dirty—everyone was tracking in snow, which promptly turned to mud. Celia wheeled her cart past seventeen varieties of cabbage, imagining the beautiful tray of raw vegetables she'd take to Lydia's, trying to decide whether to buy parsley or kale to garnish it and deciding on kale because it was tough and she could rinse if off and cook it later. She wondered whether to splurge on baby carrots or just buy whole big ones and cut them into sticks. She was admiring the purple gloss on the

eggplants and the white sheen on the parsnips and feeling better and better and staring at the lemons in their beautiful pyramid of yellowness when a feeling of pure joy washed over her
and she realized why. Bruce Springsteen was blasting all
around her. They were playing "Glory Days." In the grocery
store!

Now, woven together into meaningful oneness by music,
the cheap vegetables and deeply discounted bruised fruit and
bins of frozen rabbits all seemed different, connected and
beautiful, even in the harsh fluorescent light. Celia knew how
deceptive music could be, full of cheap harmonic tricks that
told you how to feel, taking you somewhere soft and melting
and then dropping you flat when it was over. She knew they
only played it to relax the customers, make them buy more, and
usually she hated it. But this was different. This was Bruce.

Celia looked around at the other shoppers, in their shapeless
winter coats, their grimy scarves trailing in the slosh on the
floor, to see if anyone else was getting the Bruce vibe. But the
playful Fulfilled People, who might have, and who might have
even—a few of them—been moving semi-ironically in time to
the music, were all across town, at the high-priced grocery store.
Here, shopping for bargain lettuce was no laughing matter.

Celia stood still. Around her, elderly, parchment-skinned
women in bright lipstick and high-heeled boots tottered behind shopping carts, trying not to slip on the wet floor while
they pawed for coupons in their cavernous purses. An adrift-
looking man with long greasy hair stared morosely at a frozen
pizza display. No one seemed to notice Bruce.

Here we are, Celia thought, stocking up on our briskets and chicken-drumstick economy packs, our septic-safe toilet paper and fig preserves, while, all around us, Bruce and Clarence— redemptive, raucous, rollicking Bruce and Clarence—were rocking out, offering heaven for the mere price of attention. She searched for someone, anyone, to share it with, but no one, not even the sweet-faced stock boys, would even look at her. What a waste, she thought, feeling vibrant and sexy, at one with the produce. She wished Peter were there, though he wasn't a Springsteen fan.

Suddenly, Celia couldn't wait to get home. For starters, she'd wash her hair. Then, right in front of her, like a sign from God, she saw Peter's absolute favorite—ripe raspberries, shipped all the way from Chile.

She grabbed two pints, then two more, and put them in her cart without even looking at the price. She had a wonderful thought then, almost an epiphany. Maybe, despite appearances, *everyone* here felt this way! Maybe, underneath *all* their tired, badly lit surfaces, their coarse bodily skins and fearful, dull eyes, there dwelled beautiful bright ageless spirits, just like hers.

Celia remembered something she'd heard on public radio. An autistic woman, who'd written a book about animals' emotions, claimed that cats were not as cool as everyone thought. Cats had emotions, too, this woman said, exactly like dogs and people, only you couldn't tell, *because they didn't have eyebrows to express them.*

Now Celia was stunned with the profundity of it. Maybe the convergence of these two facts was the secret of universal love: 1. On the outside they all had dried mucus crusted to the ends of their noses and were wearing sweatpants and unbecoming hats. Soon all their bodies would die, but/and 2. None of them was what he or she appeared to be! Inside they were all wild and alive! Like her! Cats had emotions, too! Then, just as Celia felt drenched with oxytocin, her spirit growing so large it was about to burst out of her body and ascend to a plane of Christ-like empathy and perfect beauty, the song ended.

The glow around the fruit vanished.

Celia stood, disoriented, in mid-fondle, holding an Asian pear. Fluorescent light illuminated brown spots on the pear that matched the ones on her hand. Someone bumped her cart and didn't apologize.

Celia caught a glimpse of her reflection in the dairy case—a tall, pale, middle-aged woman with strange hair and bad posture, wearing an overcoat with a drooping hem, blocking the aisle with a cart that contained four tiny plastic cartons of overpriced raspberries.

She put the raspberries back. They weren't locally grown; Peter would disapprove.

An ugly new song began to play.

~ellee~

The autistic woman was right, Celia thought, later, driving home. Appearances were deceiving, but it went both ways. She wanted to talk to someone about this, though she couldn't imagine whom. She couldn't think of a single person who would listen all the way to the end, and not turn it into a joke (her sister) or end up feeling sorry for her and giving her advice (Lydia). Not Peter, that's for sure, not anymore, maybe not ever.

Though at least he was polite enough to sit quietly while she talked, Celia reminded herself. She appreciated that.

People thought women only wanted to talk about sex and love, and, when they branched out, shoes and children and gluten-free diets. They thought women only thought of their bodies and their tender little hearts. But you could talk with anyone about those things, Celia thought. It was having someone to talk to about these other things that women craved. Or she did, at least.

Celia missed Lydia, though she'd see her tonight.

Lydia: 1:30 P.M.

Lydia was setting out dishes, a mismatched assortment left over from multiple aborted flights into domesticity. She *liked* things that didn't match, she told herself. At least she thought she had. Now that this might be the last party she wondered if her sunny spin on all this old junk had been another accommodation to good-enough that she shouldn't have made. Whatever, tonight nothing would match: the food, the chairs, the plates, the silver—partial sets of which had been handed down through death by various female relatives from a time when anyone who could afford silver had it, and polished it regularly. Her guests wouldn't care, she knew, but maybe she should. Or should have. Too late now.

She didn't set a place for Spence. He was going out for the evening, by agreement, and if he showed up later they'd fit him in. Though he never would fit, really. These women were her friends, not his. Of course they'd sided with her after the divorce, and when he moved back, when he had nowhere else to go, they'd disapproved.

Though most of them had softened since. *As has much else, ha*, she imagined saying to someone, to Celia.

Mostly she didn't mind it, this softening. She liked the blunting effect of aging, the way things that once seemed so important had revealed themselves not to be, or not to be any longer. She liked knowing that so much difficult terrain was behind her, in the rearview mirror and shrinking fast. And she liked these accumulations—things, traditions, people, contrasting layers of friends and routines. She told herself it was just a particular version of her body that she missed, though she knew it was more than that. What she really missed was the feeling she used to have that anything was still possible.

Do not wallow, she told herself.

Again, Lydia reminded herself to let go. Everyone said, forget the bad and move on, simple as that. Even the Bible: ". . . forget those things which are behind, and reach forth unto what is before." Something like that. (Even as a child it had seemed funny to her, being made to memorize a verse about the value of forgetting.) Forgetfulness was the secret to happiness, people said now, in magazine articles.

Lydia wasn't sure about happiness, but she knew that, sometimes, willed amnesia was the most you could pay toward a debt of forgiveness.

She cleared a counter, put out empty bowls and platters for the food her friends would bring. She set out ladles, wide serving spoons, big serrated knives for cutting bread, little blunt knives for spreading soft cheese, tiny pickle forks. It was more than they'd need but she enjoyed handling these things. It felt good to have too much; they always brought more than they promised. She set out a stack of plates, what was left of her wedding china mixed with the chipped remains of her grandmother's Haviland porcelain mixed with garage sale treasures mixed with some cheap terra-cotta she'd bought in Mexico on a whim between relationships when she was yet again redefining herself. Thank God that was all over now, she thought. It was another thing to add to the column of good things about aging.

Impulsively, and because she felt weak, Lydia sat down at the kitchen table and began to make a list on the yellow tablet there. "Good Things About Aging," she wrote at the top of the page. She kept a yellow tablet on most flat surfaces, and now she reminded herself to collect them and put them away before the party, so no one would happen upon an especially embarrassing list, although at this point there was probably little left to shock her friends.

That was a good item number one, she thought, and wrote it down on the first line.

1. There's little left that shocks your friends. They know the worst and don't seem to care (as much as they used to).

On the next line she wrote:

2. Friends (women).

On the line after that she wrote:

3. No more waiting until a relationship ends to
    redefine yourself.

On the following line she wrote:

4. You don't feel (as) embarrassed going to the movies
    alone. No one notices anyway.

On the next line she wrote:

5. Men leave you alone. She crossed it out.

The kitchen timer went off. Lydia abandoned the list and
went to the stove. She had forgotten she was boiling potatoes.
At the last minute she'd decided to make potato salad, though
she couldn't remember why. It was hard to judge how much
food you'd need when you no longer had an appetite.

Jayne

Jayne was driving to Lydia's house past a wasteland of strip malls—Vietnamese nail shops, currency exchanges, Chinese carry-out restaurants, vacuum cleaner repair shops. God, what an ugly neighborhood, she thought. Jayne was actually not going directly to Lydia's house—not yet, anyway—but was on her way to visit Wally, her father-in-law, whose nursing home was roughly in the neighborhood. Usually Douglas went on Sundays but she'd offered to relieve him this week, since she'd be in "the provinces," as they called the neighborhoods far from the lake.

Not that visiting Wally was a chore—Douglas was uncommonly devoted, and Jayne loved Wally, too—but the place smelled bad and the drive was unpleasant, through this dreary nonscape. Jayne preferred not to drive at all and seldom did—trains and cabs were her usual modes of transportation—but unless you transferred to a bus, which Jayne did not consider an option, there was no other way to get there from where they lived, on Lake Shore Drive. Although almost any place, compared to where they lived, was, well, unpleasant. Until his father had gotten too frail, Douglas had picked Wally up every other weekend and brought him back to their lovely home, so he could spend time with Little Walt, his grandson and namesake. He'd stay overnight, in his own room, on the twenty-sixth floor in their three-bedroom condominium, in the stunning building where they lived, where even the guest room had parquet floors and a view of the lake.

"Now look at that," Wally would say, sitting on the couch while they made dinner, gazing out the window at the sailboats. They had one, too, but Wally preferred dry land.

She forgot how nice their place was, sometimes. Coming out here reminded her.

She'd brought Wally the usual bottle, plus some Hershey bars. For years she'd tried to convert him to better chocolate—expensive, dark, Belgian, with and without nuts—but one of the aides finally admitted he gave it away, to her. Hershey bars were what he longed for, she said. They reminded him of the army, K rations—a pleasant memory, apparently. As for the bottle, it was against the rules at the Baptist home, but Wally liked his midday "snort" and everyone liked Wally. As long as he didn't flaunt it, they looked the other way.

Jayne was dying for a smoke. Something about going to see Wally, then her old friends, whom she loved but seldom saw—Elaine, Celia, Lydia especially—put her in the mood. She supposed it was the thought of passing time, reversals of fortune, all that, that unsettled her. Jayne was anything but sentimental, but driving through these neighborhoods made her a little sad. She'd moved on, why hadn't Lydia?

She was thinking maybe when she got to Lydia's she could bum a smoke from her, or from Celia, if one of them had started again. She couldn't keep track of who was on and who was off. Lydia used to smoke like a fiend. She'd made it look so attractive they'd all wanted to do it, all that nervous turning of the head and flicking of the ash, all that picking of tobacco from her lipsticked lip. Men were crazy about it, lurching out of their seats to hold a match close to her mouth while she smiled at them, a little cross-eyed, through the flame. Or maybe men were just crazy about Lydia.

"Don't you think she's attractive?" Jayne had asked Douglas, early on when they were first going out. It wasn't exactly what Jayne had meant. Of course she was. Maybe what she'd meant was *Do you think she's beautiful?* Women discussed it—was she, wasn't she?

Jayne waited to see what Douglas would say.

Thinking like an art historian, Jayne had always thought that what Lydia really was, was *intermittently* beautiful, like some painting in a dim niche in some church somewhere in Italy with one of those timed lights you could drop coins into— beautiful when lit, when attention was paid. Beauty happened to her sometimes, then flickered out. Usually it had to do with men. At the beginning, she'd lit up around Spence.

Jayne had gone to gallery openings with them—Lydia and Spence—in the old days, back when they were a new couple. Afterward they'd go to dinner, though Spence wouldn't eat if he had a gig later. He'd played in a band then. What a pair they'd been, so attractive, well matched, dressed all in black, like the world's cutest, hippest salt and pepper shakers. He'd been so handsome in those days—those chiseled features, his musician's hands. They'd just fit, both of them with that jet-black hair. It wasn't until they broke up that Jayne found out Lydia's true color was medium brown. Jayne remembered the night they wore matching velvet coats.

Cute as they were, they'd brought out the worst in each other, too, Jayne thought. She supposed the marriage was doomed, really. Though when she saw how they both kept repeating versions of it after, with other less suitable partners, she wondered if they shouldn't have just stayed together and fought it out.

"Very attractive," Douglas said, finally. "But not my type."

"Meaning?" Jayne said.

He'd put his hands on her. "I like this."

"No, really." Jayne knew he did. And she was glad, but she also knew there was more to it than breast size.

He'd shrugged, let go. "She's one of those, you know. *Women*." He'd flapped his big hands.

"Elucidate," she'd said, pinning him down with a pillow. They'd been in bed.

"You know," he said. "Addicted to the chase. Tragic. I don't know." He wouldn't elaborate.

Jayne supposed Lydia had been flirting with him. She knew what he meant, though. He meant like his ex. Douglas had already been through one divorce when they got together—and a hellacious child custody battle—and he didn't want any more of that. They'd both been ready to settle down. Work and raising Little Walt, his boy, part-time, were demanding enough, they both felt.

Over time she'd come to know how much he liked knowing she wasn't going to leave.

She also knew how much he would have hated knowing she was going to smoke tonight. Which she was, she'd decided. Though if no one else was, she'd be out of luck. She should stop and buy a pack now, she thought, just to be safe. She could pull over at that bowling alley, right now. It looked like the sort of place that still had a machine.

She'd always preferred buying cigarettes from a machine. She liked the privacy of it, in a back hallway, usually, in some urine-stinking alcove near the men's room where you could stand alone and think about what you were about to do. *Think about what you've done*, the teachers used to say when they'd done something bad. She liked the clandestine feeling, that guilty anticipation, then the sound, the good soft thump when the surprisingly hefty little pack dropped into the gutter at the bottom. The sound of relief, Jayne thought. You'd pull that big silver knob—there'd always be some resistance, that last second when you had a chance to change your mind—and then it would give, like a gear, and out they'd drop, attainable bliss, into the smooth silver groove. Then came the ritual opening, the thrilling crinkle of staticky cellophane, the folding back of the cardboard lid, the tearing of the foil and then, ah. That sweet burst of smell. Tobacco.

Douglas, who'd grown up near a reservation in Wisconsin and still had relatives there, though he didn't want people to know that, once told her the Oshkosh considered tobacco sacred. It was the opposite around here—strictly déclassé. They were converting cigarette machines into art vending machines now. You put in a token and out came a little origami sculpture instead. There was one at the Cultural Center. Just the sight of it made Jayne want to light up.

She wouldn't be thinking this way if someone hadn't offered her a cigarette at the park this morning. She could still smell it on her fingers. She'd put the butt in her coat pocket and rubbed it now and then, then sniffed her fingertips. Now, alone in the car on her way to the Baptist home, she wanted another.

It had been a sin of opportunity, really, not one of volition. On weekends she walked Horatio to the park in the morning, and if no one was there she unclipped his leash and let him run. This morning he'd galloped ahead, crashing through the deep snow, checking for new smells. They were all the way across the field when he'd stopped and turned, then raced back to the entrance. Someone, thickly bundled in purple, approached. Jayne knew he hoped for another dog. She watched him go, feeling guilty. She and Douglas had left him alone while they worked long hours. Now he was old, still trying to make up for a puppyhood he'd never had.

Jayne trudged back through the snow, hoping the woman didn't have some tiny dog inside her coat that she couldn't set down for fear of Horatio, who only looked fierce.

. . .

Jayne smelled the cigarette before she saw it. The woman had taken off one of her big mittens and was wearing a thin leather glove on her smoking hand. She blew a mouthful of smoke and cold white air out of her pink lipsticked mouth. "Sorry," she said, turning her head and blowing toward the street. Jayne smiled to show she didn't mind. "Actually, I like it," Jayne said. "I used to love to smoke." She wanted the woman to know she didn't disapprove.

The woman nodded. "No one knows I do this." She raised her chin to blow more smoke. "Can't, at home. Kids." She rolled her eyes.

Jayne nodded. The woman was holding the cigarette behind her back. "Sorry," she said again.

"Really," Jayne said. "Don't apologize. I love the smell. I miss it."

"You want one?" the woman said.

The question came as a small shock. Did she? She hadn't thought so, not especially, though it did smell divine. Except for the occasional communal lapse at a party, Jayne refrained, for Douglas's sake. Douglas's sister had died of lung cancer. He thought it was repulsive, a deal breaker, he'd called it. Besides, she'd never been a morning smoker. Her favorite time had been at night, after dinner, preferably with a glass of wine, sitting outside on her balcony in the summer, in that funky apartment she'd loved, flicking ashes over the railing. Or in a restaurant, with a man, pre-Douglas. What a pleasure that had been, after dinner in some outdoor place, on a summer evening just as the day began to cool, at a table on the street, watching the late commuters hustle past, the hungry-looking men in suits scanning women's faces for an instant of illicit eye contact. Funny to think that such a simple pleasure was illegal now.

The woman waited for Jayne's answer, tilting the pack in her direction, a pleasantly neutral expression on her face. She shook the pack slightly. One cigarette slid invitingly out.

Jayne felt touched, by the graciousness of the gesture. Just right, friendly but not pushy. Nicely anonymous. No names had been exchanged. If interrogated later, neither could say who the other was. The woman continued to hold the pack tilted toward Jayne, not looking at it.

"I never buy them," the woman was saying. "I found these." She tapped her cigarette once, as if in punctuation, and the ash fell off in the snow. "In the break room, at work."

What little Jayne could see of the woman, between her hat and her scarf—a stripe of glossy brown forehead, flashing brown eyes, pink lipstick—smiled. Stuck to one of her straight white teeth was a single fleck of tobacco. She took another deep, thoughtful drag. "They're not even my brand," she said, exhaling.

"They're mine," Jayne said.

The woman crinkled her eyes at that. Like the devil, Jayne thought. Debonair. As if she already knew they were Jayne's brand, and had conjured them, for her pleasure. This is how these things start, Jayne knew. Half of temptation was social obligation. At this point it seemed rude not to accept.

The woman shook the pack again as if reading Jayne's thoughts.

"Thanks," Jayne said.

Jayne placed the cool papery cylinder between her dry lips, the fruity smell twice as sharp in the cold. Even unlit it was delicious. The woman clicked her lighter and a flame sprang up close to Jayne's face.

She inhaled cold and hot at the same time, feeling dizzy as the familiar poison spread. The women smiled at each other. Jayne had forgotten what a good, clubbish feeling this was, this sisterhood of nicotine.

They smoked in silence for a minute, focused on the pleasure.

"My husband doesn't know I smoke," the woman said, holding her cigarette up and addressing it as if it were a small person who ought to be included in the conversation. Jayne nodded.

"He won't smell it?" she said. The woman made a smiling frown and shook her head. Then she patted Horatio, tossed her lipstick-stained butt into the snow, and turned back in the direction she'd come.

"Have a nice day," she said, over her shoulder.

When Jayne got home she brushed her teeth. Now she pulled into the bowling alley parking lot.

Lydia: 3:00 P.M.

Lydia went upstairs, to her office, to get a fresh yellow tablet. She wanted to make a list of everything left to do, but as soon as she entered the room, its lulling chaos, the piles of out-of-order personal history, surrounded and sedated her. She sat down—just a minute's rest, she thought—and looked at the little patch of desktop she'd cleared a few days earlier. The neat spot comprised only a few hundred square inches but seemed huge, an oasis of order amid the palimpsest of creative dead ends heaped around it.

Lydia merely had to reach her arms in any direction and stir paper to uncover years' worth of false starts—half-read clippings, sketches for paintings, course proposals, notes for unfinished essays. Beneath that was other, harder-to-look-at stuff—letters, postcards, the dreaded and ever-present mementoes. What was one supposed to do with these things? The letters, especially, gave off residual sparks of the emotions they'd first aroused, and not only warmth. Guilt sometimes, or envy. Or that old standby, regret.

She'd been cleaning, or trying to, but she'd only made things worse. Every object, every slip of paper, called up a world of possibility within a world of too many possibilities. She didn't know what to do with any of it so she set the paper down and picked up another. Not a single scrap was meaningless. Or rather, not a single scrap was any more meaningless than any other. She couldn't throw out any of it or, if she did, she might as well throw it all out. What to do with a charmingly designed teabag wrapper from a trip to Wales, that had traveled back to Chicago in her blue jeans pocket and showed up when she went to do the wash? She'd stashed it in a drawer; now, enhanced by time, it reminded her of when she and Spence were happy. Or a ticket stub from a pleasant evening of outdoor music, or a subway map for a city she hadn't been to in eleven years, or a stone from a beach in Wisconsin? She had friends who would put it all in labeled drawers, but they were a different sort of person than she was. To Lydia, that was tantamount to burial.

Burial. The thought brought her back to the present, the looming possibility that had made her think it was time to put things in order in the first place. She needed to organize her effects for those who would take over when she was gone, if such a thing happened, lest they throw it all away. Which she supposed is what would happen anyway. Probably the most decent thing to do would be to save them the trouble and throw it out herself, now, she thought. The rudeness of not doing so, of leaving someone else to confront this mess, made her feel embarrassed, but the thought that there were things here that someone might actually want had delayed the process.

If only she were more decisive, like Elaine, Lydia thought, recalling the ceremonial pitching of the blue books.

Lydia plucked a rubber-banded stack of years-old, unanswered Christmas cards from a pile and dropped it—bravely, decisively—into the wastebasket. There, that wasn't so hard, she thought. She had been meaning to sort her things for some time now, years, honestly. But while she waffled, things kept piling up. Unread books, old letters, birthday cards. Recipes, to-do lists, photos of friends with their children or their beloved animals, photos of Maxine. It was all a depressing reminder of the passage of time, not to mention a reminder of her inability to place one thing in importance over another, a trait that had gotten her where she was today, she knew.

Lydia opened a drawer. Here, under a little packet of rubber bands, was a valentine from her mother, dead for thirteen years. She couldn't throw it out now. Drawings, drifts of them, sat on the floor gathering dust. A cliché for a reason, she thought—it was literally true. Her drawings, which used to excite her, had gathered actual dust and made her sneeze.

Just last week she'd forced herself to start to sift through them. She'd spent Sunday afternoon with a pile on her lap and another pile on her drawing table, sorting them into more piles—good, bad, and indifferent—but there were so many other ways to see them that soon she had eight piles, then eleven, each a different category. Soon they covered the floor and she'd had to set little notes on each pile with the name of the category written across it—*Store. Recycle. More interesting sewn together with colored thread? Better as poems? Shred!* She stopped altogether when she came to her Irreducible Truths.

She'd worked on them for the better part of a year, every morning at dawn, before she walked Maxine. For forty-five minutes a day, she'd written over and over on a single dated page. She'd set a kitchen timer and started at the top and when she got to the bottom she went back to the top and continued, until the page was torn and illegible and the time was up. At first she just wrote as if she were keeping an ordinary journal. The genius in that was that if Spence found it he wouldn't be able to read it. But that soon came to feel meaningless, not only because the overwriting obliterated the text but in the way that all journals do, with their forced philosophy and endless fretting. Lydia wanted to move beyond that. She began to think of the writing as a meditation, written chanting. That's when she came up with the idea of irreducible truths—writing one true thing over and over.

After that, every day, she wrote a new irreducible truth for a set amount of time. She wrote until her hand hurt and the words were illegible, until the pen tore through the paper. As she wrote she counted. Sometimes she wrote the Lord's Prayer, or a verse from the Bible, or a line from a poem, or just something she thought was true. On the back of each dated page, written lightly in pencil, she recorded that day's truth and the number of times she'd written it. *Animals are perfect. 78X. Be here now. 117X. In the beginning was the word and the word was with God and the word was God. 153X.* Now she had piles of what must be hundreds of them, all looking like gibberish. She'd imagined she was working toward a show, to which she planned to invite Norris, or at least toward enlightenment, but she'd had to stop. Her hand started to cramp.

Now it just looked crazy. And what did any of it amount to anyway, Lydia thought, looking around at her piles of dusty paper. Why had she wasted her time? What had once seemed meaningful was no longer. Lydia gathered up her Irreducible Truths and dumped them in the trash.

Elaine: Mid-Afternoon

Elaine was cleaning the kitchen, as she did every Saturday afternoon. *When in doubt, throw it out* was her policy.

She knew exactly how the party would go. Sometime between the second and third glass of wine someone would want to talk about politics. Then they'd start to argue. They, not Elaine but the others, felt it was important to be *passionate*. What a load, she thought, tossing that day's newspaper into the recycling bin without even taking it out of its plastic sleeve.

The one item Elaine most wanted to throw out, she couldn't. She averted her eyes from the glossy real estate brochure, the one for the Florida retirement "village" where her sister lived and into which she was trying to install Elaine. Now that their mother was dead, her sister pointed out, there was no reason for Elaine to stay in Chicago. Elaine didn't know how to tell her sister that even if she had wanted to leave her whole life behind to move into some sweltering swamp of a country club where she was expected to learn how to play cards, which she most certainly did not want, that she couldn't. She couldn't move to a place where they didn't allow pets. Someday she might want another dog. Besides, how could she move away from here and leave their mother alone in that snow-covered cemetery? But Elaine couldn't throw the brochure out until she'd composed some kind of placating reply.

Paradise, it said on the cover, in thick, loopy orange type that Elaine knew was intended to subliminally suggest a sunset. Sunset Village. The note her sister had stuck to it said "three still left with causeway views!" Elaine slipped the glossy thing out of sight, between the well-thumbed pages of her old paperback copy of *Middlemarch*, which she'd been rereading at breakfast, and went back to tidying up.

It happened every year, these political arguments. That's when she used to volunteer to walk the dogs, though she didn't dare now, in her state, on this ice. Maybe tonight she'd take the opportunity to load the dishwasher instead. The running water should drown them out nicely.

She didn't want to hear about it, their politics. Didn't believe in it anymore. She'd come to think of it as a man sham—that's what she called it in her imagined conversations with her mother. *It's no choice at all, Mom*, she imagined saying to her. *It's just a bunch of suited-up men of the fortunate class, flapping their silk neckties at each other.*

Elaine had supported Hillary, when she ran in the primaries, in 2008, though her younger friends had laughed at her. Gender was a red herring, they'd told her. Hillary would be more of the same. Elaine wasn't so sure. At least she would have liked the chance to find out.

. . .

Fact was, all that interested Elaine anymore was women.

She couldn't remember when it started. Without even noticing, she'd let her friendships with men lapse—or maybe the
men had. She'd never married. As for romance, she hadn't been
on a date in eighteen years. Even in politics, it was only women
that interested her now and not even the politicians, usually,
that bunch of pantsuits. She was more interested in watching the dragged-along wives, with their sly lipsticked smiles.
She wondered what they were thinking, standing there looking
so pretty and so stifled. She suspected them of the same sub-
versive thoughts she would have been having, though she never
would have been there in the first place. Not nearly pretty
enough.

Elaine imagined saying this to her mother, who wouldn't
disagree, but would take a big slurp of coffee and nod. Facts
were facts as far as she was concerned. She was just as happy
Elaine hadn't been a hit with the boys. *Look where pretty got her*,
she'd said once, to Elaine, pointing out some sad-faced former
homecoming queen at the grocery store, pushing a cartful of
squalling kids.

None of the others who'd be there tonight had any patience
for this sort of thinking, Elaine knew. *That's not politics, that's
gossip*, Jayne would say, whenever Elaine wondered about the
wives. Elaine didn't care, though sometimes even she wondered why she was so interested, never having been a wife herself. She liked to read about women bureaucrats, too, the

anonymous workers who once in a blue moon showed up in the news, looking like opossums when you turned on the porch light. It was the sort of job that would have suited her, Elaine thought, if her father hadn't railroaded her into becoming a teacher. She'd ended up an English teacher, of all things, as if she cared whether the great unwashed ever learned how to punctuate a sentence. Truly, she didn't.

She would have liked to work for the government, she thought. She would have worn a navy blue suit and a white blouse every single day. Brooksley Born—now there was an interesting woman. If she'd been a man they might have listened to her; there might not have been a mortgage crisis. Though if there hadn't been, Elaine thought, she wouldn't have an excuse to not move to Florida. As it was, she could always claim she couldn't move until she sold her condo.

Of course, the one who interested Elaine most was Hillary.

But she is *a suit*, everyone had yelled, back when Elaine still bothered to voice an opinion.

Elaine didn't care. She'd voted for her. She'd even, in her one and only moment of political activism, campaigned for her. True, she'd been younger then. Walking door-to-door wasn't the ordeal it would become, even two years later. At the very least, she'd thought, trudging along with her briefcase full of pamphlets, she was burning calories. But it had been a commitment, too, making enemies like that. People had slammed doors. The difference between doing it and not doing it was everything, she'd realized, then. It changed you, and when you lost, that changed you again. She was too old to lose now. She didn't recover, didn't forgive. And now she didn't care.

She kept her mouth shut about all that now. Everyone under a certain age looked at you sideways if you admitted you'd voted for Hillary, young women especially, like Norris. They thought there was something off about you, like tainted milk, that you were past your expiration date.

What Elaine didn't tell anyone was that she'd cried the night Hillary suspended her campaign. Silly, she thought—some old bag in bed all alone, crying over an election. She'd surprised herself. Who cried anymore about anything, at this age? Why bother? It only made things worse.

That night, Elaine dreamed about her mother. They'd been stranded together at O'Hare. Their plane couldn't take off. Elaine had woken up in a sweat thinking, *We can't get off the ground*, then felt relief—it was just a dream—and fell back to sleep. But there she was again, back in the airport, and there was her mother, still waiting for her on the other side of sleep, in one those plastic airport chairs with her little zippered fake leather suitcase on her lap and her knee-high stockings drooping around her ankles, trusting Elaine to get her on a plane and off the ground. But Elaine couldn't do it. It made her sick to think of all the ways she'd failed her mother.

⁓ℓℓℓℓ⁓

Hillary had grown up in a Republican suburb north of Chicago, not that far from Evanston, where Elaine lived now. Elaine had driven out of her way, more than once, to pass the house, back when it looked like Hil could win. Once she'd parked outside. She'd taken a road map out of the glove compartment and sat across the street with the map in her lap, like she was lost, in case she looked suspicious, if that were even possible in a Subaru. She'd sat there under the special street sign that said Rodham Corner—posted up high so it wouldn't get stolen—trying to imagine the young Hillary carrying her schoolbooks up the front steps. After a while she'd driven around the block, twice, hoping for a glimpse into the backyard, but the yard was fenced and there wasn't much to see. She'd driven into the little suburban downtown, then parked her car and took a walk.

Not much there, either, just the usual banks and chain restaurants, boutiques selling expensive, useless stuff. Most of the shops looked new, like they wouldn't have been there when Hillary was. Elaine peeked in the window of the oldest-looking place she could find, a coffee shop connected to an old movie theater. She wasn't hungry exactly, but she wanted something, some excuse to stay and soak up whatever Hillary essence she could. Hillaressence.

The place was empty, but there it was, the Sign of Hillary, behind the cash register—a framed photograph of her with Barbara Walters, both of them coiffed and beaming, in pantsuits, posing with the restaurant staff. There'd been a television interview there, according to a plaque posted beneath the photo.

Elaine had taken a seat in a cracked vinyl booth by the window, in view of the photo, and waited. After a while a man came out of the kitchen and looked at her, then went back into the kitchen. Then a girl came out and walked to her table and set a greasy water glass down in front of her and handed her a huge plastic menu.

Elaine had ordered the Hillary Burger. The thing that made it different from a regular burger, according to the menu, was the topping—a little mound of chopped green olives. *I wouldn't call it tapenade*, Elaine imagined saying to her mother, imagining that she was sitting across from her. Her mother would have grunted and scraped the olives off.

The burger was all right, a little dry. Elaine thought they should have made more of an effort, a special sauce, maybe, tangy mayonnaise at least. According to a blurb in the menu the place had been Hillary's "favorite haunt" when she was a girl, and the olive burger her "favorite treat." She liked to go there after a double feature at the movie house next door, the menu said. It seemed unlikely to Elaine, Hillary wasting her time that way, but you never knew.

Elaine ate three-quarters of her Hillary Burger and more French fries than she'd intended, waiting for her coffee, which never came. Finally she put money on the table—even the cashier had disappeared—and left for the movie theater next door, looking for something more.

The place had once been fancy, she could tell. It had a newly restored Art Deco marquee, a jewel box ticket booth. Inside the booth a girl with purple hair and an eyebrow ring sat talking on a cell phone. Elaine glanced at her. When the girl didn't respond, Elaine opened the big heavy door.

Not much happening there at 4:30 on a Tuesday afternoon. The restoration project that had spiffed up the marquee hadn't yet made it to the overlit lobby. High-wattage bulbs illuminated dirty stucco and ancient stained carpeting. Elaine tried to imagine the teenaged Hillary, standing on that very carpeting, in line at the refreshment counter, waiting to buy an Orange Crush and a box of Jordan almonds, or Raisinets maybe. She'd be wearing an expectant expression and a turquoise plaid A-line skirt, snug over her girdle.

Elaine felt sure on this point, that she'd worn one. Everyone had. Hillary was younger than Elaine, right at the cusp, at the end of the age of the girdle, but in those days, it's what girls still did, wore girdles, so their undulant bottoms wouldn't roll around and excite the boys. Elaine's mother had explained it to her. At least, nice girls wore them, Elaine thought, girls like her and Hillary.

Elaine opened another door, peeked into the dark, empty theater. It smelled of sweat and salt and disappointment, also that fattening butter-like concoction they put on popcorn. She couldn't picture Hillary sitting there any better than she could see her eating an olive burger next door. When she imagined Hillary at fourteen or fifteen, she saw her already dazed with optimism and ambition, eager to move on, her sense of destiny propelling her away from places like this, telling her to stay out of the dark, to not get blindsided by fantasy and false dreams, the way other girls did. *You go, girl*, Elaine telegraphed to her, back through time. Though she felt a little envious, too, wishing she'd been even half that driven.

. . .

The place was empty except for a couple of kids in greasy poly-ester uniforms getting ready for the first show—vacuuming, making popcorn. Elaine walked around, trying to look like she had some business there. She read the movie posters in the lobby—the coming attraction was something called *He's Not That Into You*. Elaine recognized the title, taken from a how-to book for women.

The book, she happened to know, told women how to dis-tinguish between men who were truly interested in their unique and lovely souls and men who weren't, who only wanted sex, if that. Elaine imagined explaining this to her mother, making it sound like she'd only heard about it, maybe in a brief synopsis on the radio, on the same AM show her mother had listened to every morning of her adult life. *Apparently the book was so popular they made it into a romantic comedy*, she pictured herself saying. In reply, she imagined her mother making a little barfing sound, for laughs.

Actually, although Elaine never would have admitted it, she'd sped-read the book in a bookstore, and it confirmed what she already knew. Every man she'd ever considered herself close to, including her high school prom date, her amorous history professor, and her two erstwhile fiancés, had not been that into her, as the common parlance went.

The gist of the book, she explained to her mother, was that you were supposed to move on from anyone who was not that into you and keep moving until you met that inevitable some-one who was, deeply. In other words, you were supposed to wait for your prince. She imagined her mother's response to this idea would be to pat her dry hand with her own even dryer one.

Elaine found this conversation deeply satisfying, even if it was one-sided. It was especially bolstering on the day of her Hillary pilgrimage, her Hillgrimage, as she thought of it. She even allowed herself to imagine Hillary there with them, all three of them laughing together over the movie poster and eating freshly popped popcorn with real butter.

I love your mom! Hillary would say, smiling and showing her teeth, giving her mother a little shoulder squeeze. It would be just the right kind of hug—respectful, not too chummy.

That night Elaine dreamed she took her mother to the movies. They arrived late and sat down in the dark next to Hillary, and when the movie started Hillary leaned over to them and said, in a loud whisper, "He's not that into . . ." but the pronoun was garbled and then Elaine woke up.

~~~~

As she got older Elaine had grown more interested in this sort of thing—presidential history, that is, first ladies. When the Lincoln Museum opened in Springfield a few years earlier, she'd talked Maura into going with her to the opening. It was a four-hour drive but it had seemed important, both to go and to take Maura. To break up the drive, they'd stopped at Steak and Shake, for lunch. The milkshakes there were excellent.

Of course, the museum was inspirational; everything about

Lincoln was. He'd freed the slaves. There was really no single thing in American history better than that, and why didn't matter. But what Elaine could not help thinking about on the drive back, pretending to sleep as Maura drove, was the hall of Mary Lincoln's dresses.

They'd seemed embarrassingly out of place, condescending somehow, as if the curator had been asked to find something good about the wife, too, and this was the best he could do. In the midst of all that somber history—the underground railroad, the gruesome facts of the Civil War, the re-creation of the death scene of eleven-year-old Willie—there was that roomful of big, hoop-skirted dresses. Posted text described how hurt Mary Lincoln felt when Washington society snubbed her, despite her pretty dresses, which they found provincial.

On the drive home Elaine couldn't stop thinking about it—Mary Lincoln, sidelined then snubbed, her husband murdered in front of her, three of her four children dead, then committed to a mental hospital by her only surviving son. She was crazy, people said. She had hallucinations. Others claimed it was migraine headaches that made her act that way. Elaine had read that some historian had posthumously diagnosed her with narcissism. Narcissism!

At her lowest, she'd tried to kill herself but eventually managed to get out of the asylum, that cagey gal, after only four months. Her sister ended up with her. As sisters often did if you weren't careful, Elaine thought, picturing herself her sister's captive at Sunset Village. Still, what a life. Elaine had nothing against Abe—quite the contrary—but she guessed that part of Mary Lincoln's problem was being married to a great man.

She hoped Maura had taken note.

Bellevue Place, the sanitarium where they'd put her, was in Batavia, Illinois, in the Fox River Valley, not so far from Hillary's childhood home. Elaine remembered going there with her parents once, on a Sunday drive, some fifty years before. They'd taken a picnic, spread a blanket on the riverbank, and eaten ham salad sandwiches out of a basket. For dessert they'd split a Hershey bar three ways, just the three of them—who knows where her sister was that day. Later they'd rented a rowboat.

The memory made Elaine ache with nostalgia and regret. She remembered the day clearly. Frankly, she'd been a pill. She remembered complaining about the flies and refusing to eat her mother's potato salad because she'd put mustard in it. *That was fun, Mom*, she wanted to say, now. *I loved that ham salad you used to get at Gerhardt's.*

After the trip to the Lincoln Museum, Elaine looked up Batavia on a map and the next Sunday she and Maura drove there to see the building Mary Lincoln had lived in. (Maura had wanted to go the movies; Elaine had had to talk her into it.) The place was an apartment house now, surprisingly pretty. They'd bought hamburgers at Culver's on the way into town and parked across the street, ate in the car. If anyone asked what they were doing, Elaine planned to tell them they were researching a book on first ladies and that the chapter on Mary Todd Lincoln was going to be called "From the White House to the Nut House," but no one asked or even seemed to notice they were there.

Elaine was sweeping the kitchen floor, imagining her mother sitting at the table, dumping sugar into her coffee. *What if there were two presidents?* she'd say to her. *A woman president and a man president, and to get anything done they'd have to agree?*

Her mother stirred and nodded.

Certainly it would slow things down. Elaine understood that. But it might be better in the long run, for women at least. And they'd have to wear robes, she thought, so there'd be no sniping about clothes and figures.

She wouldn't bring it up tonight, though. People always laughed at her ideas. They thought she was kidding.

Lydia: 4:15 P.M.

Lydia took Maxine for a walk around the block. Neither of them wanted to go far, in this cold. The walk was a preparty routine, started when the dog was young and rambunctious, to settle her. Now it was to energize her, though she just looked exhausted. A neighbor they'd met on the street the other day had said, *Poor Maxine, she's getting so feeble. How old is she?* Lydia had wanted to kick the woman. People had no idea how much that hurt. Lydia wanted them to see how beautiful she was, how dignified, wanted them to remark that she was aging gracefully.

When they got back, Maxine plodded up the stairs behind Lydia, her legs shaking a little at each step. The dog sprawled on the floor while Lydia checked her e-mail, for the seventeenth time that day. Now Celia and Maura were discussing whether they needed more bread. Celia was bringing Peter's bread and thought Maura's offer of store-bought bread was superfluous. Celia also reported that Peter had made chutney and said she'd bring that, too, if there was anything to put it on. Elaine said to remind her what chutney was and Maura, who actually liked chutney and thought it would be good on the ham but was offended that her offer of bread had been rebuffed, said she didn't care for it. Betsy said chutney might be good on Ted's meatballs, and Jayne replied to the earlier e-mail about ice. Norris was absent from the conversation. She was probably on the road by now, Lydia thought.

Lydia clicked out of her e-mail and checked the news. The world was falling apart, as usual. Fat people were being barred from adopting Chinese orphans. Heroin was cheaper than beer. Tomatoes had lost their flavor. Signs of cannibalism had been discovered in a basement in Detroit.

She was about to log out when a headline caught her eye: *Are You Depressed or Just Disappointed?*

Good question, she thought. She was tempted to read further, but why bother? The headline said it all.

Lydia: The Letters

Lydia thought she would have heard from the doctor by now. He'd said he'd call as soon as he knew something, maybe Friday, but certainly by Saturday afternoon. Lydia was waiting to revise the letters, depending on what he said. She hoped she'd left enough time, though what she really hoped was that she could throw them out.

She supposed now that's why she hadn't bought fancy stationery and matching envelopes, made from pulpy paper flecked with rose petals and butterfly wings. Preparing that well would have made it too real. All she had was cheap printer paper and #10 business envelopes. Not a very splashy way to say good-bye, she thought, but it would have to do.

She still needed to double-check to be sure each letter was in the right envelope. There would be a plot twist, she thought. She could imagine the headline now—*Wrong Letter Changes Woman's Life*. Not that there were any secrets exactly, but each letter was different.

She'd written them last week but they needed revision. Not the plan, just the language.

The first part was the same to everyone.

Dear (insert friend's name here),

As the great Warren Zevon, who died at fifty-six, once observed, life'll kill ya.

I guess we all knew that but unfortunately my time has come sooner than I expected. After fifty-four years of more or less perfect health and a few months of troubling symptoms, the details of which I won't impose even on you, my tolerant and sympathetic friends, I finally went to see a doctor and was informed that I am in the final stage of pancreatic cancer, which either has or has not spread—update on that to follow. Hence my newly sleek silhouette. Unless he's wrong, or a cure is discovered in the next few weeks, I'm probably a goner, which makes this the last Bleak Midwinter Bash I'll throw. I hope someone carries on the tradition. It's a good time of year for a party.

That being said, I want to take the opportunity to clear up a few questions, ask a few favors, and disperse some things.

First, I want to tell you all that your friendship has been the great boon of what I thought was my midlife. I'd like to express my love and gratitude to each of you. I know I wasn't always great at being close. I've often been preoccupied, with men, frankly. That may have been a mistake and I know

some of you agree. But that's the point. That's why
you all have meant so much to me. You've allowed
me to be your friend on my own awkward terms.
Enough sentiment.

Second, I'd like to share with you my recipe for
chicken stew, the one I serve every year, which, over
the years, most of you (not Norris) have said you
wanted. I didn't mean to be mysterious. I never gave
it out because I never wrote it down because it
changes every year because I never got it right. I
thought I'd wait and write it down when I perfected
it, but it looks like I won't get the chance. So I'm
enclosing that, and I'll leave it to you to figure out
what it lacks. The so-called secret ingredient is not
okra as many of you thought although that's in
there and does ooze that viscousy goop. The
ingredient that supplies the creamy binder everyone
wondered about is simply mashed potatoes, gobs of
them, made with as much cream and butter as you
please. Now you know. Carbophobes,
beware.

The next thing I want to tell you is that, unlike
Edith Piaf and her ilk, the ones either valiant or
brazen enough to claim they have no regrets, I do.
I have regrets aplenty. Some are best left
unspoken—trust me—but others I'd like to get off
my still ample chest, which, I might note, is—
are?—still hanging in there, the last vestige of my

formerly voluptuous self. Maybe you will figure out
a way to avoid making the same mistakes. If not,
c'est la vie, as the little sparrow would have said.

I will attempt to be transparent, a new thing for
me. I see now that I've led my life too privately and
now I want things to be known. You might even
say that I want to be known. Please indulge me as I
plan to ramble.

It seems to me, now that I'm contemplating
regret, that there are two kinds—regret for things
we did and wish we hadn't and regret for things we
didn't do and wish we had. Had done. Would have
done. Did do. I'm tangled in tenses already—it
proves how slippery time can be. Or is. Which, I
guess, is the point of regret. Was it Nabokov who
said the prison of time is a spiral? Or did he say the
spiral of time is a prison?

Lydia wondered if she should stop and look it up but decided
not to. She liked not knowing.

Now that I'm dying, I find myself dwelling on
these things, on what I did and didn't do, and
wondering which is worse.

I used to think it was worse to regret something
you'd done—something stupid, something cruel
or destructive—but I'm beginning to think
the opposite. I'm beginning to think that leaving

something good undone is worse than
doing something bad. Something regrettable is
still something, an act, a scrap of energetic
material that can be sewn into something else, an
action the momentum of which can be harnessed
and redirected. Reversed, possibly, in some kind of
existential judo. A thing not done is nothing, no
thing at all.

Lydia wondered if the bit about judo was too much but decided to leave it in.

She set the paper down. If this weren't a letter but a lecture,
Lydia thought, say, for Art 101, that wonderful old chestnut of
an art appreciation course she used to teach, she would now
click on a slide of an Ivan Albright painting, the one of the
funeral wreath hanging on a door. She'd tell them the title and
they'd write it down: *That Which I Should Have Done I Did Not
Do (The Door)*. Date: 1941. Style: Magic realism—Gothic, scary,
obsessively detailed, theatrical. *This is a painting about regret*,
she'd say, and the studious ones would write *about regret* in their
notebooks. After a suitable pause and, she hoped, some awed
silence, she would click again, and there on the screen would
appear *Into the World Came a Soul Called Ida*. She wouldn't be
surprised to hear a gasp or two.

She'd give them time to take it in, the faded beauty with her
bare legs exposed, legs that no doubt were once quite shapely
and smooth but now are chunked with fat, pitted and pocked

with cellulite, and sickly pale under unforgiving overhead light. They'd all look at Ida, looking at herself in a hand mirror, seemingly unfazed by her own ravaged appearance.

Then, to set the horror, Lydia would click again and up would come *Flesh (Smaller Than Tears Are the Little Blue Flowers)*. She would watch as they gazed in subdued silence at this new expanse of creased and corrugated female flesh, another of Albright's studies in female beauty gone to ruin. Then she'd go back to Ida. Really, she thought, it didn't get much worse than that.

Aren't you curious to know what she sees in that mirror? Lydia would ask the darkened classroom. *Don't you wonder if she sees what we see? And wouldn't you like to know who the model was and how she felt when she saw this painting? If so, you may be interested to know that she was twenty years old when she sat for this.* Here Lydia would pause for dramatic effect. *Your age*, she'd say, looking into the dark at the students, sensing she'd gotten their attention now. *It wasn't time that did this to her. It was the artist's imagination that ruined her looks.* She'd lower her voice. *Don't you wonder why? Why, when he looked at this young woman, he imagined all this broken-down flesh? Was this fatalism? Some harsh kind of realism? Was it an antidote to lust? Or was this the artist's apology for it, after the fact?*

There would be dead silence by now.

And what's this? Lydia would say, clicking her electronic pointer in the dark, making a little arrow of light flicker around the dollar bills on the table. *Why is there money here? Is she a prostitute? A waitress? Are those tips we see on her little vanity table?* Lydia would lean a little cornily on that loaded word, "vanity." *It's not much money, even adjusting for inflation. Or is it just change from her pocket, a reminder of how transitory earthly wealth is? Because as you all know*, she'd say, if they were a roomful of silent, rapt twenty-year-olds, *beauty is a kind of wealth, yes? Its own kind of currency, right? A commodity, even. And we all know what people do with commodities, right?* She'd wait a beat, two, to let it sink in. She had them now. *We trade them, don't we?* There was always some pretty child up front that nodded, usually a girl but not always.

Does it remind you of anything else? Lydia would ask then. *All this beauty gone to rot?* And some bright one among them who'd paid attention all semester would say, *The Dutch vanitas painters?* And Lydia would say, *Very good! And what was their subject?* And the bright one would whisper, *Death?*

But they weren't her class. They already knew all this. She'd dragged them to see Ida at the Art Institute the day they'd celebrated Elaine's fiftieth birthday, years ago. They'd sneaked in a little flask and stood together in front of the painting, passing the flask around. Each one took a sip. A toast to decrepitude, Elaine had called it.

She'd been the first to turn. *Like a dead leaf*, she'd said, sarcastic even then, though then they were young. Celia had taken a big swig and started to cry in front of this very painting. When they went to dinner afterward, at the Berghoff, Betsy refused to eat and proceeded to get drunk—on Riesling of all things—and tell them things about Ted they would rather not have heard. *That* was the painting Lydia was talking about.

. . .

Albright was underrated, Lydia thought, setting the paper down, sick of proofreading the damned letter yet again. Most people didn't know he was a twin. Lydia liked to tell her classes about his identical twin brother, Malvin, who was an artist, too. The story went that when they came of age they flipped a coin and determined that Ivan would be the painter and Malvin the sculptor, except nobody ever heard of Malvin again. *Imagine*, she'd say, to a darkened classroom of uncomprehending eighteen-year-olds. *Imagine having an identical twin with an almost identical career and for that matter an almost identical name. No wonder the poor man obsessed over what he didn't do.*

Eppie Lederer, also known as Ann Landers, had been an identical twin, too, another of those souls forced to watch her parallel life lived out beside her. She'd also concerned herself to an unusual extent with what to do and not to do, as did her twin sister, Popo, better known as Dear Abby, who also wrote an advice column on morals and manners. Lydia happened to know they'd had a double wedding, then a falling out. They were estranged for decades. Imagine being at war with your own twin self, Lydia thought. These things were strange. Elvis Presley was a twin, too, though his brother, Jesse, died at birth. Some people said it's why he was lonesome.

Lydia knew all about it. She and Spence talked about it sometimes. He had a theory about brilliance coming in twos. He thought things came in pairs, that the universe supplied two of everything it needed, in case something went wrong. It was part of his larger theory about the vastness of the universe, the generosity of nature making up for its carelessness and cruelty. *Think of the garden*, he'd said, gesturing toward the backyard, when they discussed it. *Think of thinning, of how many promising seedlings you have to kill to get one strong plant.*

The last time they'd talked about it he was coming off a fast, eating one of his radish, ginger, and tahini salads, and he was brandishing his fork, with a homegrown radish stuck on the end. Lydia remembered him standing at the kitchen counter in his spandex bike shorts, looking gaunt and anxious, his neck ropy from tension and not enough food.

Nature anticipates death, he'd said, a little frantically. *It supplies extras!* He was almost shouting, slapping his free hand on the Formica counter—they'd meant to put in granite but never got around to it. He slapped the counter again, angry that the world didn't take his theories more seriously. *Think of Rembrandt and Jan Lievens*, he'd said, his agitation accelerating, *Shakespeare and Marlowe, Bell and Gray, Edison and Tesla, the Beatles and the Stones!*

Yes, she'd said, trying to calm him. She didn't disagree.

There has to be a parallel universe, he'd said, looking like he might cry. *It's how things work.* He was on a roll, manic that day.

Lydia agreed it was a fascinating theory. Maybe they'd talk about it tonight, she thought, at the party, though it presupposed intelligent design, an idea she knew some of her friends despised. Or maybe it was Spence they despised. She wished they'd get to know him better, after she was gone, if it came to that. *Ask him about his theory sometime*, she wanted to say. It would give them something to talk about at the funeral.

. . .

She returned to the letter.

> I don't plan to list my sins of commission here.
> I'm more concerned with my sins of omission, or
> not even sins, failures. My failure to act. So here's
> my list of regrets.
>
> My first regret is that I didn't do more with my
> painting. I became discouraged. I lost my nerve. I
> stopped when I should have kept going.
>
> My second regret is that I didn't go places I
> wanted to go.

It pained her. Lydia had thought she'd travel more later, when she had time. Now it was too late. Not that she hadn't already taken wonderful trips—she had! Or some had been wonderful; the others made good stories. But now she wished she'd taken more. More, more, more! She felt greedy in retrospect, for what she might have had. It was a strategic error she wanted to advise them not to make. She'd wanted to ride a bathing train in Japan. She'd wanted to see Alaska. *Don't bother*, people told her, *it's boring*, but she didn't care. She'd wanted to see the Globe Theatre, the northern lights, the Hermitage. Whales, bears in the wild.

And never mind exotic locales. She'd wanted to attend a full season of the Chicago Symphony Orchestra and always assumed she would, one day. Her parents had taken her when she was a child, and that enveloping world of refinement had been a revelation. The velvet-covered seats, the subdued dissonance of the orchestra tuning up, the excited silence punctuated by a few nervous coughs, and then, that first sweet note, so full of promise, not only for music but also for the lull in her parents' lifelong argument.

The first time, that first note, had been a defining moment. Art lulled them, she saw. Harmony begat harmony. It's why she'd signed up for cello, though she'd dropped it when she realized she'd never be good. It was why she'd become an artist, or tried to. She could have afforded season tickets—why hadn't she?

She'd wanted to have lunch with her mother at the Walnut Room, at Marshall Fields, on State Street. Her mother had always said she'd take them. Lydia didn't figure out until after she died that it was she who should have initiated the lunch. It wouldn't have been hard at all. Now, Marshall Fields didn't even exist. It was Macy's now. Lydia regretted that, all of it.

Once you opened these gates, Lydia thought, every petty thing came flooding through. It was a mistake, but now she couldn't stop. She'd wanted to eat at a fondue restaurant—silly, but true. Early on, Spence hadn't been interested. Later he gave up dairy out of sympathy for cows. But she could have gone with someone else. Celia would have been happy to go, if only to make Spence look bad. Though she would have made too much of it, Lydia thought, dragging along Peter and Griffin, to show Lydia what she was missing.

Lydia knew what Spence would say about all this—

dissatisfaction increases in proportion to available choice. He called it the BCAD, the breakfast cereal aisle dilemma.

Lydia supposed most of her regrets were laughable, but the point wasn't her idiotic whims. The point was all this wanting and wishing but never acting. She meant to tell her friends that if they had desires, however trivial, perhaps they should consider fulfilling them now, while they still could, so they could check them off their lists and get back to living their lives.

My third regret is that I wasn't more kind.

Lydia preferred not to go into detail here but she knew some of them remembered the thing with Dennis. That was terrible. The police had assured her it was an accident, that he'd just run off the road. Happens all the time, they said. Still. She regretted that.

My fourth regret is that I didn't sing more.
My fifth regret is that I wasted so much time worrying about men.

And why? Why had she done that? Why hadn't she spent more time alone, simply enjoying her life? Or better yet, with her friends? Lydia set the letter down. She felt a little sick.

She'd go lay the fire, she decided. That always cleared her mind. Her father had taught her how, and she remembered his instructions exactly. *Leave room for oxygen*, she heard him hector when she piled the wood too tight. He was unimpressed with enthusiasm. He wanted results. *If you build it right, one match should do*, he said, always a genius of thrift. He'd boasted that his scoutmaster had called him One-Match Dick.

Lydia knelt on the ashy hearth. First she set crumpled newspaper on the floor of the fireplace, then more in the grate along with the last of the dry evergreen boughs from the mantle, left over from Christmas. This was her innovation. Her father would have considered it cheating. Over those she lay kindling, small sticks she'd collected from the yard, arranged in a teepee over the paper and the evergreens, then added larger sticks to that and small logs leaning strategically on the skeletal teepee. Then a couple of big dry logs balanced against that. When she was done she hauled more wood in from the porch and set logs to lean against the fireplace to dry.

Lydia sat back on her heels and brushed off her hands. Even a chore as simple as this exhausted her now, but it was satisfying work and she didn't get to do it much. These days, Spence made their fires, when he was around, and when he wasn't she mostly didn't bother. He'd taken over the fireplace when he moved back and now he left his brown paper vegan potato chip bags and dirty paper towels in the grate and called it recycling. When it got to overflowing he'd ignite the pile with one blast from the butane torch he'd bought for caramelizing desserts, before he gave up sugar. He kept it on the hearth now, next to the fireplace tools. *Please don't do that*, Lydia said when he blasted flame across the room. She said it in the quiet voice a parent used on a volatile child. She meant for her politeness to overrule his angry love of fire but it only incited him. *What's the problem?* he'd say, lobbing an empty pasta box onto the pile from across the room, to make the fire flare higher.

What was the problem? Where should she begin? For one thing, there was the unsightliness of his garbage, piled in the living room, and for another there was the flame shooter. Then there was the fact that he was there at all, living in the basement. The idea had been that it would be temporary. She thought they'd agreed. Then there were the other, more immediate problems, for instance that when she got down on the floor to check the flue she had trouble getting up. Which might be related to that other little thing, cancer.

Be grateful for small pleasures, Lydia told herself. At least she'd laid a perfect fire. Her father would be proud—Lydia felt sure it would ignite with a single match.

Just then Maxine, who'd watched the fire-building proceedings quietly, walked to the fireplace, stuck her nose into Lydia's carefully constructed pile of combustibles and extracted a big, chewy stick, causing the teepee to collapse. The bang of the hard oak logs on the cold stone hearth startled the dog. She jumped back, into the end table that held the wilted tulips, knocking them to the floor.

Maxine glanced guiltily at Lydia. *Bad dog*, Lydia said, not meaning it.

She scraped the soggy tulips off the floor and tossed them into the fireplace. She wasn't any more effective in getting Maxine to cooperate than she was in getting Spence to. It was another thing Lydia regretted, this failure of hers to make her desires known.

While Lydia wiped up the spilled water, the dog stood just out of reach, waving the stick, the stub of her tail and the stick going in opposite directions, like some weird arthritic metronome. Lydia knew Maxine was trying to start a game of tug of war, her old favorite, but Lydia didn't have the energy. She was weighed down by dark thoughts, her bitter attention now focused on Spence's bad fireplace manners.

It was yet another thing to regret, this unforgivingness of hers. Better to let it go, she told herself. Focus on the party.

~eelee~

Upstairs, Lydia made another attempt at finishing the letter. She'd keep the ending short, she decided.

> I'll close, dear friends, with a plea concerning
> dogs. Indulge them. Cook them eggs on Sunday.
> Take them on road trips, unless of course it makes
> them vomit. And comb them often. It gives them
> so much pleasure that to deny this just seems cruel.
> Also it keeps shedding down. Finally, just love
> them. Their lives are so short.

Norris

Norris had left Jay in bed, pretending to be asleep. She knew he was pouting, the little fool. His feelings were hurt. He'd wanted to come along, like a dog. He should know by now, Norris thought. She didn't like dogs.

His little tantrum had made her late, and when she finally got out of the house it was snowing again. She'd had to reshovel the driveway, and by the time she got on the highway it was getting dark.

Norris almost called Lydia, to cancel. She would have, if she could have been sure Jay was gone, but the possibility that he was still there, and that she'd have to throw him out, made her keep going. *Take charge and take advantage*, she told herself, as she did a dozen times a day. She clicked on cruise control, put her *Speak Like a Native (Italian)* CD in, and steered into the snow, dreaming of Venice. Her plan was to be fluent by the next Biennale.

The weather made the drive even longer than usual. Norris stopped only once, at Calumet Fisheries, the little one-room shack and adjacent smokehouse that clung to the banks of the Calumet River, on the far south side of Chicago. She stopped there sometimes when she drove around the lake. With no tables and no bathroom—you took the food home or ate in your car or, in hot weather, sitting on the curb—the place was a throwback, Norris's one concession to nostalgia.

It was a south side thing. Her family had gone when Norris was little. Her uncle Jack took all the cousins every year, the day after Thanksgiving, for fried smelts. He'd been a school janitor, his vacations were the same as theirs. It seemed pathetic and kind of funny to Norris now, that smelts—oily little fried fish with bones—was her family's idea of what to give a child for a treat, but she still craved the taste.

Norris's plan was to pick up fish for Lydia's party but, now, standing in line, absorbing the stench, she wanted to flee. The place reeked—of smoke and fish and grease and the smell of the river in the cold. Norris wasn't used to waiting in line. She didn't even want to go to this party, she thought. She surely didn't need to take anything. The rest of them would show up with enough food to last a week.

This ceremonial eating of theirs seemed more repulsive to Norris every year. She hadn't actually been to Lydia's party in at least three years but she saw the e-mails. Not to mention that it was a colossal waste of time—the planning, the shopping, the cooking, the endless negotiating over e-mail about who was taking what, then the setting up, the trading of recipes, and afterward, the cleaning, the storing, the dividing of leftovers. You'd think they were a bunch of Amish housewives.

And all that gooey food, mounds of cooked flesh, mayonnaise, butter, cheese—it made Norris queasy just to think of it.

Except for Lydia's party, Norris made a point of avoiding occasions like this. If she had to eat at someone's house—a collector, say—she brought her own food. Rice cakes, almonds, blueberries. A Ziploc bag of spinach she'd empty onto her plate and eat raw. She had some with her right now. She used to say she had food allergies, but now she didn't bother to lie. She didn't care if they were insulted. The way most people ate was disgusting, she thought. They were better off knowing that. Norris had a soft spot for Lydia, but she had the feeling this would be the last time she'd go to this party.

Lydia: 5:15 P.M.

The letter, Lydia decided, was ridiculous. She crumpled it, and, late as it was, started over.

> Dear Friends,
>   I had planned to write a searingly honest letter that would shock us all into living more intensely, with individualized private endings for each of you. I thought it would be my legacy, in case I die, something I could leave to the world in the absence of exceptional children or good paintings. And I did try to write such a letter, but it ran long and rang false.
>   So here is something more succinct and true: I have stage-four cancer and maybe I'll die soon. Probably I will. You are my best friends and I want to give you something, in thanks.

It was too dramatic, probably, Lydia thought. But wasn't that what the proximity of death was supposed to do? Shock you into appreciating life? Though so far, she thought, it had only seemed to stall her. Onward, then.

> But now I can't think of much to say other than thank you. And carry on. Your lives look brave and beautiful to me. Also—be kind, to animals and to one another. What else? Enjoy your lives. There's nothing new here. What I mean to say is that I regret I haven't done these things or haven't done them enough. If I get a chance I'm going to change my ways.
>
> There are questions you probably want to ask. Cel wants to know if I regret not having children— she assumes I do but the answer is not really—and whether I regret that I didn't remarry. Also, and more firmly, no. You all probably wonder if I'm afraid—a little, yes—and if I have regrets. That's the point, really. I do. I wish I'd done more of what I wanted to do when I wanted to do it. I wish I hadn't said no so often.

There, Lydia thought. That at least was something true. The effort of having made herself confront it made her tired. She looked longingly toward the daybed across from her desk. Would succumbing to another nap, just a little one, be so bad? Would it be another *no*—to consciousness, to life itself? Or was it a *yes*—to the pleasure of sleep?

Whichever, there wasn't time. They'd want examples, of

course, of what she'd said no to, but Lydia didn't have the heart to list them. She knew they'd sound trivial, pathetic even. How could she tell them she wished she'd gone to the Valentine Ball in high school, when she was invited by Bill Strong—twice!—instead of staying home, claiming she wanted to finish her encaustic painting of skulls in time for the art fair when really she'd been afraid to go, afraid she'd have to dance. And it would just seem odd to admit after all this time that she wished she'd gone to New Orleans on the bus with Elise Neuberger that time, when Elise had suggested it, when they were eighteen. Lydia remembered why she hadn't. Elise had been bossy and she could be tiresome, but the real reason was some boy Lydia had hoped to see that weekend. She hadn't wanted to miss out by being away. Now Lydia wished she'd said yes more, to all sorts of things.

Lydia could hear Celia, only pretending to be joking, say, *More? Didn't you say yes entirely enough?* Celia would mean men, but Lydia meant everything. She wished now she'd taken more from what was available, or at least paid more attention to what she did take. Maybe that was all it was, she thought. Maybe she'd had plenty—trips, men, friends, *life*—if only she'd paid more attention to what she'd had.

Though couldn't attention be retroactive? Lydia wondered. Wasn't that what memory was?

Lydia tried to test the idea, tried to remember something important, relive it right then, to appreciate it after the fact, but the only things that came to mind were inconsequential, not the orchestrated events, but their unphotographable edges. The way Spence's hands had looked one night, polishing his boots before a show. A tuna sandwich in a train station. A song heard with particular intensity in a hospital waiting room. Lydia suspected these edges were where she'd lived her real life. Now she wished she'd paid more attention to those.

Lydia felt a warm weight on her feet and looked down. Maxine lay across Lydia's socks, and had rolled her head back, to stare up at her. Now, there was attention. Maybe love and attention were the same, Lydia thought, reaching down to rub Maxine's pink belly. Maybe she remembered loving things simply because she remembered them.

Much of what now seemed worthwhile, more than Lydia would have thought, was of the body. The obvious, of course—food, sex, music—but other, plainer things, too. Just running, as a child, pretending to fly, arms out, legs pumping, throat and chest burning with air, was a pleasure she'd rarely equaled since. Or weather, the wild smell of it, every day something different—that alone was enough to live for. Or so she thought now. She wished she'd thought of it sooner.

Maybe smell, or the memory of it, was love itself. Lydia remembered how her father's suits smelled, giving off clues to the mysterious masculine world outside the house, newsprint and pipe tobacco and something vaguely medicinal—gin? On summer weekends his brimmed felt hat, which he wore to cut the lawn, smelled of sweat and sweet mowed grass. Her mother's scent was subtler—domestic and intimate, with notes of bacon grease and blood and stale face powder mixing with the fine, feminine smell of Jergens hand lotion. She'd kept a glass bottle of it beside the kitchen sink and smoothed it on her hands after washing the dishes. Much later, Lydia learned the name of the fragrance—Cherry-Almond. She'd happened on it once in a discount drugstore—in a plastic tube now, no longer in a pink glass bottle with an elegant black pump. Lydia had squirted some on her shaking hands right there in the store and her mother had appeared as if summoned, younger than Lydia by decades and pretty in her shirtwaist dress.

Now that Lydia had opened the gates of smell, the memories wouldn't stop. Bingo, her childhood dog, smelled of his own oily fur, a zesty, outdoorsy, insouciant, slightly ammoniac scent, the thought of which made her choke back tears of longing for the sheer huggable corporeality of him, his thick chest around his fast-beating heart. She smelled the old wood and furniture polish of her grandmother's quiet house, and the hard, thick bars of lavender soap she kept in her upstairs bathroom. The feel of a porcelain handle on a bathroom fixture in an old building somewhere could activate the memory of that smell, which was the smell of being four and standing on a box to wash her hands before Sunday dinner.

Maybe memory is where everyone really lived, Lydia thought, not the present, or not only the present. Never only the present. Or at least it was where she lived. She didn't even know what she felt until after it was over.

Did it all come down to the body? Lydia wondered. She tried to remember loftier pleasures, moments of platonic love or intellectual insight, but she couldn't get away from the senses. She was back riding at eighty miles an hour in the passenger seat of Spence's green Camaro, through the Smoky Mountains, listening to Bob Seeger on the radio and drinking cold beer out of a bottle while a certain piney forest smell rushed through the open car windows. They'd been to the beach. Lydia had unhooked her wet bikini top and held it out the window like a flag, to dry it. Or this—early-morning hot summer smell and walking Arlo, a curly-haired foundling, past the open window of a collapsing paint-peeling house at dawn, some fifteen years before. She'd heard a woman singing scales in an operatic soprano, and it made up for a lot that was painful that summer, at least for a minute. Or this—a certain moment sitting in the kitchen of a third-floor apartment, on the top floor of a Victorian house where she'd lived alone with almost no furniture for two years. It was early, 4:30 or 5:00 in the morning, and she couldn't sleep. She was sitting at her one battered table smoking a cigarette, naked under a cotton robe, boiling water for tea. She remembered that when the kettle whistled she stood up to turn it off and turned toward the window and saw the sun just rising over the tree line, dark and red. Her robe had fallen open and she looked down then, just to pull it closed, and there was her body on fire. Her body was red. It was orange and gold. Like she'd swallowed fire. Like she was fire. And for just a moment Lydia had thought she was in flames or that she'd changed in some unimaginable way and was seeing herself, resplendent, in that split second before pain or explosion, and she'd waited for it and when it didn't come she realized it was the sun on her skin.

She was happy then. That feeling that minute that morning—that's what Lydia wished she'd had more of.

She heard a soft lapping sound. Malcolm the cat had arrived on her desk to drink from her water glass. Maybe the whole world was encompassed in the present, she thought. Maybe that morning and her thinking of that morning and that light then and this indifferent light now and Maxine lying across her feet and Malcolm lapping water from her glass were all one.

Lydia didn't know and it was too late to figure it out now. She had a party to get ready for.

Norris

Now Norris's clothes, and the inside of her car, reeked of smoke and fish. At least the smell would cover any trace of last-minute sex, she thought. She'd been trying to get out the door when Jay pulled her down.

"Now you've made me late," she'd said, after, pulling layers of black clothes back on.

He'd been sitting in the middle of her bed with one of her Hudson Bay blankets wrapped around his bony, boyish shoulders, smoking a joint. He smiled then, as if he'd been complimented, glad to have had an effect.

"What happens when I'm left sitting in a cold puddle halfway to Chicago?" She'd said this to the top of his head, standing over him with her boot in his lap. He was dawdling—if she wouldn't take him along he'd do what he could to make her even later. He'd offered to tie her boots, then pulled out the laces. Now he was relacing them.

She'd nudged him under the chin, poking his soft neck with her hard toe. "Huh? What then?"

He'd dodged the boot, snaking his supple neck to move his head out of the way. "Then you'll think of me," he'd said, keeping his eyes on the elaborate knot he'd begun to tie.

Only a boy can be so cocky and so sentimental at the same time, she thought. It was scandalous, she supposed, what she was doing, robbing the cradle this way. Though no one would think twice if it were reversed, if she were a man. And Jay was of age, old enough to make his own choices.

It was his *big boy choice*. That's what they'd called it with Sam, when he was little, when she and Andy were trying to trick him into doing something he didn't want to do. He'd learned early on it was flattery, not a real choice. He'd stand there trying not to cry, torn between what he really wanted and his *big boy choice*, the lousy grown-up alternative they were pushing on him, usually for reasons that had nothing to do with him. Jay's big boy choice wasn't so bad, Norris thought, not by comparison.

She kept it quiet, though, for Sammy's sake mostly, not that he'd ever find out. Jay and Sam might as well have lived on different planets. Sam, safely tucked away in his fraternity house in Ann Arbor, was as insulated from Jay's world as if he were still in kindergarten. People like Jay existed for Sam only on television, or in the movies, as colorful outlaws, and Norris planned to keep it that way. Though they were so close in age that Norris sometimes felt in danger of conflating them, of confusing Sam's baby sweetness with this tougher almost-boy, especially now that Norris could see how young he really was.

She'd thought he was older at first, but now that he'd dropped his act she could see he was almost as young as her son.

He'd started hinting lately about taking her to some kind of family function, his cousin's wedding. As his date.

"Oh, sweetie," she'd said, trying to be nice for a change. "I don't do weddings. I barely made it to my own." She'd made a joke of it though it was true. She hated weddings.

He said he wanted her to meet his family.

Norris couldn't help laughing. Then he'd looked hurt, so she said, "No, you don't."

"Yes, I do."

"Darling, I could be your mother."

"No, you couldn't." He'd said it automatically, a child's defense. But it was true. He was from some town out in the sticks where they got knocked up in high school. She was probably older than his mother. Norris supposed it was time to end it.

She was driving up LSD now, as the natives called it. Lake Shore Drive. Old joke: How did you get here? I took LSD. Her car stunk of fish. She didn't mind—that old fish shack was one of the few things she missed about the city. People said, *Don't you miss the culture?* Please, she thought. If she wanted culture, which she didn't, she'd go to New York. The only reason she was here, in January, was to check out the space for her show. At the last minute she'd decided to leave a day early, stop in at Lydia's party. And not for the party, which was tedious, to put it mildly. For Lydia.

Norris could see the lake on her right, a big black nothing except for where the moonlight glinted a weird silvery color off the ice. The sky was that awful orange streetlight color the city had adopted in the seventies. It looked like poison gas now, caught in the mist.

Norris missed Michigan already. It was too cold to be in the city. It wasn't any warmer there, but cold in the woods was different, less sinister. There she had her big stone fireplace. She liked to power walk the path around the pond, listening to the crunch of her boots breaking rhythmically through the frozen snow and leaves and cracking sticks, hearing her own breath, panting inside her scarf. When she got back to the house she, or they, when she let Jay come along, went inside and at first the house seemed oppressively hot, cloyingly domestic after the wildness and danger of the fresh, clean cold. The house always seemed to smell of old soup and toast and coffee then, no matter what she'd eaten that day, and she'd feel a jolt of revulsion. But then she'd get used to it and they'd take off their coats. Jay, when she let him, would pile oak logs in the fireplace that were so hard and cold they banged almost like metal when he dropped them on the hearth. Then she'd light a fire and they'd take off their boots and sit. Jay wanted to talk then but Norris discouraged it.

Somehow the cold there, while Norris knew it was dangerous, felt less ugly. Cold there seemed like part of some larger order. It seemed necessary, meaningful. The woods needed to rest, things needed to die. Here it just seemed cruel.

Norris drove past a man with no gloves holding a sign that said, "HELP mE I'm Homeless and Hungry GOD BleSS yoU." For the briefest moment she considered slowing down, handing the guy a package of smoked fish, along with her gloves. She had a small fortune in food sitting next to her on the passenger seat, each type of fish packaged separately and wrapped in white paper. All she had to do was roll down the window and hand one out. She could give him two and still arrive with too much—she knew at the end of the night most of it would be thrown out, or fed to pets that were already overfed.

But what was the point, Norris decided, speeding up. He was probably just some alcoholic who'd puke it all up. It was best not to encourage them.

Goddamn everything, Norris thought. She hated the city. Except for setting up this show, she had no reason to come back, not even to see her dealer, Natalie. They handled everything by e-mail. Norris skipped the openings, usually, shipped the art. She paid Jay to drive in the small work, the drawings she didn't trust to shippers. That's how she'd met him. He'd answered an ad she placed for an art courier. Later he claimed he thought it was a euphemism for gigolo. Not that he'd used that word, euphemism. *Secret babe code*, he'd called it.

What a child, Norris thought. And what a cad he'd grow up to be when she was done with him.

Except for Lydia and Natalie, everything was in Michigan now. Norris's parents were gone, and the less she saw of her brothers and their wives and their hordes of children, the better. The only thing that had kept her in the city was Sam, and now he was in Michigan, too. Even Andy's parents were there, still in the old house outside Traverse City. Sweet little

white-haired Betty and Hank, who'd retired from the post office sixteen years ago. It had never occurred to them to move
away, go someplace warm, or even to stop working. Hank ran
a lawn mower repair business in his garage now. In the winter
he worked on snow blowers. Norris supposed Sam had inher-
ited his sweetness from them.

Betty had cried when Norris told her about the divorce—
Norris had made sure she got to them first. Betty had said she
and Hank would always think of her as their daughter. Andy
never did tell them what happened. He didn't want to turn
them against her, he'd said. He thought she was coming back,
Norris realized, later. He didn't tell them later, either—too
embarrassed, she supposed. Now they were closer to her than
they were to him.

Her doing, that, partly at least. *You subverted their affections*,
Andy had yelled at her, almost crying, back during the worst of
it, when they still bothered to fight. She'd alienated them from
him, he said. It seemed like an ugly thing to say at first but she
saw he was right. She hadn't even realized she was doing it and
then, after she thought about it, she thought, yes, exactly, and
kept doing it, on purpose. Though they were easily enough
bought off, she thought, with adorable grandchild visits. When
he was younger Sam had spent a month with them every summer and Norris had made sure she was the one who ferried him
back and forth, as if he were her personal gift to them.

Norris was making good time now. She knew she should slow
down, on this ice, though she doubted she'd crash—her reflexes

were excellent. If a cop stopped her she'd be tempted to tell him that. Laws were for people who lacked sense, or self-control, she'd want to say. She knew what she was doing.

Most people couldn't help failing, Norris thought, passing some idiot with his flashers on, doing forty in a broken-down car. They were so sorry, they always said, after they'd made some colossal mess. They had tried to do better, but they just couldn't. It seemed like whining to Norris, but maybe it was true. Maybe most people couldn't help being weak and stupid. Who knew why? All she knew was she was the opposite.

Certain people, people like her, Norris thought, should be licensed to drive faster. They were better at it, and they really did need to get where they were going sooner than everyone else. It would be like diplomatic immunity, she thought, except this would be immunity for people who were smarter. Superior. It was just a fact. Some people, like her, were, and in a few years, she was pretty sure, they'd figure out a way to read it in someone's DNA and be able to issue a special driver's license that granted privileges. She didn't plan to roll over people, Norris thought. They just lay down in front of her. What was she supposed to do—stop? Slow down? She didn't think so.

Sometimes Norris thought she'd wasted herself on art. Maybe she should have done more, gone to law school and become a prosecutor or a judge, run for office, not because she wanted to but because she'd be so good at it. She had the temperament—ruthless, she was told. Most people weren't. Even people whose job it was to be ruthless usually didn't have the stomach for it, though it was what the world needed more of. Balls. Someone had to be strong. The job fell to whomever was able, and willing.

It had been so easy to win over Betty and Hank, Norris thought. Presents, flowers, compliments. Remembering their birthdays, for God's sake. Holiday visits with Sam. Norris thought now they must not have resisted much, must have sensed what a little weakling their son had turned into and preferred to be on the winning team. Most people did, given the chance. Not that Norris had given them a choice. Once she made up her mind she was hard to resist.

A force of nature, Andy used to call her, meaning it as a good thing in those days. Norris remembered how he'd say it in bed, worshipfully. *I like strong women*, he'd say. Arm wrestling had excited him; he'd liked it when she won. He had no idea what he was getting into, Norris thought, and even she hadn't realized how mismatched they were, until it was too late. Norris only wished Sam had gotten more of her in him, more of whatever it was that made her capable of heartless force when necessary.

She was going over seventy now—even Norris thought it was too fast, in this snow. She needed to slow down, calm down. She switched her thoughts to the house, always a palliative. It was hers now, the exquisite glass-and-steel box slung low in the trees along the lake, with its bleached oak floors and stainless-steel kitchen and 360-degree views. An all-glass enclosed walkway led to the studio, where she'd installed twenty-foot ceilings and skylights and an interior balcony with a clerestory. There, the seasons surrounded her. There was nothing else to see.

Don't you miss culture? Some fool had asked her that at an opening when she first moved. What a joke. She spent all day, every day standing at an easel. When she got tired she read a book, listened to music. She had a lifetime supply of culture in her head. What she craved was nature. And what a poor substitute for nature culture was anyway. People who asked if she missed culture meant did she miss people. Parties, openings. God, no. Never. She preferred her trees, and silence. What a gift it had been to herself, to move there. And it wasn't even that silent. There was the sound of water, birds, small wildlife rustling in the underbrush—the gray squirrels skittering up and down the tree trunks, screeching at each other over mulberries, in summer the bees. At night she heard owls. What was she doing in this city, she thought, dodging a pothole in the narrow one-way street as she drove through the filthy slush.

Won't you miss us? Someone had said it at one of these parties, after she and Andy split up and she announced she was moving north. Who was it that said that? Someone she didn't expect sentiment from. She'd laughed, then felt sorry, realizing how cold she sounded. But they were so provincial, clinging to their little routines. Didn't it ever occur to them to leave?

She'd always planned to leave, and she planned to go much farther—part-time at least, when Sam graduated. She was looking into property in Panama for a winter studio. She figured she'd earned as many houses as she wanted. She'd worked harder than anyone she knew. She'd made art and raised Sam and managed Andy's money and she'd been good at all of it, and now she was just beginning to do her best work. Or she was ready to begin, she amended.

Norris wondered if nature trumped everything. She was driving past a row of crumbling apartment buildings now. Certainly it trumped this shit, she thought. Probably it even trumped art, but who cared about that. It was the kind of discussion people had in art school. Such abstractions had never interested Norris. Certainly art trumped friendship, for her, at least. People called her a careerist, like that was so bad. What was wrong with that? Friendship seemed like a waste of time, by comparison. All that *chatting*. Though Norris had tried, with Lydia.

Won't you miss us? It was Lydia who'd said it—Norris remembered now. *I won't have to*, she'd said, dodging the question. *Nobody has to miss anybody. You can visit. We can e-mail.* She was surprised they cared.

She'd even meant it. She even threw a divorce party—for collectors, mostly, but she'd invited Lydia and told her to bring along the whole bunch of them, and they came, in someone's SUV, like a busload of geriatric tourists, brushing snack crumbs from their laps as they climbed out of the back.

It was the only time they visited, though, and Norris couldn't say she was sorry. She knew the place made them uncomfortable. Envy was hard on friendships. She didn't think she'd ever had one that hadn't faltered on it somehow. If not envy over her success, then envy for her body. What a laugh— all these paintings and all they saw was how thin she was, thinner now than twenty years ago. It was no mystery, how she did it. Anyone could, with a little self-discipline. She starved. It sharpened her senses, too. She channeled hunger into work. She knew she'd be the only one tonight not gorging like a child at a birthday party.

They all had theories about her success, Norris knew. It could never just be that she'd earned it. They couldn't bear to think that. They hinted they thought it was *who she knew*. What a joke, Norris thought. Who did she know? Everyone now, sure, but no one then. Or they thought it was something about that residency all those years ago, as if that made any real difference. Her favorite theory was that she was successful because of her name.

She'd changed it, that was true. She'd been named after her mother—Marie Norris O'Heaney—and dropped the corny Irish O as soon as it was legal, when she was twenty-one. She'd already dropped Marie, as soon as she got to college, desperate to distance herself from her mother. She saw now that it probably hurt her. She was a little sorry about that.

Professionally, though, her instincts had been exactly right. It hadn't hurt her personal life either, to have a man's name. Men, she'd noticed, liked that little hint of androgyny.

Lydia: 5:45 P.M.

Lydia was trying to proofread the latest version of the letter but her eyes kept closing. The only thing that kept her awake was the sound of Spence in the kitchen, sighing. She could hear him all the way downstairs, getting ready to go out, to leave the women alone.

He'd spent the day in his office, as he called it, the big room in the basement where he slept now and where he kept his guitars, his comic book collection, his letters from old girlfriends he thought Lydia didn't know about, his work that she wasn't supposed to ask about. He was upset the party was disrupting his routine and he was protesting by occupying the kitchen.

Spence was sighing so loudly, actually groaning now, that she could hear him through the door she'd just closed, as she was supposed to, she knew. He was registering his complaint that a) generally, life was hard, and b) specifically, she was having a party for women who'd gone on record as not liking him, though she'd told him he could join them for dinner, if he wanted. It was only fair, he'd helped her clean the house—she was so tired now, he'd done most of it, really—but she knew he wouldn't stay. He was going to some club, would probably end up sitting in on the last set. Or Lydia hoped so. It would cheer him up, and keep him out of the house.

She knew he felt frustrated—she sympathized! The market for restored guitars, let alone banjos and ukuleles, was just not that strong these days, the economy being what it was. It had been a great idea—she'd been all for it, tired of being the breadwinning wife of a session musician, which is what he was doing when they met. She'd backed the business a thousand percent. The city was teeming with musicians, resident and visiting both, and Spence knew or at least had met most of them. Had sat in with a lot, too.

"Best damn guitar restorer in the city," the *Chicago Reader* had said. "And not a bad picker either." Ten years ago, but still true.

When Lydia bought him out of the house, after they split up, Spence sank every dime in the business. He'd moved in with their accountant by then, Julie, and even she agreed it seemed like a great idea.

I feel like I made a wrong turn somewhere, he said sometimes now, holding his head in his hands. For a long time Lydia had reassured him that he was on *a path*, but lately she'd been too tired.

He'd feel much better, she thought, when he found out she'd willed him the house.

Her brother would disapprove, of course, if it came to that. He'd expect everything to go to his girls. *They already have everything*, she would tell him, if she had the nerve to discuss it

with him, which she didn't. Or not even nerve, just forbearance. She knew what he'd say. *If you had children you'd understand.* Understand what, though? Rampant greed?

When she was younger, she'd told her little brother everything. Six years her junior, he'd been the perfect, precocious
confidant, but after he got married she'd had to stop. He'd become an instant expert on marital bliss and, full of advice, he
wore his happy home life like armor. All he could talk about
was how *amazing* his wife was, how *outstanding* his kids were.
How *blessed* he was. It could all be hers, too, he implied, or used
to, if only she'd *settle down.* "Family first," he liked to say, fixing
an unctuous eye on her. He'd claim that by family he meant
her, too, but she knew he didn't. He and Liv and the girls were
a walled kingdom.

She should tell Spence about the house, she knew, to set his
mind at ease. And she would, but she couldn't quite make herself, yet. She didn't want to see his gratitude. She heard him
groan again. *Who is the one with a deadly disease here?* she wanted
to shout downstairs, but she couldn't. She hadn't told him that,
either.

According to the shit-detector quiz Lydia had taken online the
week before, this reluctance of hers to tell people how sick she
was was yet another sign of her withholding nature, proof positive that she was officially, measurably, untrustworthy. The
person who'd made up this quiz, which appeared in a popular
women's magazine Lydia read only at the hairdresser's, main-
tained that all forms of discretion and privacy were actually

signs of untrustworthiness. Lydia wasn't sure she agreed but, just to be safe, she was trying to make amends. She'd planned to tell Spence today, before the party, so she could at least say he was the first to know, but now it was too late. She'd heard the door slam. She should have told Celia, too.

Lydia went back to the letter. Maybe she'd been right the first time. Maybe what she regretted, or should regret, is not what she didn't do but what she did. Wasting so much time writing this crappy letter, for one thing, she thought. Her life with men, for another. She'd been skirting the issue. Spence was the least of it. She was thinking of Dennis, of course. That was terrible.

There were others, too. Poor mixed-up Ted. Celia, back when they talked about this sort of thing, said she thought letting Spence move back after the divorce was a misguided effort to make up for the others. Lydia said, *Couldn't it just be wanting to help an old friend?* Celia had given her a look that said no. That was around the time they'd stopped discussing these things.

Maybe she should write Ted a letter, too, Lydia thought. Or give him something, at least, maybe her grandmother's cast-iron pot. Lydia looked at the clock. She was running out of time. What would she even say? *Dear Ted, I'm sorry for my part in what happened all those years ago, for adding to your confusion.* She would never write such a letter. What if Betsy found it?

Lydia had to lie down. Here at least was bedrock, though, real regret, and the nausea that went with it. Or was that the cancer, this acid tang of vomit rising in her throat? Now that she'd hit on something real, it was amazing how much else came gurgling up to lodge there, like undigested meat. She should have planned a preparty for men, Lydia thought. She could have met them at the door with a list of talking points and a tray of drinks and a stack of their left-behind T-shirts, starched and folded, like laundry in a hotel.

So Miss Congeniality is admitting to feeling a little hostile after all? It was Celia's voice in Lydia's head, again.

Where was Celia when she needed her? Lydia wondered, though she knew. Celia was at home, waiting on a boy who was old enough to take care of himself. She should be here, Lydia thought, in a sudden fit of petulance. And not the complacent judgmental married maternal Celia, but the old raunchy one. Lydia wanted to talk to her.

Celia

Poor Lydia, Celia thought, wrapping cellophane over the big turkey platter she'd mounded with chopped vegetables. She had no real family. Though in some ways Celia envied her, too, having that whole house to herself. Or at least she would have it to herself, Celia thought, when she finally kicked Spence out.

Celia was organizing herself to leave the house. Peter had already wrapped two loaves of herb bread and put them in the car, side by side on the passenger seat, bundled in dish towels and smelling of flour, like newborn twins. He'd turned on the engine so the bread would stay warm.

"One should be plenty," she'd said.

"Tell her to freeze the other one, if it doesn't get eaten," he'd said. He meant it was a gift. Celia liked this about him, his generosity. It was clearer to her now, now that they had less. Before it had sometimes seemed like showing off.

The ragged remains of Celia's grocery store epiphany had followed her home and settled around Peter. Now that she was leaving the house for the evening, she'd started to miss him.

Poor Lydia, Celia thought again. She had no idea what a happy home life was.

"What are you going to do tonight?" Celia said.

Peter was standing at the kitchen counter reading the newspaper. Griffin was at some kind of overnight retreat and Peter had the house to himself. On the kitchen table was a stack of movies he'd checked out of the library, on the way home from dropping off Griffin, all choices he knew didn't interest Celia— three James Bond titles and underneath those something called *Bicycling the Wine Country of France.*

"Making risotto," he said. A bag of arborio rice and a little pile of oyster mushrooms sat on the counter, along with two neatly peeled cloves of garlic and a hunk of pecorino cheese. He was waiting for Celia to leave before he started cooking. Adam, Peter's big white cat, was skulking back and forth on the counter, rubbing against Peter's sleeve. Ever since Eve died, from feline leukemia last spring, Adam had been keeping close to Peter. Male bonding, Celia supposed.

"Have fun," she said, postponing her exit. She wanted him to look at her, but he'd started making a salad now, and Adam had stopped his skulking and was sitting on the counter staring at the radishes Peter had scrubbed and lined up in a neat row. He seemed distracted, and Celia could tell from the way he was acting that there was something he wasn't telling her. His evident impatience at her slow departure made her hang around longer to try to tease it out of him. Finally he said, "Don't you have to get going? The roads are icy."

"I suppose I do," Celia said, buttoning her coat and giving him a peck on the cheek. As she leaned over to kiss him she saw the telltale package from the deli, which he'd pushed out of sight, behind the olive oil. He'd bought prosciutto and he was hiding it. He was planning to put it in the risotto and eat it all himself. He was cheating on their budget.

Just like she was, she thought, thinking of the bakery cupcakes she'd left in the car. She decided not to mention the prosciutto.

Peter held the door open and Celia teetered onto the ice with the big tray of vegetables. "Say hi to everybody for me," he said, to her back. She turned carefully on the ice to wave good-bye but by the time she'd safely rotated her body, along with the huge platter, to look back at him he'd already shut the door. Through the window, which glowed with yellow light in the dark, Celia saw Peter and Adam butt heads over the kitchen sink.

Married life was so complicated, she thought. These negotiations were so delicate, these secrets so strange but necessary. Who knew what else there was. She'd learned not to ask.

It was something else she and Lydia would have discussed back in the old days, when Celia could trust Lydia not to judge her for the compromises she'd made. Now they had as many secrets from each other as they did from men. Although, Celia had begun to notice lately, Lydia seemed to have more.

Lydia: 6:15 P.M.

Lydia was getting dressed now, laying her options on the bed. Would a purple scarf look playful, she wondered, or would it just seem forced? Past the mirror, through the bedroom window, she saw stripes of falling snow, illuminated under beams of noxious orange streetlight. She watched the little crystals spin and twinkle.

Lydia was thinking about joy, whether it was possible in the midst of this, whatever this was. Dis-ease. Resignation. Grief, even, over the death of some version of herself, now gone. She was a little surprised to see that it was, that joy was exactly what she felt right now, looking forward to seeing her friends. Those manic little crystals insisted on it.

Joy as opposed to happiness, Lydia thought. They were as different as silver and gray.

Lydia ran a lint roller over the pants she planned to wear, removing bits of Malcolm's fur. She remembered how Betsy had told her, during her trial separation from Ted, that her only criterion for dating a new man was that he possess a capacity for shared joy. CFSJ, she called it. She'd written a paper on it for a professional journal.

Lydia and Betsy had met for breakfast at a pancake house, on a Sunday, so there'd be no danger of running into Ted, who was singing in the choir that morning, at church. A waitress had just set plates in front of them when Betsy told her this.

"Makes sense," Lydia had said, buttering her toast.

"Unlike Ted," Betsy added, to make her point.

Lydia looked up just in time to see Betsy's eyes darken. "Ted doesn't have that?" Lydia had already forgotten the name of whatever it was Betsy thought Ted was lacking, and she knew she was on shaky ground now, but she wanted to know.

"CFSJ? No. It might seem like it," Betsy said, stabbing her omelet with a fork. "But not really, not in the full-bodied, self-actualized way that makes for real sharing. His joy's all in his lungs. His stomach. Not his heart. Or, you know. Elsewhere." So that was it, Lydia thought. She hadn't argued.

Now Lydia pulled on one of the sweaters she'd set out on the bed—it would have to do—and went back to her office. She picked up the yellow tablet. *Write something true*, she told herself. She wrote, *My real regret is that I have lived a small, fearful life.*

Lydia picked up the letter. Even that was tentative and small, she saw now. Rewriting it would take hours, weeks, possibly the rest of her life. She crumpled the paper.

She'd make an announcement, she decided. She'd speak in the simplest terms and tell the truth, with an optimistic spin. She'd say she hoped to recover but, whatever happened, she was grateful. Now she wanted to lighten her life and planned to go the rest of the way without baggage. She wouldn't say she wished she'd done it long ago.

Lydia felt relieved. The close call, of having almost distributed this maudlin letter, energized her. She crumpled all the copies and made a little pyramid and counted the crumpled balls to make sure she had them all and then gathered them up in her sweater, like apples in an apron, and walked them down to the fireplace, where she deposited them one by one in the midst of the collapsed pile of logs. Then she rebuilt the little firewood teepee over them. They'd make excellent fire starter.

Back upstairs to deal with her hair, Lydia felt another list coming on. Just one more, she thought, to calm her nerves. She wanted to write down what she'd leave to whom. She pushed aside the pile of books she'd meant to bequeath, meaningfully, with a note inside each. There wasn't time.

She'd have them take books tonight, then. She'd give them shopping bags and let them help themselves. If they refused, she'd tell them anything they didn't take would be grabbed by her two cheerfully avaricious nieces, though it wasn't really true. The girls wouldn't want her books any more than they'd want her jewelry, which was the other thing she planned to give away tonight.

. . .

She hoped it wouldn't seem pathetic. There wasn't much. Or rather there was much, just not much of any worth, but Lydia hoped that once they got over the awkwardness it would be fun. She'd get someone to help her bring the apothecary cabinet, which she used as a jewelry box, downstairs. She'd bought it years ago, on a whim, in a hopeful mood when jewelry seemed like a good idea. Its ninety-nine small drawers were crammed with who knew what. Her plan was for everyone to take turns choosing drawers, sixteen apiece, contents sight unseen. The other three they could divide up however they pleased.

Lydia had taken out a few things for her nieces. Her mother's pearls, Ariel might like those, and her mother's engagement ring, though the diamond was tiny. Liv might have to explain its value to whichever one of them got it, that it was a *symbol*. One of them might like her grandmother's locket, Lydia thought, if she could ever find the thing. But mostly not, they already had so much. Privilege had been poured over them like water over a full sponge. Lydia wanted to capture the runoff and give it away. Not that her friends needed these things, either, but they might enjoy them. At least they would appreciate the gesture.

The girls wouldn't, and they wouldn't want her stuff. They'd been taught to Accept Only the Best, Get the Most Out of Life, Hold High Standards. Their education so far had cost twice what Lydia had spent on her house, and they were far from done. They'd scoff at her dingy trinkets.

Lydia was not a mean-spirited aunt, she told herself. When the girls were small she'd embraced the job. She'd had them over for tea parties and marshmallow roasts, sleepovers and Easter egg hunts. She'd observed their birthdays and graduations with carefully chosen gifts and whimsical parties—Spence had once dressed as a rabbit—albeit not on the scale to which they'd already become accustomed. Her observances, she saw now, must have only seemed small.

Lydia's brother's girls, adorable as they were, had turned into Amazons of entitlement. The time she'd taken them on vacation was a disaster. She'd thought a road trip would be fun—they'd take the Circle Tour, spend a week and drive around the lake, stay in knotty pine lodges and rent canoes. They were younger then, still malleable, or so Lydia had thought. But she'd brought them home early, at the girls' request. The motel pillows were synthetic, they said. The sheets were scratchy. They'd expected her to fix it somehow. The food wasn't right. *Auntie Liddie, we aren't allowed to eat fried food,* they'd said, politely but with an edge. They seemed to expect her to scold the waitress. They wanted sushi. Organic ketchup. *Girls,* she'd said, *this is Wisconsin. Fish fry is considered a delicacy here.* She took them to a bowling alley and they complained that people were smoking. The younger one cried.

"Of course people are smoking, honey," Lydia had said, kneeling in front of her, trying to keep the irritation out of her voice. "We're in a different kind of place now. A place where people smoke! Isn't it fun? Let's try to have fun and be tolerant. OK?"

"But smoking's bad!" the older one said, coming to her sister's defense, her exquisite little face trembling with outrage. As if she'd taken them to a cockfight, Lydia thought.

Their righteousness was exhausting; their perfectionism made Lydia feel shabby. She took them to a thrift store in Ludington, though by then she should have known better. She thought it would be madcap—they'd try on hats, buy costumes. "My grandma—your dad's grandma!—took me to a thrift store once," she told them, outside the store, knowing her brother had inculcated family pride in them. They had to like this, Lydia meant. It was a family tradition. "That was your great-grandma," she'd said, to remind them that, odd as it seemed, she, their aunt Lydia, was in fact their blood relation. The older one had smiled indulgently, so Lydia forged on, pretending she believed the child's pretend interest. "I was eight years old," she said. "She bought me a charm bracelet and a used ouija board and a green sweater. Because I needed one!" Lydia threw that last part in as a little hint, about how different their lives were from most people's, how lucky they were, but Lydia could tell they didn't care, that they were hoping she wasn't going to buy them any used green sweaters.

They'd followed Lydia through the store, their faces screwed into sad little moues of forbearance, hands tight at their sides, careful not to touch anything. She kept them too long, but she'd been trying to show them it was fun. "Look—want a hat?" she'd said, plopping a sombrero on Amelia's head.

"No, thank you," she said.

They wouldn't let Lydia buy them a thing. Clunky jewelry?

No thanks. A Hawaiian shirt? No. Afterward she agreed to take them for pedicures but they couldn't find a nail shop so they just went to lunch. Hot dogs were out of the question. Hamburgers were as low as they'd go.

Not that they weren't wonderful girls. They were! They'd grown up to be principled, talented, confident, strong. They were athletic and smart and graceful, with bouncing gaits and long, effortless strides and powerful tennis arms and the posture of well-trained dancers, which they were. Well-spoken, well-read, and well-traveled. Between them they knew five languages and, thanks to Lydia's brother's good job and his wife's inheritance and the elite education that naturally ensued, the girls had traveled six continents. They'd herded goats in the Andes, taught English to blind children in China, restored frescoes in Florence, sung in traveling choirs across the Ukraine. And they were gorgeous, of course, each nearly six feet tall now, with thick ropes of long, swinging gold hair and flat bellies and rosy skin and necks like columns and thick, muscular legs. You wouldn't want to be kicked by one of these girls.

How did they get this way? Lydia wondered sometimes. They'd had Barbie dolls, like everyone else. Though she recalled Amelia once using hers, dressed in an evening gown and sparkly mules, to drive a nail into a picture frame she'd made that summer at outsider art camp. Sometimes they seemed like mutant representatives from the future, forerunners of some conquering female race, destined to figure out a way to reproduce without men. At the very least, they were a new breed of girl.

. . .

Lydia had to admit, she felt a little envious. She was proud to belong to the same gene pool, but she wished she'd been given so much, encouraged to be so bold.

And never mind me, Lydia thought. She was envious of her nieces on her students' behalf—the tentative, hulking boys who hadn't a clue where they belonged in the world, half in love with any female who'd look them in the eye, the closed-faced girls, trooping off to their multiple part-time jobs. Most of all, she worried about the returning students—veterans just back from Afghanistan, old before their time. The single mothers who left class early, to pick up children, in broken-down cars. They worked night shifts and lived with their parents, their grand-parents, had no money for books or supplies. They bought them at the end of the semester, when it was too late. Lydia gave away her desk copies but there were never enough. Every semester now, she lost students when their financial aid ran out. At first, she'd told them to come to class anyway. *Just come*, she'd say, *I don't care*. But they didn't. They were embarrassed. And what was the point, if they wouldn't get credit.

It wasn't fair, Lydia thought. They worked so hard for a fraction of what her brother's girls so thoughtlessly took. Lydia wished her nieces well but they'd been given enough for one hundred lifetimes. Her things and her money went elsewhere.

Lydia made a list of what she was giving away, and to whom.

M—Elaine?

It pained her, but Lydia was thinking about asking Elaine

to take Maxine. They might be good for each other, Lydia thought, though Maxine wouldn't live much longer and Lydia hated to impose that sorrow on Elaine again so soon. And Lydia wasn't sure Elaine could walk her, even as far as Maxine was willing to go now. The truth was, there was no right person to give her to, really. Spence would keep her, if it came to that, but Lydia didn't trust him to adore her in her old age the way she deserved. She'd need someone to nurse her through her grief, then through her final days, make the inevitable decision not too soon, not too late.

Malcolm would stay with Spence.

Silver—Celia.

It was a mismatched jumble, but she and Peter gave dinners, or used to, and Celia didn't have her own. Lydia had thought about giving it to Liv, for the girls, but Liv already had some, and her mother's, and her grandmother's. The girls would get that, though Lydia couldn't imagine they'd ever use it. When the time came, their guests would eat with chopsticks, or spears.

Art supplies—Celia.

The tubes of paint were dry and cracked and most of the brushes were stiff, but there was a closet full of other perfectly good stuff—watercolor paper and canvas, boxes of chalks and colored pencils. Celia should get back to work, Lydia thought. What she didn't want she could donate.

What Lydia really wondered was whether she should give Celia part of her investment account, the one she'd expected would carry her comfortably through retirement. If so, she'd need to do the paperwork soon, before this thing went any further. She was running out of energy.

Lydia had decided to set it up so that when she died, whatever funds were left would go into a scholarship fund for returning students. She'd been musing about the idea for years. Only recently, belatedly, had she acknowledged to herself that it was time to make an actual plan. "Call abt. fund," Lydia wrote on a Post-it. She stuck it on her computer. She'd had one exploratory meeting with the dean already, but now, to make it happen, she'd have to come clean about her circumstances. And she needed to hurry, before the kid she had in mind for the first award gave up and dropped out.

Though the student Lydia was thinking of—Rochelle Smith—was a little older, not really a kid. She'd been in Lydia's art appreciation class, and the next semester she'd signed up for drawing. Lydia knew from her first paper that she was bright.

Lydia always started the semester by getting them to make a list of ten beautiful things—not to be graded, just to make them think. Rochelle had begun her list with "My son Bryan." Numbers 2 through 4 were "sunsets," "Twinkles our cat," and "Gale Jordan my mother." But then it got interesting. Number 7 was "the sound of a bee." The list ended with *Untitled* by Mark Rothko.

Lydia had to go back and read the paper again to be sure. At first she couldn't account for the leap, but then remembered: the painting appeared as a color plate, in the textbook. Rochelle had actually bought the textbook, and had been boning

up, or at least paging through, before the semester even started!
In the section where they were supposed to say why each thing
was beautiful, about number 10 Rochelle had written, "I like
how it makes me feel peaceful and also dizzy." Affixed to the
paper was a photograph of Bryan in a Santa hat, tightly holding
Twinkles. The boy's eyes, behind thick glasses, didn't quite
focus.

Rochelle had started hanging around after class. Lydia
learned she lived with her mother, and worked as a dancer at a
place called the Pony Club out by the airport. (Her stage name
was Amber.) She wanted to be an art therapist, she'd told Lydia,
or if that didn't work out, a dental hygienist.

Lydia planned to make sure Rochelle got the money, and
got to keep it, no matter what they found out about her. The
dean wanted to make it a contest, set up *criteria*. Grades, con-
duct, letters of recommendation. Qualifying essays. After that,
progress reports. Bull*shit*, Lydia wanted to say. Then she remembered it was her money and just said no. But the fact the
dean had even brought it up made her sick. That was exactly
the sort of filter designed to keep someone like Rochelle out,
the fork in the road that would shunt her finally and forever
into the won't-get-any lane. This had to vault over all that, be
a gift, out of the blue, with no sucking up or showing off required.

There were only two criteria, in Lydia's mind: need and
desire. Plus that other little thing, whatever it was, that Rochelle had that Lydia could sense. Lydia wished she could survive, just so she could stay around to keep an eye out for that.

She couldn't think of a single person at the college she could trust to do it for her, after she was gone.

Lydia remembered the time Rochelle, wearing jeans and gym shoes, had come to her office to talk about an assignment. She'd been on her way to catch the bus, to work. "Oops," she'd said, on the way out, grabbing the nylon tote bag she'd set down for a minute. "Better not forget my uniform." She'd allowed herself a little one-sided smile then. Lydia had pictured the contents of the small bag—a wisp of lace spandex, maybe, a pair of platform heels. Probably a wig, too, given the usual state of Rochelle's hair. She'd heard soft clinking coming from the bag when Rochelle turned to leave—cosmetics jars knocking against the shoes, Lydia guessed.

But probably Celia could use an infusion of cash, too, Lydia decided. There were signs that they were worse off than she let on, though Lydia didn't want to insult her by asking. Peter's business was doing *fine*, Celia always claimed. And she'd gotten that library job, whatever that was. That was good, wasn't it? Lydia had been too distracted lately to really pay attention to the details.

Best just to rearrange it and add her. She wrote "Add Celia" to her "Call guy abt. finances" list. What a pain, though, to have to think about money at a time like this.

Cookbooks—Maura, Peter.

Raspberries—Norris.

It was the only thing of hers Lydia could think of that Norris might want—Norris had admired them once. She'd have to dig them up herself next spring. Lydia would put Spence on notice to expect her. He wouldn't mind—they needed to be thinned, and Norris was the only one of her friends he liked.

Lydia hoped she'd replant them in Michigan. Roots were what Norris needed, if she was going to stay. She should have some of Chicago with her there in the soil, whether she liked it or not, a reminder of this place and the raspberry cobbler Lydia used to make. Not that Norris ever ate any.

Car—sign over to Spence.

Organs.

At least that was in order. She'd already signed the form. At the bottom she'd written, *Help yourself.*

Art—Jayne, Betsy, Celia.

Jayne might like the paint-by-numbers German shepherd, Lydia thought. She'd bought it at a thrift store in East Los Angeles and now it hung, in an enormous gilt frame, in the downstairs bathroom. Jayne collected what she still called outsider art, though the term had been debunked. Betsy might want the photos, for her office. Lydia thought she'd give the signed Kandinsky drawing to Celia.

Lydia had never liked it. It reminded her of Garrett, who she'd watched haggle for it, in French, at a flea market outside Paris. She'd been in love, and she'd been impressed. Afterward he'd given it to her, then taken her to some adorable bistro where dogs were eating from their own plates. He'd spent the whole lunch staring at some girl at the next table.

"You sure have known some assholes," Celia said when Lydia told her this, years after it happened. They'd been sitting at

Lydia's kitchen table, drinking beer and munching on Cheetos, when the subject of Garrett had come up. Celia was married by then. She'd felt qualified to dis Lydia's ex-boyfriends.

"The things we do for love," Lydia had said, quoting that awful song, thinking it was clear she was being sarcastic, meaning that it was OK, funny even, and that Celia should back off. It was during a bad patch with Spence. Lydia felt proud somehow, that she'd survived him and Garrett and all the others, the rough-and-tumble of love, and that they'd mostly survived her, stayed friends, even. She was proud she hadn't caved to something tame and sweet and painstakingly negotiated, the way Celia had. Celia had gotten so complacent.

"The things *you* do for love," Celia had said, in that superior tone she got, popping another Cheeto into her mouth to punctuate her point, then popping one into Maxine's for good measure. Maxine had been younger then, she'd eat anything.

"Does it work for anyone?" Lydia had said, forgetting for a minute that it seemed to be working for Celia. Celia had raised her eyebrows and shrugged, avoiding Lydia's eyes.

It had stung, Celia going all smug like that.

"The thing to do," Lydia had said, yanking the pop-top off another beer. "I don't mean now, it's too late. But if I had a daughter? I'd tell her the thing to do is just do what you want." Lydia squared her shoulders and took a gulp. "At least then you'd have that. Act like a man. Go be an architect in Budapest or something. Keep your sex life on the side, the way they do."

"It seems you did," Celia had said, though she hadn't meant

to let herself be drawn in. "Besides, it's not that simple. What if what she wants is to fall in love?"

"Then she's fucked," Lydia had said, flinging the pop-top in the direction of the sink. She felt betrayed. It wasn't fair that Celia was the one doling out advice on love.

Lydia didn't want to think about it, even now. She should have given that drawing away years ago.

The phone rang. Lydia stared at it. She'd been waiting all day for a call but now she was afraid to answer. Lydia tried to read the number but something was wrong with her caller ID.

The phone continued to ring. A part of her liked not knowing who it was. It allowed her to believe, or to *visualize* as she'd been told to do, that it was her doctor calling to leave a message, to tell her the tests were wrong, that the spots on her pancreas, which more recently had appeared on her liver, were gone.

Lydia imagined calling him back. *But how, why*, she'd say. *I don't know*, he'd say, and she'd say, *What does someone in my position do now*, and he'd say, *There is no one else in your position so do as you like*, and she'd try to imagine what that would be. Or maybe he'd say, in an intimate tone, *Which position is that?* She allowed herself to visualize him inviting her to dinner. He'd be wearing his stethoscope, a loosened necktie. He'd roll up his white sleeves and pour them each a glass of wine.

Lydia spotted Spence's boots in the corner, then, and felt

embarrassed. She'd been trying to invoke the positive power of visualization but already it had backfired, as these things so often did. Embarrassment was first cousin to shame, which, everyone agreed, fed cancer. Guilt, too. Also grudges, hate, resentment, remorse—all killers. Regret was the worst, they said.

Listing her regrets had been making her sicker!

Hope and gratitude, then, Lydia thought. That's what heals, they said. Love. Though the thought of that loaded word deflated her somehow, made her feel unloved. A disapproving voice in her head—but whose? Her father's? Some ex?—said, *Not being loved, you idiot, loving*, so she tried to visualize that. She reached down and buried her hand in Maxine's thick coat, though maybe that didn't count, it was so easy. Lydia thought about her friends then, already on their way to her house, and how good it would be to see them, how she would savor the evening after the doctor called to tell her she wasn't dying.

She made a quick deal with the god she wasn't sure she believed in—if that happened, if she got a reprieve, she'd give away everything. Already she felt better! That's what she'd announce tonight, after she got her good news—her newly formed plan to remake her life. She didn't have time now, but she was already looking forward to a new list: How I'll Change My Life After My Miraculous Remission.

Lydia picked up the phone to see if there was a message, but whoever had tried to reach her hadn't left one. Then the phone rang again. This time she grabbed it.

Celia

Celia got to Lydia's house early, hoping for a chance to talk before the others got there, but when she arrived, Lydia was on the phone and wouldn't get off. She didn't seem to have finished dressing. Her face looked strange—maybe it was the overhead light. It was odd, though, Celia thought. She wasn't that early and Lydia didn't like to be seen looking bad. Even when she was a mess it was usually for dramatic effect. But now Lydia really was a mess, and agitated, holding the phone with her shoulder, gesturing to Celia to put the food in the kitchen, then turning her back so Celia couldn't hear what she was saying.

Celia set the food down, hung up her coat, then sat on a kitchen stool and waited. After a few minutes she opened a bottle and poured herself a glass of wine. She looked around for Maxine, to give her the treat she'd brought, but the dog was in the next room, lying sideways at Lydia's feet, staring into the middle distance. Maxine looked worried.

Celia heard Lydia say, *No, but thanks, I'll be all right. Thank you for calling to tell me.*

Lydia: 6:50 P.M.

Celia stood at the foot of the stairs, suspicious. "Are you sure I can't do something?" she called up to Lydia.

Lydia was standing in front of her mirror, trying to think of what to do. "No," she called back, wishing Celia would just leave her alone. "Or, open some bottles." That should keep her busy for a while. Celia was terrible at opening bottles.

Now would be the time to pray, Lydia thought.

Though what would she say? *Please God, don't make me extinct, and forgive me for wasting my life.* Or *Don't make me extinct yet.* Or *Please, God, make what I know isn't true, true. Exist. And while you're at it, reverse time.*

She didn't think she could. Prayer was for children, or believers, on the fast track to heaven. *Yea though I walk through the valley of the shadow of death*—all that. She thought again of how comforting it would be, at a time like this, to believe. Who wouldn't like to have a little chat with Jesus right now, that all-forgiving best friend, that big boyfriend in the sky?

Ye who are weary, come home.

But she and Jesus had drifted apart. As she had from all her friends, if truth be told. A queasy feeling washed over her. Even she and her body had drifted apart. Or rather, it was drifting from her.

Lydia was remembering Sunday school. They'd prayed out loud, together—*Our father, who art in heaven, hallowed be thy name.* She'd even sung in the choir, if quietly and out of tune. Every year she'd tried out for the Christmas pageant. She remembered praying then, for a speaking part, but she always ended up as an angel. Her name wasn't even in the program, but it didn't matter, they said. Every voice was precious to Jesus. Every voice raised in praise made Him glad. Or so they said, and she'd believed it.

She'd believed it all—Baby Jesus and eternal life and that mercy was better than vengeance. It wasn't that she was gullible. She knew it defied logic, but she'd liked that. She'd liked the riskiness of believing in something so outlandish, and when her nonbelieving friends took His name in vain she'd felt a pang, real pain. She wasn't even Catholic but she'd stared at her palms and hoped for blood.

Now she stared at her face, grotesque and yellow in her magnified makeup mirror, and hoped for—what? Not blood. Who needed that, she thought, brushing on a little more powdered blush. Time—that's what she hoped for now. She squinted into the mirror. Time and smaller pores.

"Lydia, are you all right?"

"I'm almost ready!"

Lydia had thought she'd go back to church when she got old. She'd even looked forward to it, to a time when the burden to fit in with the secular world would be more easily shucked off. She'd looked forward to the privacy of old age, when she could become strange in her beliefs and no one would notice or care. She'd thought as she approached death that she would rediscover faith, had planned to include in her practice some of the more exotic beliefs the early Christian church had dumped in favor of the harsher, more simplistic system it later adopted. The Gnostics believed in reincarnation.

But here she was, as old as she was going to get, and abruptly she'd lost interest. When she needed belief most, she couldn't summon it. Was that possible, even? Wasn't the well of faith supposed to fill from below? But it was the physical world she wanted to hold on to now, even as it ran out of her, away from her, leaving her high and dry, between two worlds.

It was the doctor who'd called. The test confirmed what he thought—the cancer had spread. He gave her six weeks.

PART
TWO

The Party: 10:00 P.M.

In a burst of wine-fueled energy, the women had pushed the couch out of the way, scraping the floors, and moved the dining table in front of the fireplace. They'd set it at an angle so it would fit, though it didn't really, and now, after dinner, the group was wedged in front of the fire, arguing about universal health care.

Platters and plates had been removed, along with the white tablecloth, after Elaine knocked over a bottle of red wine, and now a whole new meal, a banquet of desserts, had replaced them on the bare pine table. Along with the desserts, any single one of which would have been enough, the table held candlesticks, wineglasses, cups and saucers, two teapots, a coffeepot, and a forest of bottles—wine mostly, but also mineral water, grappa, and an old bottle of Fra Angelico someone had unearthed and brought along for laughs. Elaine was dribbling some in her coffee.

"I don't care how much it costs," Celia was saying. "A society is only as moral as how it treats its weakest members." Jayne passed a tin of homemade candied grapefruit peel to Elaine.

"Ah. What would one of these evenings be without petrified sour fruit rinds," Elaine said, to Maura, who'd brought it. She might as well rip out her teeth with pliers, Elaine thought. Everyone else was laughing at some story Betsy was telling now, about her clients and welfare fraud, but Elaine couldn't shake her dark mood, and thinking about her dental problems didn't help. She could hardly afford to have teeth.

Maura smiled, as if she hadn't heard the insult. Maybe she wouldn't bother to make candy next year, she thought. Her grandmother had taught her how, but the only people who'd ever liked it were all dead now. Roy had loved it. Of course, he was of an older generation that appreciated that sort of thing, she thought. They'd eaten it in bed—the tin balanced on her belly, sugar dropping onto her breasts, like snow. They'd done it every year, called it their own private Christmas. He'd spent his actual Christmas with his family.

When the tin came to her, Lydia took a piece and nibbled on the end. "Delicious," she said, setting it down. Elaine picked up the uneaten candy and made a show of slipping it under the table to Maxine. When the dog refused it, Elaine tossed the thing into the fire. The sugar set off sparks.

"Opa!" someone said.

Lydia watched her guests. Everyone was talking at once now, even Elaine, even Norris, about grass-fed beef, the best place to vacation in Mexico, homelessness, Afghanistan, aging parents, Greek yogurt, college tuition, sleep apnea, the nutritional value of kale, the surprising satisfaction of silk long underwear,

Botox, some novel everyone had read but her. Lydia was happy they seemed happy, but she felt exhausted.

Lately, in the midst of some gathering or the middle of a conversation, Lydia noticed she wanted to disappear. She'd make excuses, go to the bathroom, pretend to hear the telephone and leave the room. In a restaurant, the feeling would come over her so overwhelmingly that she'd need to get up and go away. *I'm sorry*, she'd say, *I need a little air.* She'd move to the outside seat or hint that she had an overactive bladder, which was less embarrassing than this other thing she didn't have a name for, this feeling she sometimes got that she would simply explode if she had to be in close proximity to another human being for one more second. Betsy could name it, Lydia supposed. Betsy could probably even suggest medication, though even if Lydia had expected to live long enough for some calming drug to take effect, which she didn't, she wasn't sure she'd want to be medicated out of this feeling. A diagnosis would make the feeling a sickness, and this felt more fundamental than that.

Lydia remembered a cat she'd had—Gladys. Two weeks before Gladys died, she'd started to leave. Neighbors would call to say she was in their garage. Someone called from a sandwich shop, four blocks away. *We've got your cat*, they said, always kind. Lydia would bring her home and give her something special to eat, but the next day Gladys would do it again. After she died, it occurred to Lydia that Gladys had known it was time to leave. Maybe, Lydia thought, that was happening to her.

It seemed a shame, though, bad timing. She'd looked

forward to the party all year and this would be her last. Now, in the midst of it, she could hardly breathe. She'd gotten stuck on the inside of the table, next to the fire. It had been fine earlier but now she felt trapped and could feel herself starting to sweat. She was plotting how to get out. She could crawl under the table, she thought, pretend it was a joke or that she wanted to pet Maxine, though that was a bit far-fetched. If she had to, she could climb over the table but that would seal it, that she was certifiable. She should just excuse herself, she thought. People did it all the time, though then she'd have to speak, interrupt Jayne, who was telling some story, to ask Celia to get up.

Lydia eyed the couch, the cool, beautiful, commodious couch, which is where she wanted to be. She wanted to lie down, just for fifteen minutes. She was trying to will herself there, where she could stretch out and be quiet and watch her friends having a lovely time. Let others talk, she thought. Let them carry this burden of social responsibility.

Are you all right, someone said. She was clawing at her neck, unzipping her fleece vest to let in air. *I think I need a little air*, she said, and they let her through.

Lydia needed to tell them, she thought, before it got too late and they started to leave.

"I need to make an announcement," she said, from the couch, but nobody heard. Celia was telling a story about Bruce Springsteen and everyone was laughing. Lydia didn't have the energy to say it again louder. She closed her eyes and waited.

Maura

Maura couldn't get over this feeling, even now, in the middle of a party, that everyone important in her life had betrayed her. She knew it was wrong to cling to hard feelings this way, and she tried not to. But some days Maura would wake up thinking about some thoughtless thing Roy said years before, and that would remind her of something Elaine said or something her mother had said when she was a child, and Maura wouldn't be able to go back to sleep and all the next day and for days afterward she'd think of it.

Just teasing, people always said, after. *Lighten up. Stop being so sensitive*. Even tonight. Elaine had just said exactly that, after she'd made fun of the candy.

She'd been clumsy as a child, it was true, also bad at gym, always dropping things. Fat, of course. Though looking at the pictures now, Maura could see she hadn't been as fat as she'd thought. Then she graduated from high school and got the job and everything changed. She lost seventeen pounds in six months. She bought new clothes, dyed her hair blond, got a perm. They were out of fashion now, but then it made a difference. When Maura saw how much difference it all made, how differently people treated her, she kept going. She got braces, then surgery. First her nose, then breast implants. After that liposuction, chin enhancement. She saved up for it the first time. Roy paid for the rest.

People misunderstood about Roy, Maura thought. They thought he was some terrible person but he could be nice, too. He called her dear. Sometimes she felt bad she'd let it go on all those years, that she hadn't done more with her life, but other times she thought what they'd had was a kind of life, too. It was their own world, secret and with many rules, but good sometimes. Once a week he'd bring over take-out food, little presents sometimes.

Elaine won't listen to this, even now. She tells Maura that Roy took the best years of her life. But Maura doesn't know what that means. What else would she have been doing? Elaine says, *Anything—don't you get it? You could have done anything.* Maura didn't know about that. He may not have been perfect but he'd treated her better than anyone else had.

They were together twenty-one years. She'd seen him twelve days before he died, of a heart attack at the age of seventy-two, on some island in the Caribbean, celebrating his fiftieth anniversary with his wife and his four children and his eleven grandchildren and his first great-grandchild. Maura read about it in the newspaper. The obituary said he died "surrounded by those he loved most." That had hurt, she'd had to admit. She'd always hoped that when he died, it would be with her.

It was his idea she go to college. He'd pay, he said. The catch was everything had to be secret, forever. He paid for the condo, too, every month. Now she owned it. *Big deal*, Elaine said, when Maura told her that. *You got a three-room condo with a view of the parking lot and free tuition at community college night school. His wife has two houses. His kids went to Yale.*

They didn't all *go to Yale*, Maura said, standing up to her, which she almost never did. But that hurt. Maura felt more jealous of his children than she did of his wife. Actually, she didn't feel at all jealous of his wife. Though at the beginning she'd wanted something more conventional. What it turned into, that was his idea. *What if we had an arrangement?* he'd said, early on, when she tried to break up with him. He was painting her toenails when he said it.

For years she didn't tell anyone. Then she told Lydia, who'd been so understanding that Maura thought it would be all right to tell Elaine. Elaine was all over her to dump him.

Maura didn't feel angry at Roy until later. Now, sometimes bad memories came back—all those holidays, alone. Somehow it was all connected—her mother, her sisters, Roy.

Elaine thought she was Maura's defender but there were times, Maura thought, she could be as mean as the rest of them, meaner, really. What was it about her that brought out the meanness in people, Maura wondered. Even now, here at Lydia's, among friends.

The Party: 11:30 P.M.

Despite the deep cold, snow had started to fall again, and the view out the window was a Christmas card, picturesque beyond all probability. *Snow on snow.* Inside, the fire, after its first hour of dangerous blaze and much overtending by the women, who'd taken turns poking and stoking it, had settled to a low, steady burn. Maxine had consumed most of the soup bone Maura had brought her, buried the rest in a snowdrift, and returned, covered with a white crust that began to melt the minute she walked inside. Now she was positioned at an angle under the table, her face as far away as possible from the occasional spark that flew past the fire screen and as near as possible to handouts and crumbs.

Norris was standing at the window, in her coat, watching the snow. She'd been trying to leave for an hour but her car was blocked. Jayne, never much good at parallel parking and now completely out of practice, had parked too close behind her, right up against her bumper. Norris had purposely arrived late so this wouldn't happen, but Jayne had gotten there even later. She'd sat with Wally while he finished his supper, then stayed until he fell asleep. Now—finally, Norris thought—Jayne had gone to find her keys. They'd need to dig Jayne out, then Norris.

Jayne started to put on her coat. "You can't leave yet," Lydia said. "Surprises are in store."

"We're digging Jayne out," Norris said, stepping outside. Two shovels leaned in a corner of the front porch. Norris picked one up and handed the other to Jayne.

Five minutes later, Jayne came back, stamping snow off her boots and asking for cat litter, for traction. Ten minutes after that, they both came in and announced the car was stuck. Norris held a cell phone to her ear. She was on hold with Triple A, she said. She pressed the speaker button and set the phone on the table. Finally, a recorded voice announced there would be a minimum six-hour wait for a plow. "What if I told you this is an emergency," she said to the human who came on the line after she pressed more buttons. "Then I'd recommend you call the police," the voice said. In the other room someone had turned on the television. It was official, according to the weathergirl—a blizzard. Everyone in a three-state radius was advised to stay off the roads.

Someone yelled, "Slumber party!" Glasses were clinked. Norris said something indecipherable under her breath.

Lydia sat in a kitchen chair, with Malcolm sprawled across her lap. Last year this would have been funny. Tonight it seemed like a bad dream. She was just too tired. Almost as soon as they'd arrived she'd been looking forward to them leaving.

Though at least now she had an excuse to postpone the announcement. She'd do it in the morning, she told herself.

"Better call Ted and tell him not to come," Celia said to Betsy, hoping to make her hurry, to keep Ted from leaving. If he was already on his way they'd be stuck with him all night. The last thing anyone needed, Celia thought, was Ted on the premises.

"He's probably already on his way," Betsy said, digging her phone out of her purse.

Celia looked at Lydia.

"What?" Betsy said, sensing conspiracy.

"Nothing," Lydia said. "Call him and tell him you're staying here for the night."

"I know you think he's overbearing," Betsy said to Celia, holding her hand over the phone while it rang. "But it's better than smug."

Jayne breezed in with a stack of dirty plates. "Stop fighting, you two," she said, though she found it entertaining. She set the plates on the counter, next to Celia, who was talking to Peter on her cell while she rinsed wineglasses. Betsy brushed past, phone to her ear, on the way to the hall for some privacy.

Lydia watched, wondering how soon she could politely retire to a horizontal surface.

Norris

Norris knew she shouldn't have come. Now she was stuck here. She'd planned to spend the night at the Park Hyatt, then Sunday in the city. She needed to check out the exhibition space at the Cultural Center and had planned to do that first thing in the morning, then see a drawing show at the Art Institute after that. If all went as planned, she'd be home before dark. Now there was no telling when she'd get out of here.

What a mess, she thought. Even a day away hurt, when she was preparing for a show. If she were home, she'd be in bed now. And back in the studio hours before anyone here was even awake. She hated departing from her perfect routine.

Norris knew people thought that was boring, but she'd noticed they were generally the same people who hadn't found something worth doing. Norris loved her routine. Every day she got up at five. She couldn't wait to get to the studio, though she made herself run three miles first, to get it out of the way.

After that, she showered, made coffee. Then she walked the few feet to her studio and went to work. Nothing felt better than that. Later she'd eat something, a piece of fruit, some yogurt. She'd had a kitchenette and a bathroom built into the studio so she wouldn't have to leave.

She drew for a while, first, to warm up—thirty minutes, maybe an hour—then she went into the painting, whatever she had going. Usually she put paint down, made moves, but sometimes, when a painting was further along and starting to get tricky, she'd just sit with it all morning. Looking, thinking. Sometimes when she wasn't sure what to do she'd sit with it until mid-afternoon. It was like a conversation that had wound down, she thought then, like waiting for the other person to speak, tell her what it wanted. Though usually she knew what to do and kept at it until she had to get up, to stretch, eat.

She left the studio then, took a real break. Shuffled to the kitchen with that light-headed feeling of leaving the real world, the work, behind. Then there was the mail, the solitary lunch, more yogurt, with nuts, or a piece of cold fish, or a boiled egg. She glanced at the newspaper, went outside for a few minutes, usually, walked to the pond. Then it was back to the studio, though afternoons were less focused. If she couldn't think of what to do she allowed herself to read then, though it felt a little like surrender. An uncertainty fell over her in the afternoon; she questioned everything she'd done. It was different from the exaltation she felt in the morning, but she liked even that, the sense of reassessment, of coming back to earth, thinking, *It's not as good as I thought it was but I know how to fix it.* Or *I don't know yet but I know I can figure it out.* Painting was a puzzle she knew she could solve, something she was always working in her head. By late afternoon when she was sure she couldn't work anymore, or was afraid the work she would do would cause more harm than good, she took another walk. After that she ate, usually a salad, then spent an hour or two on the computer. Sometimes she drank a glass of red wine then, just one.

Jay came over sometimes after he got off work and let himself in. Norris had given him a key so he wouldn't bother her, ringing the bell. He knew not to disturb Norris when she was in the studio. Sometimes he made dinner and had it waiting for her—she'd taught him how to broil fish. Norris allowed it as long as he didn't come near the studio. She didn't ever want him there, except when she needed him to help her move things. He was a distraction, which was his purpose, but only when she wanted to be distracted. And he came to the house only when she told him he could, about twice a week.

She made him wait, not to tease him, but because twice a week was what she wanted, and when he stayed overnight she made him sleep in the guesthouse. He understood to let himself out the side door in the morning, so she wouldn't see him. A few times he'd fallen asleep in her bed, or pretended to. *Oh no you don't*, she'd say, waking him up. *You know the rules.* And he'd leave, like the obedient child that he was. Norris didn't want to see him in the morning. It spoiled her routine.

The new paintings were big, bigger than ever. She was just finishing the twelfth, and probably the last, in a series of birch forests. She'd flown to Norway to do the research, hired a guide to take her around so she could take photos. She'd stayed all of four days—that's how eager she'd been to get back and get started. Each painting was nine feet square, nothing but tree trunks and light, and, in a few, snow. No sky, no ground. The work was laborious and time-consuming but it didn't take as long as it used to, now that she knew what she was doing.

Some critic had accused her of *cranking them out* but he was an ass. Even Natalie, who'd made a fortune off her reliable productivity, had suggested taking a break. But why? She'd never felt so herself.

Though lately even Norris had the nagging feeling she should change it up a little. Do something else, throw in a monkey wrench to keep from getting stale. She was looking at the women here tonight and wondering. Here could be her next show.

It was an odd thought. She hadn't painted the figure in twenty years, and the complication of starting now, having to negotiate with actual living subjects, was tiresome even to consider. It was just that they were so, so what? So *vivid* tonight, Norris thought.

She was looking at Celia's hair. It was a fuzzy halo. She was wondering what color it was, how to make that color, and thinking she'd start with Naples yellow and add a lot of white. And something else—some red, but which one, so it wouldn't turn orange?

Sometimes change was like that, Norris thought. It just happened, with no transition, for no discernible reason. Being stuck here, which was the last thing in the world she'd wanted, was having a strange effect on her. She'd always sworn she wouldn't paint people, but she was starting to think she was going to paint these women.

She could almost see the show already. The painting of Lydia would be the anchor. She'd aged a lot since Norris had last seen her. She looked gorgeously decrepit tonight. She'd be the centerpiece, facing the door, and to her right maybe Elaine, the odd piece that made it all tremble and keep trembling, the disturbing element that activated beauty.

People assumed ugliness was the opposite of beauty, but they were wrong, Norris knew. Prettiness was. Who was it who'd said that thing about beauty? Norris thought it was John Graham, the artist who'd made that obscene drawing of the woman with the gash in her neck, at the Weatherspoon. *Beauty is the beautiful expanded to the verge of ugliness.* Something like that. That's what they were, Norris thought, looking around. That's what these paintings would do.

She was getting one of those vision rushes now, the kind she usually got only in the woods, that state she used to fall into as a child that made her feel so strange—happy and mute and totally disconnected from other human beings. It's what made her want to paint in the first place, that sheer pleasure in looking. When she got that way, in high school, her parents thought she was high—she could hardly make out what they were saying—and she was, but not on drugs. She'd look at them— through them, they said—like they were talking objects.

In those days, she'd wanted to look more than make; sometimes she still did. Making, looking—either way, she thought, it was all about pleasure. All this blather about art as a higher good missed the point. Or was intentionally false. Art was pure selfishness. The rest was just talk.

Norris scanned the room. The candlelight on the bottles—my God, she thought. The stiff pink icing on those ridiculous cupcakes, the constellation of dark crumbs littered across the honey-colored table, Elaine's small, fat fingers resting on a silver knife, the moon of her cuticle, greasy from something she just ate, glinting in the firelight, the fire glinting off the silver knife with that low pearly glow that looked like a seventeenth-century Dutch sky. The moon on the snow, out the window.

My God, how beautiful it all was, Norris thought. Almost too beautiful, too Vermeerish, though the women themselves were clownish, too, more like a scene out of Jan Steen. Norris wouldn't make the paintings this beautiful—too corny. She'd pull it back a little. But she saw it, and she supposed this was her version of love. Appreciation was the best she could do, she thought, though if they knew how well she appreciated them, this minute, they might forgive what they thought of as her coldness.

She wondered how many of them would be willing to sit for her, nude. She could make photos instead of drawings, if she had to, to make it easier for them, so they wouldn't have to sit around embarrassed and bare-assed in her drafty studio all day.

Although it might be companionable, sort of, Norris thought, if they'd promise to shut up.

What odd thoughts she was having. An hour ago she didn't even like these women. Now she was imagining her friends—suddenly they were her friends—coming through her studio one by one and taking off their clothes. Unless she had them come in pairs. They'd like that better, she was sure, they'd feel less embarrassed, though she'd have to be very strict about her no-talking policy. Maybe she could pay them, Norris thought. Maybe that would make them take it more seriously, but no, they'd be insulted. She'd have to bribe them some other, more irresistible way. Dinners, wine—they loved to eat and drink. She could pay Jay to cater it. The cold studio would be a problem, though. She'd have to crank up the heat.

Unless she waited until summer. Put them in the water! How beautiful that would be, she thought—each standing calf-deep in the lake with ripples running out from her legs, her feet distorted by water. She'd put them in the little cove, standing on the stones. Norris wondered for a minute what Jay would think when she traipsed them through. *Be careful what you wish for*, she'd tell him.

She saw it now, the whole show, each painting seven feet tall, each woman a little larger than life, the stones under the clear water, the pond life at the edge, the ferns and frogs and turtles and schools of minnows and then the pale flesh of the women, their hair streaming down. Little yellow leaves lying flat on the water. She could start now, she thought, get their permission tonight. Then she remembered—she had her cameras in the car.

Celia walked past, wineglass in one hand, cannoli in the other, her soft hair a cloud around her head. Norris saw her as she'd paint her, long-necked and flat-chested, a tall, graying Botticelli nymph. Norris had no idea what she'd see when they took off their clothes. She'd protect what they most wanted protected, but some of it, the real shape of them, needed to stay. They were more beautiful than they realized, than she'd realized. She was beginning to see every painting. All she had to do was do it.

Norris got up and grabbed her coat. "I'm going to get my camera bag," she said. No one heard her. Betsy was in the middle of one of her faux-naïve stories, the point of which always seemed to be the discovery of her own carnal nature.

A shriek went up. Now that no one had to drive, they were getting really drunk. Even Elaine was laughing, for the first time all night, with her head in her hands, tears streaming down her face. They were wiping their eyes with napkins, choking on cupcakes.

Good, Norris thought. They'd be relaxed, for the photos.

The Party: Midnight

Norris was moving furniture. Fiddling with lights.

"I'm not doing this," Elaine said, to no one in particular. She was sunk into the couch, arms crossed over her chest.

"What if you just photograph us with our clothes on?" Lydia said, thinking that ten years ago this would have been fine, even last year she would have gone along with it. But not now. "I think that would be interesting enough."

"Interesting enough is not the idea," Norris said, adjusting her tripod, not looking up. But she knew it was the best she was going to get, tonight at least. They needed to get used to the idea. She'd get them to come up later when the weather got warm so she could experiment, inside and out, nude and clothed. Take her time.

Maybe there were two shows here, or more, over time, every few years the same women. Maybe she should put them underwater, she thought. She saw each one in the pond submerged up to her breasts or her neck or deeper, up to the eyes maybe, the scalp. Maybe she'd paint them lying on their backs in the water with their clothes rippling out around them.

Maybe she'd stand on the dock and photograph them floating on their backs as if they were dead.

Underwater. It was an idea rich with possibility, she thought. Norris heard the word all the time now. Mortgages. Homeowners were *underwater*. Thank God she didn't have to worry about that. She, not some bank, owned the place. She owned the whole thing—the house, the studio, the guesthouse, the boathouse, the barn, the six acres of surrounding land—and she kept a nine-millimeter Beretta in her bedside drawer to make sure she didn't have to share it with any surprise visitors.

"Whoa. What's this big boy?" Jay had said, hefting it, the first time he saw it. He'd been snooping, looking for matches, he'd said.

"Put it down."

He'd waved it in front of his face like a movie gunslinger. Squinted through the sight. "I thought ladies like you kept big old nasties next to their beds. Not some sweet piece like this."

"I said put it down," Norris said. "And don't say *ladies*."

"Why not?" He'd turned to look at her, his mouth still open.

"Because it makes you sound like a hick," she'd said. "Now hand it over."

He'd closed his mouth. "So what's it for?"

"Scaring off little hicks like you," she'd said, grabbing it.

Thinking about it now, she was sorry she'd hurt his feelings—a little sorry, at least—but it was true. He was a hick.

· · ·

Norris checked her light meter, thinking that posing them in water would allow them some privacy. It might even be a collaboration, she was thinking now. Let them choose their pose, how far underwater they wanted to be. It already was a collaboration—Betsy, Maura, Jayne, and Celia had each picked up a corner of the table, still covered with food and bottles, and carried it back to its rightful position so she could set up. She'd moved the big leather armchair to face the fireplace and had thrown more wood on the fire to make it blaze. She wanted to capture the flush she saw on them now.

Collaboration wasn't her usual mode but here was an opportunity to try it. She thought of the art dealer's daughter, that ridiculous name. Tiny Fabulous. It was some joke about art world vanity, she supposed, about people like her, some hipster parody of artists who held themselves apart. Who cared? Who said she was unwilling to experiment?

"OK, Betsy," Norris said. "Sit up straight, more toward the front of the chair." At the last minute Norris had shoved the big leather armchair out of the way and replaced it with a straight-backed kitchen chair. Better not to let them get too comfortable.

Betsy was sitting nervously, fluffing her hair around her shoulders and practice-smiling in her tight little way. She'd already been to the bathroom to primp, put lipstick on, some goopy crap around her eyes. *Less is more*, Norris wanted to tell her but Betsy wouldn't have understood.

"This is not a yearbook photo, Betsy. Relax."

She didn't want to direct them too much, though. Self-presentation would be part of it. If Betsy wanted the world to see her in blue eye shadow then so be it. Norris could change it later, tone it down or better yet heighten the color to truly grotesque levels. Besides, these were just studies, reference. The important thing, she thought, looking through the lens, the thing to preserve was this awkwardness, this edge between the fake self Betsy was trying to project and the other Betsy that Norris saw beneath it. Norris let her pose and mug, flashing her big, gummy high school smile, with the cute eye crinkle and shoulder roll. Norris kept shooting, waiting for Betsy to tire, trying to time her clicks to catch the uncertainty that came between the smiles.

"Do you suppose you could take off a few layers, around your neck? I need to see where it attaches." Betsy frowned but went to the bathroom and emerged wrapped in a scarf, her pale sternum exposed.

"That's it." Norris said. "Now try not smiling. Think about something sad. Think about Ted."

Norris photographed every woman, and Maxine and Pud. Lydia posed with Maxine—the dog wouldn't sit on the chair alone—and then by herself with the new orange pot. Norris lowered it into her lap, on a towel because it was still warm. "That's really quite beautiful," she said, from behind the camera. "It reflects up under your face."

"It's not really my color," Lydia said, thinking that orange reflecting off the underside of her chin didn't sound good.

"You look fine," Norris lied. The truth was that Lydia looked ghastly—it occurred to Norris she'd never seen Lydia look ghastly before—but it was going to make a wonderful painting. "Just think of it as kind of an Alfred Leslie look."

Lydia's face went blank and then, as memory supplied an image, changed to alarm. Norris said, "Good, do that again." She clicked several times more and stood up. "I got you at least."

"Get me out from under this pot," Lydia said. She felt weak.

Elaine went last. She held a plate of cupcakes for several shots. Norris said, "Why are you holding that? Did you make those?"

Elaine said, "No. I thought I was supposed to hold a plate of food."

Norris said, "Well hold what you made."

"I can't." Elaine said. "It's gone, eaten."

"Didn't you bring that dairy crap in a can?" Norris said. "Hold that." So Maura, who'd been watching this exchange, wishing she had the guts to speak to Elaine this way, went to get the can of whipped cream and Elaine held that, smirking and rolling her eyes.

"If you don't cut it out I'm going to paint you like that, with your eyes rolled back in your head." Norris spoke from behind the camera.

"Go ahead," Elaine said. "Make me look like the cadaver I

feel myself to be." Norris clicked some more, getting Elaine's belligerence. She looked to Norris like an old bull, considering whether it was worth her trouble to charge.

"What about you," Lydia said to Norris as Elaine staggered up out of the low chair with a hand from Maura. "Want me to do you?"

"I've got it," Norris said, producing a cable from her pocket. She sat straight on the hard chair.

"You need an attribute," said Jayne, thinking of the medieval saints. Norris had already thought of it. She held up a fish skeleton. She held it in two hands, like a banner, and just before she clicked, with her foot, Malcolm, who'd smelled fish, appeared from nowhere and levitated neatly onto her lap. Norris clicked a few more times—woman, cat, fish. A portrait of two predators, she thought. Perfect.

"Done," she said.

The Party: 12:30 A.M.

Betsy had started calling Ted around 11:30 but hadn't been able to reach him. She was worried something had happened to him but then they heard him on the front porch, stamping snow off his boots.

Celia went to the door. "Well, here you are," she said, sorry to see him. "What's the problem—afraid your wife's a flight risk?"

Ted bowed. Snow fell off his hat onto the wood floor. "Delighted to see you, too," he said.

Norris patted the little chair she'd set up in front of the fireplace. "Hey, Ted, come sit. I'm doing portraits. Bring your meatballs." She couldn't believe her luck. She hadn't even thought of Ted. He was the perfect counterweight.

"Shouldn't I comb my hair?"

"You look fine," Norris said, pushing him into the chair, pulling off his scarf. He was wet around the ears. There was snow in his beard. She yanked his hat off and his wavy gray hair sprang out, soft like a boy's. Only his beard was still red.

"I like it when you're rough like that," Ted said.

"I don't think you would." Norris was talking from behind her camera, trying to provoke him. "Sit still. Look at me. Stop smiling. Think about meat. Meatballs, meat loaf, pot roast, roast beef, beef stew, short ribs, long ribs, tournedos of beef, beef liver, goose liver, emulsion of duck gizzard, roulade, tapenade . . ."

"Tapenade isn't meat," Ted said.

"Good," Norris said. "Do that again."

The Party: 1:45 A.M.

The women, the dogs, and Ted all stood at the bay window watching the storm. They could hear the wind through two panes of glass. Snow was blowing horizontally. *Snow on snow.* Someone had turned the television back on to monitor storm reports. There'd been a four-car pileup on Lake Shore Drive. Three people had been declared dead and two more were still in the wreckage.

"*Oh, the weather outside is frightful . . .*"

"Shut up, Ted."

Celia and Lydia piled bedding and pajama-like garments on the couch. "You all know where the flat surfaces are," Lydia said. "Make yourselves at home." She looked at Celia.

"I'll handle it," Celia said. "You go to bed." Tired as she was, she was happy to take over, though she wondered what was wrong. Lydia had been acting strange all night.

"Good night," someone called out as Lydia headed upstairs, like a child, she thought, being sent to bed in her own house. She heard an outburst of laughter. Elaine, who'd earlier fallen asleep, sitting up on the couch, was wide awake now and retelling her therapy story, by popular demand.

"I thought it would be like going to confession," she was saying. "But the therapist was too, I don't know. Involved."

A shriek went up, drunken laughter.

"What's so funny about that? Every week I'd tell her about my life and instead of telling me what to do she'd start to cry."

Another louder shriek. They knew the story but they loved to hear her tell it. Maura was wiping tears from her face with her napkin.

"Did you cry?" someone said.

"Hell, no. I went stone cold."

"That's so sad," Jayne said, her face on the table. She could hardly speak for laughing.

Lydia slipped off to bed unnoticed, glad her guests were having a good time.

Sunday Morning

Before she'd gone to bed, Lydia, with Celia's help, had brought extra bedding into the living room, along with two sleeping bags and a stack of T-shirts, sweatpants, and pajama bottoms.

Lydia had told Celia to give Betsy and Ted her bed. She'd take the daybed in her office, she said. It was too short, even for her, but she didn't want anyone else in there. There were plenty of other places for them to sleep, accommodations left from the days the house had been a stopover for Spence's traveling musician friends. He'd crammed a queen-size bed into the closed-in back porch; now Lydia called the awkward space the guest room. The couch opened into a double. Spence wasn't going to make it home tonight—anyone willing was welcome to his futon in the basement. There was a ratty couch down there, too.

The party wound down in a boozy haze. Ted, who hadn't eaten a proper dinner, he said, helped himself to everything. The women wandered in and out of the kitchen to wrap food in cellophane and load the dishwasher, then lingered to pour themselves glasses of water and more wine. They opened the wrapped food to eat one more brownie or one more meatball and set plates on the floor for Maxine and Pud, then rewrapped the food and stuffed corks back into the few bottles that had anything left. By 2:30 most of them had dispersed throughout the house to various beds and sofas, and by the time Maura went off to squeeze into the still-made guest bed next to Elaine, who was flat on her back in the middle, snoring through her open mouth, Celia and Jayne were the only ones left in front of the fire. Jayne was smoking one last cigarette.

Lydia lay on the daybed, wide awake and fully clothed under a pile of blankets. She'd been too tired to undress and now she couldn't sleep. She couldn't get comfortable, though she was happy to have given up her bed in return for keeping everyone out of her office. Soon she'd have to give up even that, she knew, but for now, with a houseful of guests and the recent prodding and poking of her body, this little room, with its slanted ceiling and piles of paper, felt like all the privacy she had left.

Lydia was trying not to panic, listing in her mind everything left to do. She needed to call her brother. She couldn't reach Spence. She supposed he'd turned off his phone. She didn't even know what club he'd gone to. Hadn't asked.

Lydia stared at the cracked ceiling. The doctor had told her to put her things in order. What a joke. What did that even mean? Sign some papers, sure. But real order?

Pray, she told herself, but all she could think of was the prayer her father had taught her—she must have been four or five. *Now I lay me down to sleep / Pray the Lord my soul to keep / If*

I die before I wake / Pray the Lord my soul to take. The possibility of dying in her sleep had seemed thrilling to her as a child, a kind of benign kidnapping, a way to go straight to heaven and skip over all the things she'd dreaded, even then. Now she didn't believe in heaven.

If only she could sleep for a few hours, Lydia thought, maybe this awful queasiness would go away. Maybe then she'd be able to think. None of her usual tricks were working, even her favorite alphabet list.

Apiphobia: fear of bees.

Brontophobia: fear of thunder and lightning.

Chronophobia: fear of time. That was a good one. She'd even memorized the symptoms and she enumerated them now, noting that she exhibited all nine.

Useless, though. Usually she dropped off around gamophobia (fear of marriage), but tonight she'd made it all the way to zeusophobia and wasn't even drowsy.

The daybed was harder and narrower than Lydia remembered, and now she'd been joined by Maxine. The dog had stayed downstairs for a while, but after Elaine let her out one last time she'd plodded upstairs—harder for her than ever but she saw it as her duty—and nudged open the office door with her nose. She was accustomed to sharing Lydia's bed, wherever that might be. Now she was curled in a black ball at Lydia's feet, forcing Lydia into a fetal ball of her own.

Two strange twin embryos we are, Lydia thought, both about to be born backwards, into death. Maxine didn't have much time left either, Lydia knew. If they died tonight they'd be discovered like this, she thought. Maybe Norris would take a picture of them, curled together in death, and make a painting of it, and when she had her next show a picture of the painting of the picture would run in some art magazine, next to a glowing review. It was an oddly comforting thought, the possibility of such an afterlife, and Lydia began to drift off but then Maxine started to scratch and Lydia was wide awake again.

She got out of bed and lay on the rug. At least there she could stretch out. Let Maxine have the bed, Lydia thought, dragging a pile of blankets onto herself. But the floor was hard, even more uncomfortable than her half of the daybed had been, and she got up and went to her desk.

E-mail, the great consoling companion of the sleepless, that little glowing gray rectangle of warmth, her window into the beyond, beckoned. The Internet never slept, and nothing there would ever die. Lydia logged on, hoping for what, she wasn't sure.

Mostly there were ads, which she deleted. Something was wrong with her spam filter, though who cared now. Lydia noticed, as she clicked one ad after another into oblivion, a weird glow of preciousness. Their promises, which on any other night would have seemed mundane, sounded almost sweet now, like overheard greetings from some quaint distant world she'd already left behind.

Say good-bye to shoe clutter. (Good-bye, Lydia thought.)

Eliminate toe fungus immediately. (Eliminate toes.)

The incredible pet nail trimmer.

It seemed to be a foot-themed evening. Or morning. Lydia could see just the slightest softening of black to gray around the edges of the window shades. Any other day, she would have enjoyed the sight, that feeling of privacy and promise early morning held.

She'd have to tell them at breakfast. Instead of the warm, fire-lit mood she'd imagined, with everyone's edges softened by wine, there would be bright light and bickering, hangovers and hard feelings and not an extra toothbrush in sight, let alone a change of clothes. When they heard the news they'd want to stay and help when all she'd want was sleep. She dreaded it.

Lydia sat cross-legged in her desk chair wrapped in a quilt, trying to conserve as much body heat as possible. She could hear Maxine in the daybed, sound asleep now, making excited little panting sounds. Lydia heard the swish of the blanket rustling around her feet. Maxine was running, in her dream. Toward what, though? Lydia wished she knew. Lydia wished she could join Maxine in her dream, and run alongside, the way they used to, along the lake.

Lose fat while sleeping. Lose fat while dying.

Use the Trust-O-Meter to find Dependable People. Too late now.

Meet your perfect mate online. Delete.

See you soon I hope? This from her boss. So this is what he did in the wee hours. She'd taken short-term disability leave and now she needed to tell him, too. She hesitated, considering whether to get the unpleasant task over with now, but it didn't seem right, to tell him before Celia, and Spence and her brother. She scrolled down.

Trust the Marines with Loved Ones Remains. She hesitated, finger poised over the mouse. Something looked familiar about the address—KMALE. Then she remembered—Kamal, ex-marine, baby daughter. He'd been her star student for two semesters, then dropped out. "It's OK, Professor," he'd said, standing up even straighter than usual, when he'd stopped by her office to say good-bye. (*Professor!* She'd wanted to cry.) "I've got plans." She hadn't heard from him in over a year.

She clicked the e-mail open. It was a press release. She scanned the text.

MARINES OF BIOTRAUMA
(DEATH SCENE REMEDIATION)

Elite team of U.S. Marines . . . trained to perform search and recovery for fallen servicemen . . . unique mission from Day One . . . hygienic cleaning . . . sensitivity to emotional trauma . . . timeliness crucial . . . readiness at all hours of the night . . . remains recovered from the field . . . Reverence for the Deceased . . . countless ceremonies loading human remains on aircraft for transport . . . Respectful Onsite Commemorations . . . decontamination . . . remediate traumatizing Incident in the home . . . Families currently clean up 82% of all Incidents.

Lydia scrolled down to the photo. Two clean-cut young men, boys really, stood in front of a garage. She recognized Kamal on the left. The boys wore T-shirts printed with matching slogans. One had a knapsack slung over his shoulder. The other, Kamal, held a mop and a bulging plastic garbage bag. Both appeared to wear blue latex gloves.

Lydia squinted. Forty-eight hours earlier she'd been at her doctor's, naked and flat on a paper-covered table. Similar gloves had encased her doctor's cold hands when he'd unceremoniously thrust them into her body cavities.

Lydia studied the photo. The boy holding the knapsack was shorter and huskier, still buff from his days as a marine. With his guileless toothy smile, he could have been on a fishing trip. His pack might hold night crawlers, his dad's old reel, a brown bag of lunch.

It was his idea, Lydia felt sure. Kamal's expression was harder to read, his posture a little deferential despite his upright bearing. He was the one with misgivings, she could tell. But what had he wanted to do? Lydia couldn't remember. Probably his buddy talked him into this over a few beers. *C'mon, man, don't you want to get rich?*

Lydia clicked on *zoom* to enlarge the photo, to read what was printed on their T-shirts. *Pain is weakness leaving the body.*

Was this someone's ghoulish idea of a joke? Lydia wondered. Whose, though? Not Kamal's. And why would anyone go to the trouble? Besides, no one knew she was dying except for her doctor.

No, this wasn't a prank. It was a business concept. Times were hard; these were enterprising boys, U.S. Marines, America's finest. *Put two and two together*, her father used to say, frowning and stabbing the air in front of her face, meaning she was being obtuse. These boys had been to war, they'd looked down the jaws of death and *had* put two and two together and this is what they'd come up with—a suicide clean-up company.

That's what all that awkward language was trying to cover up. They were mainstreaming their military skills. Death is a mess, they'd learned, especially when you did it yourself.

DIY. Do it yourself.

It wasn't the first time she'd thought of it. Why wait until the bitter end, *until the last dog is hung*, as her father used to say, with a morbid glint in his eye. Maybe it would be better to handle it while she still could, rather than wait until the doctors took over. Or some awful nursing home. This is when a husband and children would come in handy, Lydia thought. Society would require them to take care of her.

She imagined e-mailing Kamal right now. Writing a check and pinning it to her pajamas. Telling him where to find her so by the time they arrived she'd be gone.

She wasn't ready, though, not nearly. And anyway, hadn't they had enough of all that, in Iraq? They were kids, her nieces' age. They should be eating pizza and writing term papers, not swabbing up brains.

Lydia heard a little rustling in the covers. Maxine. Lydia had forgotten all about her, but sensitive Maxine had woken up and intercepted these disturbing thoughts. Had been, Lydia knew, reading her mind and now was regarding her suspiciously from her post in the daybed. Maxine did not allow this sort of thinking on her watch. She rotated her ears in Lydia's direction and growled at the danger she sensed.

Just kidding, girl, Lydia said, climbing back into the daybed and kissing the dog between the ears, then nudging her onto the quilt she'd spread for her on the floor. She'd get back in, Lydia knew, especially after the shocking material she'd just uncovered, but before she did, maybe Lydia could catch thirty minutes of sleep with her legs not completely cramped. Thirty minutes would help a lot. She hoped when she woke up the e-mail would be gone, would turn out to have been a dream. She had half a mind to e-mail Kamal right now, tell him to let people clean up their own messes, tell him to go back to school. Although, how? The GI Bill didn't cover child support.

Lydia was dreaming. A young marine wearing blue latex gloves was mopping her kitchen floor. She was sitting on the counter, wearing baby doll pajamas, watching him and swinging her legs like a child. "Sign here," she said to the man, handing him a contract. "Everything's paid for, even a laptop. All you have to do is reenroll." She noticed the man's shoes were polished to a gleam. "Move over, Lyd," the marine said. "Let me in."

She tried to tell him to just sign the form and reenroll but he kept telling her to move over, and as she woke up she realized the marine was still there, was now in her bed, but that he had morphed into a fuzzy, corpulent, middle-aged man who smelled of garlic and red wine and barbeque sauce. The man was wearing boxer shorts and a T-shirt and his long, bare, fuzzy legs felt cold folded up against her back.

"Jesus, Ted."

The daybed that had been too small for Lydia and Maxine now held Lydia and the vastness of Ted, who was nearly three times Maxine's ample Rottweiler size. Maxine was awake now, too, and on her feet, at the foot of the bed, with her nose resting on the mattress and her eyes fixed plaintively on Lydia. She was making a rumbling sound low in her throat. It was one thing to let Lydia have the bed to herself for a while, but no way was she giving up her spot to this foul-smelling interloper, whose scent she remembered well and with no particular fondness.

Ted was trying to spoon, with half his body hanging off the edge of the bed and one thick, hairy arm around her waist.

"What are you doing?" Lydia whispered.

"I'm lonely," Ted said. "We never talk anymore."

"You want to talk, now."

"I want to be friends again," he said. "I thought it was the perfect time."

Lydia felt something press against her back. "Ted, stop it. I thought we agreed."

"You agreed. I didn't say one way or the other. I miss you."

Lydia pushed backwards with her feet and the half of Ted that wasn't already hanging off the daybed slid onto the floor with a muffled thud.

"Oof," Ted said, though it wasn't much of a fall.

"If you want to talk, stay there."

"Why are you always so mean to me?"

"I'm tired," Lydia said, curling up her legs to make space for Maxine, who heaved her big body up into the space Ted had vacated. "Make it fast. I need to sleep."

"Don't be like that," Ted said. "Tell me something. Like in the old days."

"What old days?"

"You know. The good old days. Har har har." Ted rolled onto his back so that he could more fully laugh his big silly laugh. He kept getting fatter, and lying there under the blanket like that, he looked like a mound of something to bury.

"Quiet. You're going to wake up the whole house."

Ted shot a wily glance at her profile. When she didn't respond he began to sing, softly at first. Lydia recognized what she knew was his second-favorite song from his third-favorite musical.

Lydia pulled the blanket over her face.

Ted continued, louder now.

"Please stop, Ted."

He paused, looked over at Lydia.

"Please?" she said.

"Not unless you say you'll talk to me. If you don't, I'm going to keep singing. I can go on all night, as you know." When she didn't answer, he resumed. "*We've gabbed the whole night through! Good mornin'! Good mornin' to . . .*"

"OK," Lydia said. "What do you want to talk about?"

"*You!*" Ted sang, finishing the line on key and rolling onto his side. "Tell me something fascinating."

"All right," Lydia said. "Here's something fascinating. I'm dying."

"Me, too!" Ted let out another of his big theatrical har har har laughs. "We all are! You gotta come up with something more interesting than that."

Lydia sighed. Reached out with her foot and poked Ted in the middle of his big belly. "Let me ask you something," she said. "And try to be serious for a minute."

"Gravitas is my middle name," Ted said. He put his finger to his head in a pantomime of puzzlement. "Or was it gravy?"

"Do you have any regrets?" Lydia said. "I mean, if you found out you were about to die, say in a few weeks, what would you do?"

"Hmmm." He looked thoughtful. "Really?"

"Really."

"Honestly? I'd buy all my favorite food and lock myself in a motel room and eat myself to death. Ho Hos, macaroni and cheese, fried chicken with mashed potatoes and gravy, Roquefort cheese, barbeque potato chips, an entire rib roast from Whole Foods with horseradish mayonnaise . . ."

Sunday: 6:30 A.M.

"I have wasted my life."

Lydia was trying to tell Ted everything she knew she wouldn't have the courage to say to anyone else, before she ran out of time, but now it was getting light. She could see pink around the edge of the window shade now.

"Frittered it away, Ted! How ignoble is that? Don't you see what I'm saying? I've lived my entire life as a sloth and a coward and a misdirected fool." She was whisper-shouting at Ted.

They faced each other in what had been the dark, Lydia cross-legged on the daybed, wrapped in blankets, Ted lying on his side on the floor like a huge curvaceous harem girl, one fleshy arm supporting his curly head and his immense hairy belly protruding between the hem of his too-short T-shirt and the stretched-out elastic of his grayish, once-white jockey shorts. A pilled pink blanket hung off his big freckled shoulders like a too-small cape.

"I hesitated, and I demurred, and I called it patience, and now I'm about to be dead and I haven't done one fucking thing that matters." Lydia dabbed a self-pitying tear from her own cheek. "As we used to say in fourth grade, what a gyp."

Ted rolled onto his back. "You may be overstating a little," he said, folding his hands on his belly. "But I get the idea. Though I wouldn't say you demurred exactly. Refused is more like it."

"Then I regret that, too," Lydia said, disappointed he hadn't disagreed more forcefully. "I regret that I refused. I regret that I lived a small refusing life. Out of inertia, Ted! I have lived a small refusing conventional life, out of fear and inertia. And consideration for others, like they gave a shit."

"Let's back up here," Ted said. "Not that conventional."

"Relatively," Lydia said, avoiding Ted's sly look. "Relative to what I imagined when I was young, relative to what's in my head. Relative to what I could have done if I'd just, I don't know. Done it."

"Oh, boo-hoo," Ted said. "I'm sorry you're dying and all but you don't seem especially inert to me. Are you sure that's it? You gave this party, didn't you? Made that nice stew? Go back to the consideration-for-others part."

"OK, you're right," Lydia said. "Maybe excessive accommodation is more like it. But whatever, now my life is almost over and I feel like it's made up of, I don't know, leftovers. Scraps. Parts I didn't have the heart or the guts to snip off and walk away from." Lydia looked at Ted. "Do you know what I mean? My life is a heap of remnants." She studied Ted's face for a sign he understood. He was massaging his eyelids with his fingertips. "Did you ever sew?"

Ted stopped massaging. "Ever sew?" His voice rose up out of the mound of him with indignant resonance. "I only made every costume for my high school production of *Brigadoon*."

"Right," Lydia said. "I forgot. So you know what I mean. How you have to trim things off. It's the last thing you do and if you don't it's a mess. And I never did. Everything I ever did is unfinished and everyone I ever knew is still hanging off me. I should have cut everything clean and started over but I didn't and now I'm a mess."

"Actually, the last thing you do is to press it," Ted said, in a tight voice. "But I know what you mean. You mean I'm one of those messy threads." He waited, and when she didn't disagree, he said, "That's me, a hanging chad of love."

"That's not what I meant."

Actually, it was exactly what she'd meant. It was no use, Lydia thought. There was no one she could talk to. There was no one who wouldn't be hurt by what she had to say.

Sunday: 9:00 A.M.

Lydia was awakened by the sound of someone saying *Oh no*.

She opened her eyes to bright, cold, unforgiving light. Blue sky, sun on snow, doubly bright. The brilliant snow—she could see it through her gapped, torn window shades—made everything inside look shabby. Daylight revealed all—her paint-cracked ceiling; dust on the windowsills; messy, useless piles on her desk; dog hair on the dingy blanket; cat hair clinging to the lampshades. Lydia hated to think what it revealed on her face.

She shielded her eyes but saw through the tunnel she'd made with her hands that more than a foot of clean, fluffy snow was piled against the windowsills, and on tree branches, and on the roof of the garage. It must have snowed all night.

Celia was standing in the doorway, one hand clapped over her mouth, like a cartoon, and comically disarrayed—her hair flat on top and fuzzing out to form an odd shape on one side, with little pieces of lint stuck in it. Her bluish ankles and veiny feet stuck out from a pair of Lydia's too-short plaid pajama pants.

"Hey," Lydia said. She lay at one end of the daybed in a cramped ball. At the other end lay Maxine in the same position.

Lydia heard something that sounded like an old-fashioned coffee percolator, but louder. She and Celia looked in the direction of the sound, and there on the floor lay the source of Celia's shock—a huge, inert mound of snoring flesh insufficiently draped with a small pink blanket.

Another death-rattle-like snore issued from the body on the floor.

"Oh, Lydia. How could you?"

"Don't be ridiculous," Lydia said. "But let's get him out of here."

"You have a crane?"

"Good point."

Celia was staring at her. "Lydia, we have to talk."

"We do. But not about Ted."

"I don't mean Ted." Celia fumbled for something in the pocket of her pajama pants. "I mean this." She held up a piece of crumpled paper.

"Give that to me!" Lydia grabbed for it.

Celia took a step back.

Lydia flushed. "Where did you get that?"

"It was on the floor, behind the big chair. Don't look at me that way," Celia said. "I was trying to pick up a little, before you came downstairs."

"Those were supposed to be burned! I put them in the fire."

Celia shrugged. "It was in a pile with Maxine's toys."

They both looked at Maxine, who dropped her head onto her paws, sensing accusation but not knowing what she was supposed to feel guilty for.

"You weren't supposed to see that," Lydia said. "It's stupid. Give it back. It's not even edited."

"Edited? Why didn't you tell me?" Tears filled Celia's eyes and balanced there, trembling.

"Oh, stop. I was going to," Lydia said. "Really. But it got too late. I got too tired."

Another rattling exhalation came from Ted. Celia looked at him, then back at Lydia. The tears that had been brimming in her eyes spilled down her cheeks. "You told him? You did! How could you tell him before you told me?"

"I said, I was going to," Lydia said. "But everyone was having such a good time."

They stared at each other, listening to Ted snore.

"I need your help," Lydia said.

Sunday: 9:30 A.M.

Broad-shouldered, long-armed, sure-footed Celia single-handedly carried the apothecary cabinet through Lydia's bedroom, past Betsy's small sleeping body, into the hallway, and down the stairs. The cabinet wasn't so heavy as it was awkward, and Celia knew that if she didn't keep it upright the ninety-nine little drawers would slide open and spill their contents, creating a rolling booby trap of a thousand little beads that would probably cause her to slip, trip, fall, and die right then and there, even before Lydia had a chance to announce that it was her intention. Where were all these goddamn needy useless men when you needed one, she thought, bumping into a wall and crushing her knuckles, trying to see over the top of the thing. Not that she would have trusted this job to Ted. Or Spence, for that matter, wherever he was. When she got the cabinet downstairs she lurched through the hall and set it with a thud next to the dining room table.

Elaine and Jayne were in the kitchen, setting out fruit and bread and platters of last night's leftovers for breakfast. They'd made coffee and squeezed oranges and filled pitchers with water and lemon slices and were setting it all on the big table along with various bottles of aspirin and other analgesics they'd found in Lydia's bathroom cabinets. Spence had reappeared— the trains were running—and he'd already shoveled the front walk and was now building a fire with last night's garbage. The dishwasher hummed purposefully. Maura was sweeping the kitchen floor.

"What's this?" Jayne said to Celia, setting a basket of stale bread on top of the cabinet. "Did you know your hand is bleeding? Are you crying?"

"Lydia has a little ceremony planned for us," Celia said, ignoring Jayne's questions. "She has something she wants to tell us."

~~~~

Lydia lay submerged in the tub of hot water and Epsom salts that Celia had drawn. "Take your time," Celia had said. "I'll come get you when things are ready. No one's going anywhere. I promise."

Lydia didn't believe her. It was Sunday morning, almost Sunday afternoon. Everyone had somewhere to go and now that the streets were clear—Lydia had heard the plows—they would dig out Jayne's car and leave. But she couldn't hurry if she tried. She wasn't even sure how she was going to get out of this bathtub Celia had deposited her in. Not that she cared. Leave it in the hands of fate, she thought. If she died in this tub, so be it. She slid underwater and closed her eyes. Almost fell asleep.

Drowning in the bathtub while your friends assembled in

your kitchen to argue about the proper way to make waffles wasn't so bad, she thought, when you compared it with turning some strange color and being carted off, in pain and smelling bad, to a hospital where you'd die anyway, hooked up to a machine. She wasn't sure she could pull it off, though. How would she stay under? She had nothing to weigh herself down. Even if she fell asleep, wouldn't she float back to the surface?

No, she wasn't ready to die. For one thing, she hadn't made anything official yet. There needed to be an actual will, Celia had told her, not just these fatuous letters and lists.

"Fatuous?"

"I'm sorry," Celia had said. "I didn't mean fatuous. I just mean your letters are wonderful but they're not going to hold up in court if there's a dispute with your, well, you know. Jayne's a lawyer," she said. "I'm going to ask her to handle it, or to find someone who can, first thing tomorrow morning." Celia felt a sense of urgency. She'd seen Lydia's body as she'd helped her into the tub.

"Jesus, Cel. Spare me the long face," Lydia had said, seeing Celia look away and thinking that the sight of her unclothed body at least didn't used to make people cry.

Now she lay in the cooling-down, grayish water. She had no idea how much time had passed. The bathroom was no longer steamy or even warm. A draft was coming through the door. Malcolm had nudged it ajar so he could hop onto the sink and keep her company. He sat there companionably, studying her jutting clavicles through half-lidded yellow eyes. At least he didn't seem repulsed by the sight of her body, Lydia thought. That was a good sign. Cats could sense these things. Though so could dogs. Maxine was an emotional wreck these days.

Her mind wandered back to her conversation with Ted. She hadn't done anything properly is what she'd meant, nothing all the way. She'd tolerated what she shouldn't have, not persisted in what she should have and never finished a thing.

It was exhausting to think of. Even more exhausting was to consider how she was going to get out of this bathtub. Why had they installed this deep soak tub? But she knew why—it was when she and Spence had first moved in, when the idea of not being able to get out of a bathtub would never have occurred to either of them. He'd installed it himself, as a surprise on Valentine's Day, an act that now seemed unimaginably distant and embarrassingly hopeful, obscenely so.

Hope *was* obscene, Lydia thought. It was wet and sticky. Forget audacity. The Obscenity of Hope was more like it. Though it had seemed sweet at the time.

Celia had left her phone on a footstool near the tub and told her to call if she wanted help, but Lydia couldn't even reach that.

"We're going to fix you up," Celia had said. "Starting today. As soon as we get everybody out of here. We're going to fix up this place and make it easy."

"Who's we?" Lydia had asked, not liking the sound of it.

"I am," Celia said, feeling more focused than she had in some time. "And Spence, whether he likes it or not. I know

Peter will want to help. Ted, your brother. Everyone will want to help."

"Please, not Ted."

"OK, not Ted. For starters, we're going to set up an emergency phone system."

"Oh no."

"It's the twenty-first century, Lydia. We're getting you a cell phone."

"Oh no. Not a cell phone."

"Yes, with speed dial. We are not your pioneer ancestors. And as soon as I leave here, I'm going to get you a cane."

"A cane? What am I, Mr. Peanut?"

"Don't argue," Celia said. "And yes, it's going to be the ugly aluminum variety from the drugstore until I can locate something cuter. Maybe I'll get Ted on the case. You know how he likes props."

Celia had been thinking she was also going to buy a walker and some adult diapers but she'd kept that to herself.

~œœœ~

Maxine pushed the door open, filling the bathroom with her good musty scent. Behind her stood Celia, holding a tray. "I brought you tea," she said. "Want me to heat up the bathwater? Or do you want out?" She stuck her hand in to test the water temperature.

Lydia dragged a washcloth over herself, let out something like a laugh.

"What?"

"I was thinking about my mother."

"I liked your mother."

"I used to watch her take baths," Lydia said. "In the middle of the day. She'd just lie there for what seemed like hours, with a washcloth across her eyes. I thought that's what all mothers did all day." Celia nodded to show she was listening. She was pouring tea from a yellow pot. "I'd sneak in and sit cross-legged on top of the toilet," Lydia said. "I tried to be quiet. If she heard me come in she'd take the washcloth off her eyes and put it over her crotch."

Celia snorted.

"Are you laughing or crying?"

"What's the difference?" Celia said.

~eelee~

Lydia dried herself, slowly. Dressed in the sweat suit and robe Celia had set out for her. Pulled on heavy socks. Slowly. Combed her thinning hair. Considered makeup, decided against it. Somehow, in one day, she'd turned a corner, aged years. Now that she'd admitted she was dying, she felt her life slipping away.

~eelee~

Lydia stood at the top of the stairs. She could see Celia below her, in the entry hall, barring the front door. In front of Celia, with her back to Lydia, stood Norris, camera bag over her shoulder. She held an orange in one gloved hand and her car keys in the other. Decked out in big sunglasses and a long white scarf, she was ready to go, if only she could get past this nuisance, Celia.

"*What* is so important that you have to leave right now?" Celia was saying.

"I told you. I have a meeting."

"On Sunday morning."

"Yes, in fact."

It wasn't a complete lie. Norris still planned to drive to the Cultural Center—it was open, she'd called to make sure—to scope out the space. She'd call the curator at home from her car. Maybe she could talk him into meeting her there. If not, they could discuss the installation over the phone, while she walked the gallery. She might even still have time for a quick visit to the Art Institute, before she headed home. Nice and neat, if only Celia would get her big, bulky, unkempt, food-reeking body out the way. Wasn't it a little late in the day for a grown woman to be wearing pajamas? Did Celia never comb her hair?

"Jayne's car isn't any less stuck than it was last night," Celia was saying.

"I'm well aware of that, Celia. But it just so happens that Triple A is on its way right now to dig us both out. Now, if you don't mind, could you please step aside? I'd like to warm up my car."

"Hey," Lydia called from the top of the stairs.

"Norris is just going out to meet the Triple A guys," Celia called up to her. "But she's coming right back in. Right, Norris?"

Norris was about to say no, but something in Lydia's face stopped her.

"For just a little bit," Norris said. "Then I have to go."

"Great," Lydia said. "I have something I want to give you."

~eelee~

Everyone was assembled at the table, which was covered once again with food, bottles, pitchers, and plates. The house smelled of coffee and bacon. There were ten around the table now. Peter had shown up with freshly baked bread, to help dig out their cars. Spence had been back for hours and had vacuumed, then shoveled the neighbors' sidewalk. Extra chairs were crowded together, plates were held in laps. Betsy, hearing that an announcement was about to be made, had opened the last two bottles of champagne, before Celia had a chance to stop her. Glasses were filled.

The party had resumed, with all the women, and Ted, wearing some version of what they'd slept in, except for Norris, who'd brought her overnight bag in from the car. She'd been up since six, run three miles in the newly plowed streets, washed her hair, and put on clean clothes. Norris looked at her watch.

Jayne tapped her fork against her glass. Betsy was yelling, *Toast, toast,* and Ted was saying, *I was going to make French toast but Jayne used all the eggs,* and Spence was raising his glass and saying *To all my friends* in his best Mickey Rourke, although these were not his friends. Maxine, who knew too much, lay sideways across Lydia's feet.

"Quiet, please," Celia said. "Lydia has something she wants to tell us."

Sunday: 11:30 A.M.

The men were in the kitchen, loading the dishwasher and putting away food. The women sat around the apothecary cabinet, dividing up the jewelry. All ninety-nine drawers had been distributed and now they were trading. Elaine, who did not have pierced ears, had gotten an earring drawer and traded the whole thing with Betsy, who'd gotten pins but favored chandelier earrings and a retro hippie look.

"I love this." Maura was holding a long string of freshwater pearls against her chest.

"Spence bought those for me, at an outdoor café," Lydia said. "Some guy came to the table with them strung over his arm."

"Wow," Maura said, looping the pearls around her neck, thinking of Roy. "I've never had pearls."

"What about this?" Norris said. She held up a sterling silver pin in the shape of a dragonfly. She'd gotten a drawer full of funky miscellany, not her style. Usually all she wore was a man's diving watch and, for formal occasions, diamond ear

studs, but she'd found the little pin among the Bakelite brace-
lets and it was the one thing she didn't hate.

"Isn't it nice?" Lydia said. "It was my mother's. Art Nou-
veau, I think." Norris pinned it near the shoulder of her black
turtleneck.

"What's this?" Elaine said, untangling something heavy
from a mess of knotted-together chains. She held up an oversized oval locket with a tarnished filigree cover.

"My grandmother's locket!" Lydia reached for it. So that's
where the thing had been all these years. She'd given it up for
lost. "I wonder if anything's in there," she said, reaching for the
locket again. She'd kept things in it, in high school.

Elaine ran her fingers over the side, looking for the release.
She found a little bump and pressed. The cover popped open.
Out fell the stub of a joint.

A cry went up, false hilarity. Celia took the roach between
two fingertips and held it to her lips, pretending to inhale.
Someone went for matches. Meanwhile, Elaine held the open
locket in her palm, plucking at something still stuck inside.
After a couple of tries she extracted the thing and held it up.

All they could see was that it was a piece of tightly folded
paper, crushed to fit. Elaine shook it a little and the paper began to relax. They saw blue ink, girlish handwriting, the ruf-
fled edge of a page torn from a spiral notebook. Lydia's list of
fears.

So that's where it went, Lydia thought. She had no memory of
having put it there, or anywhere—though it made sense, the

locket had been a hiding place—and no memory of having put the locket in the apothecary cabinet decades after that. For a second, before anyone knew what it was, she thought of grabbing for it. It was bound to be embarrassing. Under almost any other circumstances she would have grabbed for it, but to do that required getting up. She felt too tired.

Besides, she thought, why bother? It was ancient history, and if the doctor was to be believed, she was weeks away from death. Maybe, she thought, at this late date it might be amusing for once to let her friends see her without trying to control what they saw. Too little, too late, maybe, but really, where was the harm? At the very least, she thought, this could provide a bit of entertainment, fulfilling her duty as a hostess by taking the edge off the morning's grim mood.

Elaine unfolded the paper, rattled it. Bits crumbled off and fell to the rug. She looked around to make sure she had everyone's attention before she began to read.

"'Things I Fear,' by Lydia Fallows."

A little murmur went up. Elaine looked at Lydia, realizing that what she was about to do might not be as funny as she'd thought. She felt kinder this morning, after a surprisingly good night's sleep, and Lydia's announcement had put her foul mood in perspective. Elaine raised her eyebrows, asking permission.

Lydia shrugged.

Elaine adjusted her glasses and began to read. Lydia mouthed the words along with her.

"Things I Fear," by Lydia Fallows

1. Dancing (in public)
2. Going to parties
3. Giving a party . . .

The group had been silent but now a little cry went up. Maura reached over and gave Lydia's shoulder a sideways hug. "But your parties are so nice," she said.

"They're very nice," Celia said.

"Do you want me to stop?" Elaine said. "Maybe I should." Lydia shook her head.

"Is it OK if we laugh?" Jayne said.

Lydia nodded. "Please," she said. Maybe it would help, she thought. Things had gone from bad to awful.

Elaine resumed. Now every item elicited some kind of noisy response—hoots, boos, gasps.

4. Diving, especially scuba
5. Driving
6. Being buried alive
7. Getting married
8. Having a baby (a. giving birth, b. taking care of it)
9. Tarantulas, snakes, some worms, large beetles, centipedes
10. Big black dogs
11. Being seen naked
12. Getting fat

13. Going to hell
14. "This one's crossed out," Elaine said, looking at
    Lydia over her reading glasses. Lydia shook her head.
15. Being abducted by aliens
16. Being forced to sing in public
17. Bad LSD trip
18. Drowning
19. Throwing up or any kind of seizure in public
20. Going to doctor, dentist, etc.
21. "Crossed out."
22. Going crazy and being put in a straitjacket
23. "Crossed out."
24. Measuring out my life in coffee spoons
25. Ballroom dancing—gym
26. "Also crossed out."

Elaine looked up. "Are you sure you wouldn't care to illuminate us?"

"I don't remember that one," Lydia said, though it wasn't true.

27. Competition
28. Dying without accomplishing anything
29. Somebody reading this list

Celia

It was late Sunday afternoon now, already dark, and everyone except Celia had gone home. Spence was outside, shoveling again—another three inches of snow had fallen—and Lydia had gone back to bed. Celia was vacuuming.

What was it that made people crave disaster, she wondered, banging the vacuum wand under chairs, sucking up dog hair and food crumbs from under the couch. Boredom? Or impatience, the wish to hurry the world to the end they knew was coming, just to get it over with? Or was it the cleansing effect of destruction that people craved, she wondered, the possibility it offered for change? Everyone had stories—the house fire that unburdened, the bankruptcy that freed, the divorce that allowed the broken parties to walk away from the unbearable complications of love. Sometimes loss was a relief.

Something rattled up the wand—more jewelry, probably, a thin gold necklace, maybe, or a charm bracelet. But who cared, now?

At the very least, Celia supposed, disaster took people's minds off their pettier concerns, made them put aside their

schemes and grudges, at least for a while. Many a minor griev-
ance had been forgotten as people stood on street corners with
strangers, on 9/11, Celia thought. She doubted many perfect
dinners had been cooked that night. She'd gone to the pantry
and found a can of mushroom soup and felt grateful for it.

Yesterday morning there had appeared again a headline on
her home page that had been there for days—*Hard Times Make
for Shabby Hair.* It had made her feel guilty. She needed a haircut and had been putting it off. It wasn't cheap. And she was
terrified of Victor, her hairdresser. He didn't listen. Usually he
did something awful. Paying him, then tipping him, afterward,
felt like humiliation. She'd go home and look in the mirror and
cry, then wait a few months and go back and he'd do it again.
Why do you go back, Peter had said when she'd told him. Celia
had said she didn't know, but she did. It was like marriage.
Starting over with someone else would just be too hard.

Vacuuming made Celia's back hurt. She dragged a heavy chair
from a corner and sucked up a little stash of cat toys. She didn't
feel like bending over to pick them up. She knew her hair was
the pettiest of concerns. "I acknowledge that," she said, out
loud, over the roar of the vacuum. Who cared if someone
heard? She was sucking dust off the drapes now with the bare
wand. She'd removed the attachment to get into the corner and
hadn't replaced it and now she'd sucked fabric into the roaring
hole. She yanked it out—it felt like a rescue.

Here's what bothered her—for three days running she'd
avoided opening the story on shabby hair in hope, yes, *hope,*

there would be some newsworthy disaster to take its place. She wanted to feel virtuous in postponing her haircut. She wanted to not get a haircut because she was thinking of more important things, not because she was afraid of another one of Victor's expensive hack jobs. She wanted to invoke that selfish bromide of her grandmother's that was supposed to sound charitable but wasn't—*Look around and be grateful, young lady. Somebody else has got it worse.* Her hair was bad, yes, but it was nothing compared with *that*.

Celia had been thinking this just yesterday morning. Now everything had changed. Lydia had given her two Ziploc bags of costume jewelry, and a velvet pouch containing her grandmother's marcasite bumblebee brooch, which, she said, Celia had once admired, although Celia didn't remember having done so. Lydia had told them she was going to die any day.

Celia jabbed at a cobweb that hung from the ceiling.

She should have noticed something was wrong. She could have helped, gotten Lydia to the doctor sooner. Though Lydia had been distant lately, it was true. Celia had assumed it was another of her dramatic reinventions—Lydia being nervous, Lydia being mysterious, Lydia on a diet, Lydia having another semisecret affair, which caused her to change shape, color, even. Though yellow should have been a clue.

Now Lydia was giving away her things and Celia didn't know how to tell her that she didn't need her family silver, that she didn't want it, that she would not polish it, that her era of dinner parties, which Lydia remembered so fondly, had been over for years. The silver was beautiful—her response had been sincere—but truly, she didn't want it. Now she had to decide whether to tell her she was going to sell it or just wait and do it after.

And the jewelry—it was too sad. They were just going to put it in drawers and feel bad when they came across it, looking for the same old hoop earrings. Maybe not Betsy, but the rest of them. And just when it seemed like the morning couldn't get any worse, Elaine had to read that list. That, as Celia's eighty-one-year-old mother would have said, was the living end.

Celia had had no idea. She remembered some story about a high school counselor and then the road trip with the guy who turned it into a song. But Lydia had made it sound funny, not sad. Celia had no idea she'd been going around reciting some list in her head for forty years. Or that she felt so strongly about such, well, such strange things. That she was suffering from all these absurd fears.

Why didn't she tell me? Celia wondered, angry now, stabbing the vacuum wand in the direction of something shiny and sucking it up on purpose this time, not caring what she committed to oblivion. Why didn't she tell me any of this sooner? Celia thought. She could have helped. Couldn't she?

PART
THREE

Norris

Celia was organizing Lydia's care and e-mailed Norris to ask if she'd help. Norris e-mailed back to say it was a busy time for her but that she'd come if Celia couldn't find anyone else. Then she wrote back and said her schedule had changed and yes, she could come.

Jay could keep track of the house, she thought. She needed to go in for the show anyway, to supervise the installation. She'd get a hotel room, to have somewhere to go when she needed a break. She'd told Celia that, that she'd need a break, that she wasn't one of those people that could just move in and be there 24/7. She said she hadn't even spent that much time with Sam when he was a baby.

She could dig up the raspberries when she was there, she thought. Lydia had said she wanted her to. *It's two degrees out*, Norris had said when Lydia told her. *After*, Lydia had said. *In the spring—get Spence to help. OK*, Norris had said. What else could she say?

Lydia's dying changed everything. Norris never would have guessed it would affect her this way. They hadn't been close in years, but now the thought of losing her, of Lydia being gone from the planet, had thrown her off. The strangest thing, Norris thought, is that this effect, of Lydia's imminent death, had begun to set in before Lydia even told them. Norris had felt something coming toward them that night—change—without knowing what it was.

When she got home that Sunday—she'd canceled her plans and just drove back—she'd gone to her computer and sat in the dark, Googling people she remembered from the old neighborhood, from high school, grade school, even.

Except for an obituary for Larry Kulick, though, who'd died in a boating accident seventeen years earlier, and one mention of Claudia Puddeliwitz, who'd shown up on a long list of donors to some political candidate, no one was there. Not one. All those children she'd loathed, who'd so loathed her, weren't anywhere to be found. It was like waking from a nightmare and realizing the ghoul in the closet was an old coat.

She'd stayed up half the night, that night, sitting there at her computer in the dark, drinking one glass of very good red wine after another, admiring the ice on the pond and listening to the hooting of what she'd come to think of as her private pair of owls. She'd wanted to feel safe and satisfied with the beauty and serenity she'd achieved, all she'd earned and accomplished, but she didn't.

It bothered her, that there was no trace of any of them—her rivals, her enemies, those mean little brats. How could they have been so vividly awful as children and then just disappear into ordinariness like that? They should have put up a better fight, Norris thought. She still would have won. But she would have felt better, knowing they knew she'd bested them.

She supposed they were leading the kind of lives that didn't register on the Internet. Like her family, Norris thought, cops, teachers. *What is your problem*, she could hear someone say. Andy, she supposed—same old argument. *Why do you always have to be such a bitch?* But why did that make her a bitch? *They'd* terrorized *me*, she thought, even the "nice" ones, and then had the nerve to disappear into nothing before she could show them the tables had turned. They wouldn't know the Venice Biennale if it bit them in the ass.

It made her feel the way she'd felt playing tug-of-war with her brother, the time he let go and she'd landed on the sidewalk and cracked her tailbone. *You try too hard*, he'd said, and walked away. He'd laughed, smug bully. Who's laughing now?

Norris didn't regret a thing, she told herself. Or maybe a few things, maybe the thing with Lydia. She was a little sorry about that, how at the end, in the interview with the director, when he asked who she wanted to invite to the mentors' panel, Norris had caught her breath, hesitated—she was good, she could have been an actor, too—then hinted, as if it were painful to say so, that she thought Lydia wasn't really up to the company.

She almost seems jealous, Norris had said, pretending confusion, surprise that someone she'd looked up to could be so petty, though it wasn't true. If anything, Norris thought, she'd been the one who was jealous. People liked Lydia.

The least she could do, Norris supposed now, was sit by her side while she died.

The Funeral

Lydia died the second week of March. She died in the hospital bed Spence had set at an angle in the living room of their octagon bungalow, with a view of the fireplace, the television, and the bay window, which gave on to the muddy mess of the front yard, not that she could see any of it at the end. Spence had aimed the bed toward the window, hoping she'd live long enough to see the tulips he'd planted, but she didn't make it to April.

She died around five on a Tuesday afternoon at that grayest of gray hours in the Chicago winter when time seems to stop between day and night and the edges of things blur into nothingness, when objects formerly known to be solid seem to dissolve in a haze. Maybe it's easier for the soul to slip away then or maybe Lydia just wanted to die when Celia wasn't there.

Maybe it was a contest of wills. Celia had planned to be present when Lydia died. She wanted to hold her hand and tell her it was OK and witness her last breath. She had wanted to sit with her, alone, after it was over, postponing the inevitable phone calls until she felt ready and, when she was, she wanted to be the one to make them. She had planned to be. She had been there through everything else. She had helped Spence move furniture to make a place for the bed and stayed every night for nine days after that, getting the hospice nurses to show her how to administer drugs and subsisting on daily food drops from Peter, also from Maura and Elaine and Ted and the neighbors, with practical help from a rotating staff of hired caregivers and Spence intermittently and visits from a stream of friends Celia had only heard of in addition to all the women from the party except for Norris at first and then later Norris, too, who showed up with a duffel full of T-shirts and sketchbooks and a five-pound bag of raw almonds and moved in.

Norris took over then. She told Celia to get some rest, and after that they traded off. Sometimes Celia, in the kitchen making coffee, heard Norris talking to Lydia in a low voice. Sometimes Celia thought she heard Lydia reply, though that wasn't possible—she was unconscious by then, wasn't she?

Elaine came almost every day. Jayne, Maura, and Betsy worked out a schedule and visited in the evening. Ted, who was working the night shift that month, showed up in the afternoon, with casseroles or little bouquets—violets, once—and moped about miserably, in the fading light, sighing and dabbing at his eyes until someone reminded him not to be late for work. The last week, Lydia's sister-in-law moved from their remote suburb into a nearby hotel and later was joined by Lydia's brother. They came and went with relatives Celia had never heard of, and toward the end a hospice chaplain showed up. He invited Lydia's friends to sit in a circle around her bed and talk to her by-now silent form about their beautiful memories of her but everyone felt embarrassed and sad and made up excuses to leave. A prayer group arrived from Ted's church.

Through all this Celia was Lydia's keeper, not Spence, partly because she seemed to know what to do but also by force of the not-so-subtle assumption she imposed on Spence that he didn't, that she was better suited to the job than he was. She sent him on errands, made him feel unwelcome, though it was his home, not to mention also his house, which, by then, he knew, having read Lydia's will, which Jayne had written. He sat by when no one else was available, but when Celia returned she urged him to leave and, not knowing what else to do, he did, holing up in the basement or going for yet another long walk.

One weekend they were joined in this mostly comfortable gloom by Lydia's nieces. Awed by their first proximity to death and thrilled to escape the frivolities of college life for something real and useful, they'd insisted on flying in to help.

Celia put them to work. They were too energetic to sit still for long by Lydia's bedside, but they excelled at singing a cappella and giving deep-tissue shoulder massages and taking Maxine on walks, when she could be pried from Lydia's side. They made grilled-cheese-and-tomato sandwiches and did endless loads of laundry and ran the vacuum cleaner twice a day with such vigor that Celia had to ask them to stop. The noise drove her crazy, though she was pretty sure Lydia was beyond hearing a thing.

Immediately preceding Lydia's death, Celia had been at the house for fifty-two consecutive hours, but when the hospice nurse assured her that death was not imminent, she went home to take a shower and change clothes and eat a frozen pizza with Griffin at her own kitchen table and read e-mail at her own desk, although she couldn't bring herself to answer any of it. She left Norris in charge, with a list of phone numbers and a little bottle of liquid morphine, and told her to call her if anything changed. Celia then lay down for what she intended to be a ten-minute nap and didn't wake up until the phone rang five hours later.

So it was Norris who was there at the end. Norris and of course Maxine, who, Norris said, let out a long low howl when Lydia took her last breath and then set her head down on her paws and died in her sleep an hour later. Everyone was relieved about that. Maxine's grief would have been too much to bear.

~eelee~

Malcolm, who'd disappeared the day Lydia died, reappeared on the front porch the morning of the funeral, holding in his jaws a perfectly intact dead mouse. Spence, not wanting to get cat hair on the new black suit Celia had told him to buy, watched from the front window as Malcolm set the mouse on the welcome mat, perhaps as a tribute. The gift, and its ceremonious placement, lent an elegiac tone to the day.

Lydia's brother and sister-in-law planned the service, with help from Spence and Celia, who was still furious she'd missed Lydia's last breath. At first, Spence had suggested a memorial at the house, but Lydia's brother didn't think it was appropriate, since they were no longer married. And he wanted a real funeral, at his church, since Lydia didn't have one. Spence understood—the arrangements weren't really his call. Though it would be far for people to drive, those who even had cars. No public transportation went there.

Everyone agreed the funeral was beautiful, tasteful. Celia and Spence gave dueling eulogies, and Ted, who'd arrived at the house as soon as he'd gotten word of the death and waited until Celia was in the bathroom to volunteer his musical services to Lydia's brother, sang "Amazing Grace," his voice cracking only once.

After the service, light refreshments were served in the church basement.

Celia and Elaine stood under an exit sign, sharing cookies from a paper plate. They were waiting for Maura to come out of the ladies' room, where she'd gone to repair her eye makeup. They planned to ride together. Lydia's brother was hosting lunch at a nearby restaurant and Peter had gone to get the car.

Celia and Elaine scanned the crowd for familiar faces, deconstructing the funeral.

"It was nice of Trish to come all this way."

"And Garrett's here," Celia said. "I don't see him now."

Elaine nodded.

"There's that girl who's getting the scholarship. Nice that she came."

"Lydia would have liked the music, I think," Elaine said.

"I hope so," Celia said. "She picked it." She had pressed

Lydia to express her preferences in all things funereal, though Lydia, at the end, lost interest even in that. "Did you see that young guy in the back?" Celia said. "Who do you suppose that was?"

"You mean the handsome one? The prince of good posture?" Elaine gestured with the paper plate. "Black guy? Shaved head?"

"Maybe part Hispanic."

"One of her students, I assume."

"A student? You think so?"

"You know Lydia. She brought out the best in the boys."

"But in that suit?" Celia said. "With that posture? I don't recall my students looking like that."

"True," Elaine said, not caring. She was studying the plate, trying to decide which cookie to eat next.

"Look!" Celia said, looking over Elaine's shoulder. "There he is—with Norris!"

"Trolling for cougars, probably," Elaine said, not looking up. "If you combed your hair you might have a chance." She selected a pecan sandie and took a big bite. Powdered sugar fell onto her bosom.

"Look," Celia whispered.

Elaine grudgingly turned in the direction Celia was staring. Sure enough, there was skinny little Norris, with her spiky short hair, in a tight black sheath and opaque black tights, deep in conversation with an enormous, square-shouldered, gleamingly well-groomed young man.

"Looks like FBI to me," Elaine said.

"Maybe," Celia said. "Maybe he's investigating a double homicide and is going to take her out in the parking lot and shoot her right now."

"We can only hope," Elaine said, brushing crumbs from the front of her black pantsuit.

PART
FOUR

January again. Two years had passed since Lydia's last party and the six women were together for the first time since the funeral, for what some of them had taken to calling the Lydia Fallows and Maxine the Dog Bleak Midwinter Memorial Bash.

The first year, no one had felt like giving a party. January had come and gone, and finally, as the anniversary of Lydia's death approached, Celia sent an e-mail, to everyone except Norris, suggesting they meet for dinner at some gloomy Mexican place someone thought Lydia once had liked. But no one had time for dinner and the plan devolved into drinks and even then only Celia and Elaine showed up. The evening ended abruptly when Elaine spotted an oversized cockroach disappearing into the vinyl upholstery on her side of the booth, in possession of a large crumb.

The following year, they swore they'd do better. They discussed the plan at length, via group e-mail, excluding Norris by mutual, unspoken agreement until the very end. They discussed decamping to the Caribbean, imagined themselves sitting around an oceanside table in sarongs and sunglasses, drinking a variety of rum drinks in Lydia's honor. They even imagined the drinks—mojitos, piña coladas, Cuba libres, margaritas—but the trip proved impractical. Jayne didn't have time. Celia, who'd lost her job at the hospital library, had time but couldn't afford it. Elaine didn't feel up to flying. When Norris's e-mail appeared, inviting them all to her place in Michigan, to see the finished work for her new show before she shipped it to New York, Celia, to everyone's surprise, insisted they go.

So there they sat, around Norris's enormous steel-and-glass table, as Betsy told how she and Ted had finally parted ways. "It's all good," she said. "We're friends now. Lyd would approve. In fact, it was her idea."

Everyone laughed at Betsy as usual, although she was different now, they'd have to admit if they stopped to discuss it. She was dating, she said. And she looked less clownish, in almost no makeup and not much jewelry, except for a pair of Lydia's earrings. She seemed like an adult finally at the age of fifty-four.

They could see she was right. Breaking up with Ted had been good for her. Everyone was laughing because Betsy had claimed that Lydia appeared to her in a dream and said, *Ted needs to go.*

"You mean she told you in a dream that you needed to kick him out?" Jayne said, in that lawyerly way of hers. "Or that he wanted to leave?"

Betsy shrugged. "Both, maybe. Who knows? That's the beauty part."

"That's Lydia for you," Maura said. "Diplomatic even from the grave."

"I took it to mean we should sell the house and split the money," Betsy said. "After that, it was easy. He was waiting for me to bring it up."

Even Betsy was laughing now, at the idea that she'd conjured a visitation from the dead to allow herself to do something everyone agreed was so obviously overdue. Most of them did not believe that Lydia's spirit had made an actual appearance in Betsy's dream life, although some of them would concede later in a group e-mail that excluded Betsy and to which Norris did not reply that maybe Betsy needed to think so. Everyone was laughing now except for Norris, who was in the kitchen, and Celia, who had an even stranger claim to make and was now considering whether this was the right time to make it. Maybe she should keep it to herself, she thought. The fact was she and Lydia talked all the time.

"This barrier between life and death," she'd said, to Peter, a few days after the first time it happened. "Maybe it's not as definite as we've been led to believe."

They'd been sitting at the kitchen table on a Sunday morning, reading the newspaper and eating soft-boiled eggs on toast. She'd been testing Peter's reaction, wasn't sure she wanted to tell him the whole story yet. She wasn't sure he'd take it seriously, was afraid he'd only pretend to, and that the resulting conversation would leave her feeling childish.

Peter had looked up and glanced at Griffin, but he was

oblivious, deep in the sports section. "What do you mean?" Peter had said.

"Maybe it's, I don't know." She looked down at her egg, poked it. "Porous." She looked up. "Or gradual?"

Peter frowned. "Sounds like wishful thinking to me," he'd said, rattling his newspaper. Then, seeing her face, he got up and went to stand behind her chair. He put his arms around her.

"Thanks," she'd said, feeling a little suffocated by his pajamas, which were covering her face. He smelled like toast.

A hug was always nice but the truth was it wasn't what she'd wanted. She'd wanted to discuss the possibility of an afterlife. But she could see he thought she was still a little deranged. And she had been—first from the effort of the deathbed vigil, then from grief—until Lydia showed up in the kitchen one morning and asked to be taken for a drive.

"Are you—a ghost?" Celia had said, to the fairly solid-seeming same old Lydia who sat at her kitchen table, after she'd recovered from the shock of seeing her, the first time it happened.

"Technically, no," Lydia had said. "I think that's something different." She looked thoughtful, as usual, and nearly as substantial, though substantiality had never been her strong suit. "I just thought I'd drop in to say hi," Lydia said. "I miss this." She gestured vaguely.

"You don't mean you miss this," Celia said, making a face. She glanced around her crumb-littered kitchen, taking in the breakfast dishes in the sink, the overflowing recycling bin, Griffin's hockey gear.

"Yes," Lydia said, looking around Celia's kitchen. "I do. I miss the beauty of the physical world. I miss you."

Celia's face crumbled.

"Do you suppose we could go for a drive?" Lydia said then.

Celia said of course and turned her back on Lydia, for just a second, to rinse her hands, but when she turned around Lydia was gone.

The next time Lydia appeared—she showed up only when Celia was alone—they continued their conversation. "You can't mean you miss *this particular* physical world," Celia said, snatching a dirty dish towel off the counter.

"I do," Lydia said. "Or most of it. Not my body." She looked down at her purple yoga T-shirt, the one that said *Embrace Change* in pink cursive across the front. "But I miss all this . . ." She searched for the word. "Corporeality. I miss weather, how it smells. I miss how Maxine smelled. Though most of the rest of her is here. There. Wherever." Lydia looked sad for a minute. "I miss looking at things. You have no idea how this all looks from here, I mean from where I am." She gazed at the kitchen counter, toward an open box of saltine crackers. "I have to tell you. I really miss food."

"I'll make you something!" Celia said, feeling a little crazy but relieved to have a task. "How about a sandwich? I have some nice New Zealand cheddar. I think I even have romaine lettuce. Or wait! How about a cheese omelet?"

"No, thanks. I couldn't. I mean, I can't. We don't," Lydia said. "What I'd really like is to go for a drive."

It took a few more visits before they made it all the way to

the car. By then the novelty of Lydia's appearances had begun
to wear off and Celia was having a bad day. "You should have
picked someone to haunt who had a better car if all you wanted
was to be driven around," she'd said, looking over her shoulder
as she backed out of the garage and into a dead lilac bush. The
brakes needed work. She'd thrown a towel over the split upholstery on the passenger's seat, before they got in, but Lydia had
waved her hand.

"Really, don't bother," Lydia had said. "I don't feel much.
This," she gestured at her body, "it's mostly for your benefit.
Though I feel the air a little," she said, rolling down the win-
dow. "It's lovely."

Celia drove north on Milwaukee Avenue with all the windows down so Lydia could feel the breeze even though it was
33 degrees and sleeting. Lydia hung her head out the window
like a dog. They passed a strip mall. Filthy half-melted snow-
drifts revealed coffee-stained foam cups and patches of bare
muddy ground. Half-frozen dog turds lay along the curb. An
angry woman in a flapping coat stormed out of a currency exchange. A man exploded out the door behind her, shouting
insults.

"Nice," Lydia said.

"Sorry," Celia replied, assuming sarcasm. "We'll be past all
this in a few minutes." She glanced at Lydia. "I thought we
could get out of town, to the dog park, maybe. Or up into Wisconsin? If you have time."

Lydia smiled.

"Or would you rather go west—Bull Valley?"

"This is fine," Lydia said. "Really, it's beautiful."

Celia glanced over and sped up. "I'm driving you somewhere beautiful but we're not there yet."

"You have no idea," Lydia said. Then, at the next stoplight, between a Burger King and a gas station, she disappeared.

The most recent visit had been just weeks earlier. Lydia and Maxine, who had started to come along on these visits, had shown up on an especially bleak winter afternoon. Celia had been standing at the kitchen sink, looking out the window at a bare mulberry tree, wondering what to do next. She'd been fighting the urge to go lie down when she'd seen a little movement over her shoulder.

"Boo," Lydia said, sitting down next to Maxine on a pile of newspapers. Between them, they hardly made a dent. Celia thought she seemed fuzzier this time.

"Long time, no haunt," Celia said. It had been months since Lydia's last visit.

"Sorry."

"So where do you want to go this time?" Celia said.

"Would you mind cruising around my old neighborhood?"

They rode in silence for a while, Maxine on the seat between them. "You're not going to disappear again in the middle of traffic, are you?"

"I'll try not to. Cel?"

"What?" Celia was distracted, making her way down a narrow one-way street, trying to weave through an obstacle course of gaping potholes.

"I need to tell you something."

"OK. Should I pull over?"

"No, keep driving. It's about Norris."

"Oh, no."

"Try to be calm about this," Lydia said. "I want you to know that she helped me."

Celia was trying to fit between a double-parked delivery truck and a particularly large pothole that threatened her back left tire. It took her a few seconds to reply.

"Helped you what?"

"You know. Die."

Celia swerved toward the truck, swerved back. Her back tire dropped into the pothole with a sickening clank. She banged the steering wheel. "I knew it!" she said. "I knew it, I knew it, I knew. I knew it wasn't time!"

"Stop. Stop being so dramatic," Lydia said. "And keep your eyes on the road."

"I knew it," Celia said again, under her breath this time, racing through a stop sign. "That murderous bitch. I knew she was up to something nefarious in there." Celia was speeding down the little side street now.

"Would you please just slow down and listen? I'm running out of light here."

"Sorry. Continue."

"I'm trying to tell you that I asked Norris to do it."

"Killer bitch."

"She wouldn't at first, Cel. I had to talk her into it."

"I don't believe you."

"What do you mean? I'm telling you that I did."

"I don't care what you're telling me. I don't believe you."

"You think I'd come all the way back to lie to you."

"I think you're protecting her. You always protected her and you're still doing it. How could you have talked her into anything? You were out of it." Celia sniffed. "I was there, too. Remember?"

"Oh, Cel," Lydia said. "Of course I remember." Here was one thing Lydia did not miss—Celia's histrionics, and having to console her. "You have to understand," Lydia said. "I was in and out of it. It's hard to describe."

Celia didn't say anything. She was staring intently at the road now, pretending to watch for potholes.

"I'm just saying, stop ganging up on her. She feels bad enough."

"She feels bad?" Celia was yelling again. "Can I disagree here? Or do you get to control the conversation because you're dead?"

"I get to control it because I'm running out of light," Lydia said. "But what?"

Celia didn't answer.

"What?"

"For one thing, just because someone asks you to kill them doesn't make it right."

"OK. What's the other thing?"

Celia went silent.

"Hurry up, Cel. This corporeal thing I've got going is not going to last much longer."

Tears spilled onto the steering wheel. Celia's voice quavered. "Why didn't you ask me?"

"Ask you what?"

"To do it!"

"Oh, Cel." Lydia was losing patience. These ridiculous emotions of Celia's were exhausting. Envy, desire, hate, love, even loyalty—Lydia had felt them all, too, intensely. Her life had been nothing but. Now they just seemed childish. "Oh, Cel," she said. "I couldn't have asked you. You know that."

"Why not?"

"Because you wouldn't have."

A few seconds passed before Celia replied.

"Yes, I would. I might have."

"No, you wouldn't. Besides, she owed me."

Celia glanced over. It was the first thing Lydia had said that made any sense. Celia began to feel a little better.

They drove in silence until Celia finally said, "Maxine, too?"

"What do you think?"

"Now, that's just wrong!" Celia was slamming the steering wheel again. "She was perfectly fine."

"No, she wasn't. She had a splenic tumor. She was dying, too. Her whole world was me."

"Elaine would have taken her. I would have. Besides, it's all so Egyptian. Throwing everyone into the tomb with the pharaoh."

"Like I'm the pharaoh."

"You know what I mean."

"Slow down. You're going to get a ticket. Listen, I want you to do something for me."

"What?"

"I want you to talk to Norris, make her feel better."

Celia made a retching sound. "Why don't you? Since you're so out and about these days."

"I tried to," Lydia said. "I can't get her attention. Over-achiever types aren't as amenable to these kinds of visitations, apparently."

Celia turned to face Lydia, really hurt now. "What's that supposed to mean?"

"Eyes on the road, please," Lydia said. "Don't argue about everything, Celia. Don't argue with a dead person. And stop being so competitive. It's tiresome."

Celia stepped on the gas.

"Just give her a break," Lydia said, after a minute. "I know you. You're all going around dissing her, not inviting her to anything. I'm just saying, let up. Maybe she's changed. For one thing, you need to go see the paintings. She made me look like something out of Burne-Jones. A wraith bound to earth by only an orange casserole."

"Ted's loving that casserole," Celia said, glad for the change of subject. Lydia had made a present of it to him the morning after the party, along with the leftover stew that was in it.

"I know," Lydia said. "Listen. Just try being Norris's friend. If she invites you, go. Make the others go, too. You weren't going to, but you should."

Celia didn't answer.

"There's something else you should know."

"Oh, great."

"That guy you and Elaine were gossiping about? Kamal? It's not what you think. He was my student and we got back in touch. It's a long story, Norris can fill you in. But that's why he came to the funeral."

"Wait."

"Let me finish. I was trying to set it up so he'd get the scholarship but he has to reenroll, which then makes him eligible for the GI Bill, which is great, but then technically he wouldn't qualify for this but he needs it because if he quits his job to go to school how is he going to pay child support? So I asked Norris to finagle it. Be his sponsor." Lydia was talking fast now, as if she were running out of time. "She's the one who brought him to the funeral, so she could meet him. Anyway, I thought you should know, if you're going up there. So you don't jump to conclusions."

"What in the world are you talking about?"

"Got to go. Thanks for the ride."

Maxine stood up on the seat and leaned into Lydia. They blurred into one.

"Wait! Where are you always going off to?"

"Aspen," she, they, said, dissolving into a flurry of swirling snow before Celia had even stopped the car.

~elle~

Less than a month later, almost exactly two years after Lydia's last party, Celia sat with the other women at the big steel-and-glass table in Norris's house. The table was covered with food, an odd assortment of offerings—the usual potluck dishes—combined with an elegant spread of appetizers prepared earlier by Kamal, who'd left the premises after setting out artful platters of steamed artichokes and homemade aioli and turning down the heat on the sweet-potato-stuffed Cornish game hens in the oven.

The conversation had moved from Betsy and Ted to Spence, who, it appeared, had stayed in the house. Someone had seen him there the previous summer, mowing the lawn.

"I heard he's working now, at that yoga studio."

"I heard he adopted a pit bull, from an animal shelter."

"Two, I heard."

"I heard he was dating," someone said.

Celia nodded. "Peter took Griffin to a Cubs game and they saw him in the bleachers, buying a hot dog for a woman who looked exactly like Lydia."

"A hot dog!" they all shouted.

Now the women were telling Lydia stories. Celia decided to go ahead and tell her story after all, absent certain significant details about Norris. When she got to the part where Lydia said Aspen, Maura gasped.

"But she never skied a day in her life," Jayne said.

"We're not talking about skiing," Celia said.

"We're not talking about life," Elaine said.

"Maybe it's a metaphor."

"For elevation."

"Heaven!"

"Oh, please."

"Snow. A clean sweep?"

"A fresh start."

"Ted told me she visited him." This from Betsy.

"That's not fair," Elaine said. "Why would she visit Ted and not me?"

"He says it has something to do with the pot," Betsy said. "You know, that big cast-iron thing she gave him that morning? He says it has to do with spiritual essences absorbed by stone. It's why they have so many ghosts in England, he says. All those stone houses."

Elaine rolled her eyes.

"Anyway," Betsy said, ignoring Elaine now, addressing the group. "He says he heard her voice, when he was making jambalaya."

"What did she say?"

"Ted, you are too friggin' fat," someone said, in a spooky voice.

"That would have been his feet talking."

"He's lost weight, actually," Betsy said.

"What did she say?"

"Just his name. He claims he was alone in his kitchen and heard his name spoken out loud. In Lydia's voice."

"That's pretty anticlimactic."

"Not the way he tells it," Betsy said. "He says he got down on his knees and prayed."

"To the ghost of Lydia?"

"To the jambalaya!"

"How should I know who Ted prays to these days," Betsy said, annoyed now.

Norris appeared with a fresh bottle of white wine. Elaine had asked for red but Norris didn't trust her not to spill.

"Let me top off everyone's glass before we go into the studio," Norris said.

Full glasses in hand, they trooped through Norris's exquisitely spare rooms. They passed her collection of Japanese erotica, shuffled shoeless across her bleached oak floors. Betsy asked for a detour through the kitchen. There, tucked behind a juicer, Elaine spotted two full bottles of cabernet. One was even open.

Elaine was insulted and took it as a license to snoop. Celia hung back, too, and as soon as they were alone Elaine opened the refrigerator. They'd expected to find a comically unappetizing assortment of vitamins and cruciferous vegetables, but what they saw was even better. Sitting in the middle of a pristine and otherwise empty shelf sat a dinner plate that held a beeswax figure sculpted in the shape of a muscular male nude.

They stared into the glowing interior. "I suppose this is what Norris plans to serve us for breakfast," Elaine said.

Celia just shook her head.

"People!" It was Norris, rounding them up.

Celia and Elaine hurried down the breezeway connecting the main house to the studio and joined the little group outside the closed studio door.

"Let me say something first," Norris said, squaring her already square shoulders. She looked from face to expectant face. "These paintings are about something I didn't realize I needed to make paintings about, something I hadn't thought about much, before."

"Other human beings," Elaine whispered.

Norris glanced at her, continued. "As you probably know, I haven't worked from the figure much lately. Or really, ever. And maybe I should have asked your permission before I went ahead. I'd meant to ask you to come up for sittings, but the photos got me started and after that . . ." Norris looked around at the attentive but not yet fully comprehending faces, then shrugged. "Memory just seemed to be the way to go," she said. "Please don't anyone be insulted."

Elaine shot Celia a dark look. Celia pretended not to notice. "I also want to say this," Norris continued. "I think of this show as a kind of tribute, to Lydia." She paused, embarrassed. "For bringing us together."

Norris turned her back on the surprised murmur and opened the studio door.

"I thought she hated us," Elaine said, to no one in particular. They all filed in.

Around the perimeter of the enormous white-walled studio stood seven seven-foot-tall, five-foot-wide paintings. Each was a full portrait of a single figure. At the far end of the studio stood an eighth painting, even larger, a double portrait of Lydia and Maxine.

"Where's Malcolm?" Jayne whispered.

Elaine snorted. "He got cut," she whispered back. "He wouldn't take off his coat."

"He's not here," Norris said. "Neither is Betsy's dog. Only females."

"And Ted," Betsy said, insulted.

"Sorry. Of course," Norris said. "And Ted." They all turned to look at the painting of Ted.

Incredibly, Norris had painted him nude. He stood, up to his ankles, in a clear pond bordered by a lavishly imagined version of Norris's hyperabundant garden. In front of him, in both hands, he held Lydia's orange pot, which mostly covered his genitals. Ted's hair and beard and the pot, also a wisp of visible pubic hair, were all painted the same glowing color, a mix of alizarin crimson, cadmium yellow, and titanium white.

Ted appeared lit from below, the orange of the pot reflected in a bright slice on the ample underside of his belly. Another slice of orange appeared under his double chin and, as if the enamel on the pot had bled into the surrounding air, orange light glinted on the pond's surface, which was broken by ripples around Ted's thick ankles. The little coarse hairs on his legs picked it up, too, as did the mackerel clouds in the sky. Ted's blue eyes shone weirdly. It took a minute for them to notice that, reflected in the twin convex mirrors of both eyes, blazed two tiny forest fires.

For once the women were speechless. Betsy looked like she might cry. "He's the only one I asked to come for a sitting," Norris said to Betsy, as if she'd asked.

After the women had recovered from the shock of seeing Ted, and so much of him, they began to mill around, sipping from Norris's big wineglasses.

"These are incredible, Norris," Celia said. There was no point in denying it. She'd returned to the painting of Ted, transfixed by his casserole-covered crotch.

"Thank you," Norris said, knowing it was true.

She knew it was her best work yet. She'd taken a risk and it had paid off. She'd put the photographs away, painted from her composite memory of twenty years, giving the women—and Ted—glorious versions of their own bodies fabricated from her rich and generous imagination.

"You gave me back my beautiful boobs," Elaine said, for once not sarcastic.

"It's how we'll look in heaven," Maura said, standing in front of her own portrait, in love with her body, maybe for the first time. Norris's version of her was better than any surgeon's. Celia glanced over to see if Maura was making a joke but she didn't appear to be.

Norris didn't know about heaven, but Maura had the general idea right. She'd meant them to look their best. The passing thought of painting them exactly as they'd looked that Saturday night had yielded to this more interesting, encompassing idea, each woman a composite of her best features over a life—the thought-sharpened faces of middle age, the smooth bellies and dense high breasts of youth. Even Ted's paunch looked firm, royal.

"This is gorgeous," Celia said. She'd drifted away from Ted and was standing in front of the painting of Lydia and Maxine.

Norris had painted them standing at the edge of the water,

with no sight of land behind them. The lake was green. Maxine was in front, body in profile, like a prize heifer, her head turned to face the viewer. Silvery water dripped, flowed from her face as if she'd been drinking from some source so bounteous that it ran out of her like a fountain. Her broad muzzle was black and velvety, as it had been when she was a puppy, her orange eyebrows furrowed with intelligent concern. Lydia, naked and lovely as some medieval Eve, stood modestly behind the dog, one pale hand resting on Maxine's broad black flank.

Celia loved it, though she didn't know what Lydia had been talking about. She couldn't see what was so Burne-Jones about it. And the orange pot Lydia had referred to was nowhere in sight. Still, Lydia had told her to go look at the painting and now that Celia had seen it she wanted it.

"It's nice, isn't it," Norris said, stepping back and squinting. It wasn't a question. It was plain truth that it was nice. Better than nice.

"What are you going to do with it?" Celia said. "I mean, after the show comes down."

Norris shrugged. "My dealer's shopping it around. A collector in Houston is interested."

"I want it," Celia said.

"What do you mean?"

"I mean I want to buy this painting."

Norris almost laughed. "Oh, Celia. Don't be ridiculous." She crossed her long arms across her flat chest. "Natalie charges a fortune."

"I understand that," Celia said. "I'm not asking for a

discount. I'll pay on installment—that's how it's done, isn't it? But I want it."

~~ellee~~

Norris sat alone in her empty studio in a shaft of mid-morning light, drinking a cup of hot water and lemon juice. The women had just left—they'd spent the night in the guesthouse, which Kamal had vacated for the weekend. He needed to visit his grandmother, he'd said, although Norris had pointed out he didn't have to leave. There was plenty of room in the main house, she'd said, if he wanted to stay, just this once.

After a long breakfast—Maura had brought coffee cakes and Betsy brought fruit and Jayne made omelets and Celia made mimosas—the women headed out en masse just as the shippers arrived to pack the show. Now the work was well on its way and the women were driving by caravan back to Chicago.

They'd decided to convoy in the driveway, on their way out, in case someone's car broke down, they said. *It's three hours*, Norris had said. *It's not like you're crossing the Rockies in Conestoga wagons.* She knew it would take them twice as long, that every time one stopped to go the bathroom they'd all have to stop and then they'd spend half an hour at some truck stop, buying snack food and aspirin. And Elaine needed cat food, she'd announced, at least a dozen times. She, with Maura's encouragement, had adopted a stray of indeterminate gender that she'd named George Eliot, and it was all she talked about.

What a bunch of old ladies they'd turned into, Norris

thought, standing in the driveway, waving good-bye. She could hardly believe they were her oldest friends. Possibly her only friends. Though, until last night, half of them could hardly stand her.

Norris stared out the window now, toward the pond. She was thinking about her trip. She was supposed to leave in two weeks, fly to New York for the opening, meet with collectors. Natalie had set up dinners.

Norris had made up an excuse when Kamal suggested he go along this time. "For moral support," he'd said, handing her a glass of freshly squeezed orange juice. As if she needed moral support.

"Why don't you be my immoral support and be here when I get back," she'd said, and then was sorry when she saw his face. But she couldn't allow that. Could she? That blending of worlds? Sam would be there, probably with his new girlfriend. He should be spared his mother's randy side, at least for a few more years, shouldn't he? Although it wasn't really about Sam. He was an adult now, with a sex life of his own. The truth was she didn't want some tagalong sycophant.

Though that wasn't fair, she thought. Kamal wasn't Jay. She felt a little bad about that whole thing. He'd left in a tearful rage one night, brandishing the Beretta, briefly holding it to his temple before she'd disarmed him. She'd grabbed his phone off the bed and threatened to call his mother. Norris knew he kept her number on speed dial. She got the locks changed the next day. Kamal wasn't like that. He was a grown-up, a marine.

Though he was starting to get restless with their arrangement, she could tell.

Men have feelings, too, Norris. She remembered someone saying that to her once. Who, though? Andy? Her mother? Lydia, of all people?

Norris looked around the empty studio and exhaled. She felt good about this, at least. It was going to be a good show. Two paintings had already sold—the one of Ted and the self-portrait. She hadn't planned to include herself but then decided to, after she figured out how to keep it from being too personal. She'd painted herself rigidly frontal and completely nude except for her face, which she'd swathed, burka-like, in a green paisley scarf. Really, the only part that was a portrait was the eyes; the body was just a pretty decoy.

Natalie had told Norris she thought she could sell the whole show. The big painting of Lydia and Maxine would bring a lot, she'd said. The thing with Celia wanting it had thrown Norris for a loop, though. In the old days she would have just laughed in her face. Celia couldn't afford a painting like that, even if she paid on installment for the rest of her life. Did she think Norris would be shamed into giving it to her? Ridiculous. It wouldn't even fit in her fussy little house. Though Norris understood what Celia really wanted, and it wasn't that painting. She wanted a memento, something of Lydia. Norris hoped Peter would talk Celia out of it.

It bothered her, these messy complications, everyone's wishes and wants and hurt feelings. They encroached on her freedom, took up her time. How was she supposed to sustain these newly deepened *relationships*—even the word made her queasy—if everyone kept making such unreasonable demands? Breakfast parties that took half your day, red wine for Elaine, who was guaranteed to spill, travel privileges for Kamal, whole paintings for Celia, sixtieth-anniversary parties, for God's sake, for one's elderly former in-laws that required the breaking of bread with one's ex and his wife.

Norris had been trying her best not to think about it. She'd stuffed the invitation, which she'd received from Sam two weeks earlier, back in its (shocking pink) envelope and slipped it under a book, but the thought of the thing lurking there nagged at her. Betty and Hank's neighbors—with Sam's help, apparently—were throwing Betty and Hank a surprise pizza-and-stuffed-meat-loaf party at the Traverse City VFW Clubhouse. Tomorrow.

Sam kept texting her, then e-mailing, trying to get her to say she'd go. The messages came in insistent little blips. "Dad and Janet will be there. They told me to tell you you should come." "Gram would love to see U." "We picked up the flat-screen TV today. I'll add your name to the card." "Shirley's gonna sing!"

According to the invitation, the Stemwinders, the seventeen-piece all-VFW-member band, led by tubaist Gil Cross, was already rehearsing. "Dancing to a selection of big band favorites" would commence after lunch. Norris could picture the sheet cake now.

How did reasonable people manage all this nonsense, and still get anything done?

Never mind, she thought, taking a sip of hot lemon water. The main thing was that the work was good. Finished, packed, and gone. And now her studio was empty again, except for two tiny photos she'd tacked to the wall.

Norris dragged her chair over to sit in front of them. One was the Polaroid she'd taken at the party, two years before— Lydia in front of her fireplace, looking jaundiced and shrunken in too-bright lipstick, with that enormous orange pot in her lap, weighing her down like a stone on a leaf. The other photo was thumbtacked next to it. It showed the second, smaller painting of Lydia, the one Norris hadn't shown them, which was still in the storage closet.

She got up and went to the closet, dragged the painting from where she'd hidden it behind a blank stretched canvas, and brought it over to lean against the wall in front of her chair. The painting looked like a smudge in the bright white studio. It was almost monochromatic. She'd ended up using all tones of gray—yellowish gray skin, bluish gray sheets—sick room colors. It showed Lydia half covered with a sheet, only her head and neck and bare wasted arms showing. Her eyes were open—conscious, staring. She was shrunken, but still herself. In the dark, hovering over her body, Norris had painted the ghost of the orange pot.

She'd based the painting on the dozens of photographs and charcoal drawings she'd made at the end, showing Lydia in bed, her by-now-colorless hair across the pillow, sheets tumbled like waves around her wasted body. Norris had asked Lydia's permission, first to draw her and later to make the photos, and Lydia had agreed to it all. Norris wasn't sure she would, and had wondered whether it would be too terrible to go ahead in secret after Lydia fell fully into unconsciousness, but she hadn't needed to. The first time Norris asked, Lydia had nodded once and said, whispered actually, "Fame, at last," then closed her eyes. The second time she'd raised her hand a few inches from the sheet, and let it drop.

In most of the drawings Maxine sprawled next to Lydia, big, solid, and black. In some, Lydia's eyes were half open, dog and woman staring out as if already from the afterlife. In one Lydia even appeared to smile a little. That really happened, Norris remembered it, though it seemed incredible now. She'd never shown that drawing, or any of them, to anyone.

What a strange time it had been, Norris thought now, looking out the window at the snow that had begun to fall. She could hardly believe now that any of it had happened, that they'd gone through that together, she and Lydia, that they'd talked that way with each other, finally, as they never had before.

Then Lydia died, and Norris put the drawings and photos away. It wasn't until she was finishing the big painting of Lydia and Maxine, eighteen months later, that she got them out again.

She'd laid them all on the floor of her studio one morning, as reference, she'd thought, and spent the day looking at them. The next morning, she started a new painting, and in a week it was finished. At first she thought it belonged in the show, as a transition piece, a hint of more to come, maybe, or just as a dark note, but in the end she saw that it didn't belong. In so many ways, it didn't match the others.

Norris had wondered, as she'd worked on the second painting, if it was too strange, too personal. She'd wondered if people would think it was exploitive somehow, if they'd understand that it had been a collaboration, that Lydia had agreed to this, wanted it, even. But there was no way to prove that, and finally Norris decided she didn't care what people thought.

She hadn't shown it to anyone yet, though. Partly it was that she didn't know what to make of it. The painting was smaller than she usually worked, and much looser, more transparent. She'd drawn in charcoal first, on the canvas, and then painted over the drawing so the charcoal blended with the paint and the turpentine and made the whole thing gray. She'd planned to add color later but then she didn't. It might be a study, she thought. Or it might be the beginning of a new series, all loose, all gray, all Lydia.

Norris turned the painting to face the wall and went back to staring at the two little photos. The double orange dots of the casserole pulsed in the all-white room.

Usually this was the best hour of all, after everything had been carted off and she was alone, between projects, on the verge of a new idea. Anything was possible now; everything was. This must be what it was like to be a virgin bride, she sometimes thought, waiting for her groom. Sometimes she started a new painting the same day.

But today felt different. For the first time in a long time, maybe ever, Norris didn't feel like working. She felt a strange new impulse, one she'd heard of but never experienced. She wanted to take a break. She felt like taking the day off, maybe the whole week. Or two. Maybe she'd take a vacation, she thought, a vacation from her life, from being Norris.

Though she wasn't sure she knew how. Always before, after she'd packed up work for a show, she'd returned to the studio immediately. That day, when possible. And it wasn't just will that drove her back, her famous self-discipline. She wanted to, looked forward to it. She always had ideas for new work, was impatient to start the next thing. Usually by the time she'd finished a show her mind had moved on to something else and it had happened this time, too. She'd started a new sketchbook midway through the painting of Ted. She'd written *Deities* inside the front cover. She was thinking of doing more figures, maybe a suite of twelve, possibly the Greek gods. She planned to use Kamal as a model.

Oprah = Zeus? she'd written under a torn-out magazine picture she'd taped to one page. She'd crossed out Zeus and written *Athena* and under that she'd written *Zeus = Bill Clinton?* She'd made a little sketch of him in a suit and tie, his face looking pouchy and soulful, holding a thunderbolt on his lap. Next to that was another sketch that showed him naked, heroic, ithyphallic.

But these were cartoons, not paintings. Nothing there, she decided, tossing the sketchbook aside.

She sat in her low, overstuffed armchair, the one she'd liberated from her grandmother's sewing room fifteen years earlier. It was upholstered in pale yellow and cream silk that had gone dingy with time, an incongruity in the otherwise stark white studio. It was the one soft thing she kept there, and the comfort of it allowed her to sit a while longer.

She imagined twelve twelve-foot paintings of gods and goddesses with Baroque lighting, maybe in flight, seen from below, like Tiepolo angels. Maybe she should go to Venice, she thought. See the Tiepolos again, get inspired. Maybe she should do it now. She could, she thought. She had time. She certainly could afford it. She could leave today, fly to Rome, catch a connecting flight, and be there by tomorrow night. Walk from church to church, stopping by the water to eat sardines in lemon juice and drink espresso. It was a pleasant thought. But even that, the thought of such a trip, felt burdensome, like entertainment, not inspiration. She didn't feel like being a tourist, even for art.

She'd rather walk in the woods, she thought. She closed her eyes. Blessed quiet. She could not get enough. Maybe it was time for a change of a different sort. A real break. Painters who taught took sabbaticals from teaching to make art. Why couldn't she take a sabbatical from making art? Though what else she'd do eluded her.

Why did people even make art, Norris wondered, her eyes still closed. She knew what she would have said before, ten years ago, ten days ago, even. Because she could. Because she was good at it.

Flannery O'Connor had said that, Lydia once told her, a long time ago, when they'd had the discussion, before it became clear that Norris was going to be successful and that Lydia was not, when they could still discuss the idea of talent and success freely, theoretically. *Why do you write*, someone had asked O'Connor, Lydia told her. *Because I'm good at it*, Lydia said she'd said. They'd laughed. It had seemed so simple at the time. Was that a good-enough reason anymore, though? Norris had to wonder.

She opened her eyes. Things were different now.

The show was done and Lydia was gone, and the thing was, awful but true, there was a part of her that was a little bit glad. Norris didn't have to answer to her anymore, didn't have to go to anymore of her parties, didn't have to look at her and feel guilty. Now the whole thing could be laid to rest.

Norris stood up and stretched. It was time for something new, she thought. Or at least something else. She grabbed a down vest from the closet, yanked a hat over her ears, and walked outside. It had been a long time since she'd taken a walk without a purpose.

~~eelee~~

Norris was on the road by five A.M., driving south into a snowstorm. She was heading for Chicago, or rather to Celia's blighted suburb, to drop off the painting. After that, who knew where. Maybe she'd keep going south, Norris thought, until she got someplace warm. Kentucky? Tennessee? She had no idea how far you had to go before it stopped being cold.

She'd decided to proceed as if the exchange with Celia,

about selling her the big painting, had never happened. Instead, she'd packed the smaller one in bubble wrap and put it in the trunk. It wasn't gorgeous, like the one Celia had seen, and it wasn't easy to look at, but it was the better painting, Norris felt sure, and she was pretty sure that Celia would know that, and would have chosen it if she'd had the choice.

Norris planned to drop it off first, before she changed her mind, on her way to wherever else she was going. Then, when the exit came up she almost didn't take it. She didn't feel like stopping, or explaining. But then she clicked on her turn signal and now she was heading west, rounding the lake toward Chicago, into the snow.

She hoped to arrive when Celia wasn't there so she could just give the painting to Peter, or even to the boy, whose name she could never remember. She didn't feel like talking to Celia again so soon. They'd need to have a real conversation eventually, of course, but Norris needed to think about what to say, not just about the painting but about the job she was thinking of offering Celia.

Norris had been thinking for some time that she needed to hire someone, in addition to Kamal. She needed someone with experience, who knew what they were doing, to archive her work, handle her correspondence, convert old slides to digital files. Her dealer did only so much. Kamal had been a help, but this wasn't a career for him. He had other plans, or he used to have. Maybe it was time to let him go.

Their relationship—that ugly word again—complicated everything. "So which is it?" he'd said, just last week, over a nice lake trout he'd poached in wine. "Are you my boss or my girl-friend?" *He* was giving *her* an ultimatum! Preposterous.

Celia would know what to do, and Norris knew she needed the money. It wouldn't hurt her to get out of the house, either. She could come every week, at first, stay a night or two, in the guesthouse, as long as she behaved herself. (Norris would just tell her: No barging into the studio. No weeping. Absolutely no talking in the morning.) She should probably come to New York, too. The rest of it they could handle by e-mail.

Norris wished she could say all this to Peter instead of Celia. He wouldn't argue, or—God forbid—cry. Men were so much easier, Norris thought.

Most of them, at least. She couldn't reach Kamal. She'd left him seven messages, saying she'd be away for a few days and asking him to call her, then telling him to, but he hadn't. When she got back she'd see if he still wanted to go to New York. He might not, she'd hurt his pride, but if he agreed, she'd tell Natalie to change the reservation, book a suite, with separate bedrooms. He'd never been to New York. He could see the sights while she was working—it could be a farewell present.

Norris felt good, though she hadn't slept much. She'd woken up at four and run her three miles in the dark, then packed fast—laptop, a couple extra long-sleeved T-shirts, fleece vest, underwear, running shoes, heavy socks, sketchbooks, notebooks, camera bag, sleeping bag. If she ended up south maybe she'd buy more gear and camp. Now, that would be something different, she thought. She hadn't done that in twenty years, not since Andy.

At the last minute she'd taken out the sketchbooks and laptop. And the cameras. Just try it, she thought. Try not working. If she couldn't stand it she could always have supplies overnighted to some hotel. All she really needed was a credit card.

She thought of her one rich uncle, the only one of her father's four brothers who'd made any money, who'd visited exactly twice and made her parents so uncomfortable, with his jewelry and his stories and his expensive suits. What was it he'd said? *Travel light and carry plastic.* He'd even winked—at her— when he'd said it and slipped her a twenty before he left. She'd followed his advice. She'd buy what she needed when she got there, wherever there was.

On her way out the door, in the still dark morning, Norris stopped. Went back to her bedroom and dug around in the drawer where she kept a small jewelry box. There she found the sterling silver dragonfly and pinned it to her fleece vest.

Norris was making good time now, despite the snow. She could see the pink sky dawning in her rearview mirror. She could die right now, she thought, on this highway, going eighty miles an hour, and except for getting this painting to Celia she'd have done everything she'd set out to do in life. Maybe after she dropped it off she'd go west instead of south, drive straight through Iowa to Nebraska, Wyoming, Idaho, Oregon. Or head north, to whatever was up there. Alberta? She'd skirt the cities—were there any, even?—and head for someplace empty of art, if there were such a place. She drove into the snow feeling better and better.

~~~

Norris was standing on Celia's collapsing front porch, waiting for someone to answer the bell, entertaining second thoughts. She could still get out of here without a conversation, she thought. She could just leave the thing, in its many layers of plastic bubble wrap, leaning against the door and split. If it weren't for all the snow on the porch, she would have already.

She took out her phone and hit redial. She'd stopped leaving messages. Now, when Kamal's recorded voice came on, she hung up. He wasn't responding to texts, either. Where the hell was he? And how dare he not answer or, as she suspected, just turn the thing off? She'd bought him that damn phone, and it hadn't been cheap.

Norris stood looking across Celia's front lawn, trying to figure out what to do. The morning light had tinted the smooth glaze of slightly melted then refrozen snow a buttery pinkish gold. The sight calmed Norris. She imagined how she'd mix the color.

Norris was thinking she'd earned the right to leave. She'd even called Celia—twice—from the road and left messages, to let her know she was coming. Celia must not be home, she thought. Unless she was, and wasn't answering. Did no one answer their phone anymore? Or was it just that no one answered when she called?

.   .   .

Just then a black dog appeared from behind a hedge and started across the lawn, making a crunching sound as its paws broke through the crust of snow. Norris saw no dangling leash, no collar, even—strange for the suburbs, or anywhere these days, she thought, everyone so up in arms about animal welfare. Didn't appear to be a stray, though. If anything, it looked overfed.

When the dog got opposite Norris it stopped and turned its head to meet her gaze. They stared at each other for a few long seconds. Norris could see the animal's orange eyebrow-like markings. Something about the dog looked familiar, but, Norris reminded herself, the eye, the mind, played tricks.

"Ring the bell one more time." This instruction entered Norris's consciousness as if someone—Lydia actually, it was her voice—had spoken out loud, inside her head. "If Celia doesn't come to the door this time, you can leave."

Norris, not usually so compliant but unaccustomed to hearing voices, pressed the bell again. Again she heard the weak plunk on the other side of the wall. Like everything about the house, the doorbell needed repair. The money Lydia left Celia had all gone to necessities for the boy, Celia had told them—his college fund, braces, camp, tutoring.

How annoying, Norris thought, out of patience now. She hated people who didn't repair things. And damn Lydia. If it weren't for her, she wouldn't be here in the first place.

One thing was for sure, though. This was the last time Norris would do something for a dead person. Once you started down that road, your life unraveled, backwards. She remembered when her mother died. She'd had to make a choice then—wallow in memory and regret, or forge on. Forge on had been her decision.

This was ridiculous. Celia wasn't here and neither was Peter and Norris was freezing her ass off and in one more second, Norris decided, she was going to turn around and walk back down those slippery lopsided lawsuit-waiting-to-happen stairs, without falling, and get back in her car—*with* the painting— and forget all this nonsense, this failed experiment in being a better person. She no longer felt like driving south, either. Or west or north or wherever she'd dizzily intended to go in the unrealistic pink dawn. Now, in the harsh true light of day, all she wanted was to get back to her studio. Maybe if she hurried she could salvage the afternoon.

Norris picked up the painting and turned to leave. There, standing at the foot of the porch stairs, blocking her way, big and black against the snow, was the dog with the orange eyebrows. It must have crept up when she wasn't looking, she thought. It didn't appear threatening exactly—maybe it was Celia's dog and it had gotten out—but neither would it budge. And it wouldn't stop staring at her. Now Norris had no choice but to stay.

Norris averted her eyes from the dog's intense gaze and tried the bell again. Stamped her feet to warm them up. Finally she heard a sound behind the door. Then the door opened a crack and stopped, caught by a little chain. Out of the crack slipped a cat. Then someone unhooked the chain, the door swung wide, and there stood Celia.

Though it was 8:30 in the morning, almost lunchtime by Norris's schedule, Celia was barefoot, and wore a robe and pajamas. She looked puffy-faced, like she'd just woken up. Her hair resembled some inventive bird's nest, with hairpins and little bits of what might be construction paper sticking out of it. A smear of something greasy clung to her face near her mouth.

"Norris? That *was* your voice I heard. Wow. I mean, what a nice surprise."

"Hi." Norris tried to make her voice sound friendly. "Is that your dog?"

"What dog?" Celia said. Norris looked behind her but the dog had gone. Celia pulled her robe closed. "You want to come in?"

"I won't stay long," Norris said, dreading what was to come.

Norris was sitting in Celia's living room on her rickety Victorian furniture. Celia had disappeared to get dressed, then reappeared with tea in a pot, on a tray, along with little napkins and a plate of oatmeal cookies left over from the party that Norris had sent home with her the day before. Now Norris accepted a cup of tea, no milk, no sugar. Celia picked up a cookie.

Norris was intensely uncomfortable. It wasn't just the hard, bumpy, scratchy velvet atrocity of a settee she was sitting on, though that was bad, digging into her back and her butt, or the "eclectic" décor—the doilies and the fringed curtains and the framed handkerchiefs and the art projects and the piles of books and the hockey stick lying on the dining room table, the dust motes and cat hair floating in the sunlight. It wasn't even this enforced coziness, or the weirdly sweet tea, although those weren't helping either.

"That was so good of you," Celia was saying. "The party, I mean. The food and the wine. Those incredible paintings. Everything was so lovely." Celia reached out and touched the dragonfly pin on Norris's vest, smiled at it. "We needed that," she said. "Or I did. I haven't laughed that hard in I don't know how long."

"Can I get to the point?" Norris said, knowing as the words came out of her mouth that her tone was exactly wrong. But she wanted to get this over with, was unable to stand even another minute of this, whatever this was. At the sight of Celia's face, though, she tried again. "I've brought you something," Norris said, trying to sound kind this time. She held out the bubble-wrapped package, which Celia had been pretending not to notice. "I'd prefer that you open it later, after I leave. If you don't mind."

"OK." Celia sounded uncertain but she took the package, set it next to her chair.

"I want to make you an offer," Norris said, then had the sudden sense that someone, and not Celia, had given her a dirty look. "I mean, I've come to ask you a favor."

Celia smoothed her hair behind her ears when Norris got finished telling her about the job. "Of course. I could do that," she said, matter-of-factly, brushing crumbs off her face. She'd start by digitizing everything, she said. Then they needed to hire someone to design a proper website. "No offense," she'd said. She'd talk to Peter about the travel part, being away during Griffin's hockey season. But she didn't think it would be a problem. Norris said OK and left soon after that.

～ellee～

Norris was standing next to her car in a parking lot a few blocks away. She'd forgotten to eat breakfast and had stopped to pick up some yogurt, on her way out of town, at a little market three blocks from Celia's house. Norris held her cell phone to her ear and kicked a big clod of dirty snow off her left front tire.

She was checking her landline messages again, and here, at last, was Kamal. There were three messages, actually. Two from Kamal had come in in the last hour. First he apologized for being "a little out of touch," then announced he was in the process of moving out. He was going back to Chicago, he said. School. Scholarship. Blah blah.

He was quitting, dumping her, was the point. Good luck with that, Norris thought, briefly furious, forgetting for a minute that it was exactly what she'd planned to do to him. Let's see how he likes moving back to his grandmother's apartment, she thought. It was remarkable, though. Once you went off script, anything could happen.

Kamal's second message, twenty minutes later, said he was leaving her phone on the kitchen counter along with her keys and that he'd boiled eggs and put them in the crisper as usual.

Taken out the garbage. Well, good-bye, he said. He sounded a little choked up. He said he sincerely appreciated everything she'd done for him.

This last part made Norris feel small. He hadn't even gotten a trip to New York out of it. She wished he'd kept the phone at least—he'd need it—but she knew why he hadn't. Now there was no way she could reach him.

Norris kicked some more snow off her tires. By then the third message had started to play but she was so distracted, thinking about Kamal standing at the stove, boiling the eggs, that she missed the beginning. So it took her a few seconds to realize that the husky voice she was listening to now was Celia's and that she was in tears, thanking her for the painting.

~eeeee~

Norris was rounding the lake again, going east this time, back to Michigan. She'd been trying to listen to her *Speak Like a Native (Chinese)* CD but she couldn't concentrate and now she was thinking that no matter how much you tried to stay away from other people, stay out of their lives—for their own good!—and tried to keep them out of yours, that you couldn't, and that when the bulwark finally burst it was all a big teary mess, now and forever after, and that maybe, though it wasn't what she'd ever wanted, she just had to get used to it. This is what Lydia had said to Norris about her own life, that it was a mess.

"I wish I'd been more like you," she'd said to Norris, toward the end. "No, you don't," Norris had said. Now Norris was becoming like her.

Norris glanced in the rearview mirror and met the eyes of
the dog. It—he? she? (Don't go there, she told herself)—had
been sitting quietly in the backseat, looking out the window
during the Chinese lesson, but now it seemed to be watching her.

Norris had been rearranging gear in the parking lot when the
dog she'd seen in Celia's yard had reappeared, trotting over and
sitting amiably alongside her car in the snow while Norris dug
around in her bag, moved things from the trunk to the backseat. Once Norris saw that the dog was harmless, she didn't pay
it any more attention. She was distracted enough, what with
Kamal's and Celia's voices ringing in her head, thanking her.
She'd slammed the back door and peeled away. Norris was already on the entrance ramp to the expressway when she'd
caught a glimpse of the dog in her rearview mirror, rearranging itself into a sitting position from where it had been lying
low, in the backseat.

The thing had stowed away! Norris almost pulled over and
shoved it out of the car right then and there. Easy enough—
and Norris was wearing pointy boots, if it needed encouragement. On any other day she would have.

She glanced in the mirror again. The dog stared back.

Norris supposed she'd take it to one of those places—just
drop it off as soon as she got back—where they'd scan it for a
chip and send it home if it had one, although somehow Norris
knew it wouldn't. Or it would and they'd call and the people
would lie and say, *Oh, it wandered away.* Then they'd promise to

come and get it but they'd never show up and the place would put it down. Norris knew—it's what she'd done with Sam's dog, twelve years before.

Where would she even keep a dog? And it would ruin her floors. She stepped on the gas.

Norris was doing seventy, seventy-five. The snow had started again. Probably, Norris thought, she should slow down. But she wanted to get past her own exit before she changed her mind.

The dog, sensing opportunity, had moved into the front seat. Now it sat next to Norris, on top of the shocking pink envelope. Just sticking out, from under the dog's haunch, Norris could see a pink triangle and a glimpse of Sam's handwriting, on the back of the little Xeroxed map that showed where the VFW hall was. There, Sam had scrawled elaborate, carefully worded directions to the free municipal parking lot—"for overflow, in case you're late and there's a crowd!"—as if he could sway her with that, as if the prospect of inconvenient parking were the reason she hadn't wanted to go. She pressed a little harder on the accelerator. Hold on, Sam, she thought. If she kept steady and didn't stop, in two more hours she'd be in Traverse City.

The snow came harder and harder now. Cars were parked on the side of the highway, lights on, waiting out the storm. Trucks barreled past, hurling piles of snow and salt on Norris's windshield, rendering her blind for seconds at a time. Someone skidded off the road right in front of her and rolled into a ditch. Finally, even Norris had to slow down. She could hardly see the road ahead of her. Her mirrors had iced over by then, and in the time it took for her windshield wipers to make a full pass across her window, more snow lodged there to obscure the view. Her side windows steamed up and the car filled with the dank, musty scent of the dog. On any other day she would have pulled off the road, given up. But she couldn't stop now.

At least her timing was perfect, Norris thought. At this rate, she'd arrive well after lunch, just in time to catch the band. With any luck, there'd be leftover meat loaf, for It. Maybe she'd even dance.

Acknowledgments

This book would not exist without the help of three amazing women. Jo-Ann Mapson, gifted writer and generous spirit, happened upon my first novel at the La Farge branch of the Santa Fe Public Library, and, although she'd never heard of me, recommended it to her agent. Deborah Schneider, now my agent, too, believed in this book, buoyed it (and me) up with unflagging zeal, and found it a home at Viking. Carolyn Carlson, my inspired, tireless editor there, understood the book instantly, then offered suggestions and insights that made it better. I cannot thank you three enough.

Thanks to everyone at Viking Penguin who helped: Clare Ferarro, who said yes; Beena Kamlani, for her smart and subtle editing; Ramona Demme, for everything; also John McGhee, Winnie DeMoya, Paul Lamb, Roseanne Serra, Nancy Resnick, Nancy Sheppard, Laura E. Abbott, and Carolyn Coleburn.

Thank you, also, to the artist residency selection committee at the School of the Art Institute of Chicago, and Shanna Linn, who made it possible for me to work in pristine quiet at the Roger Brown House in New Buffalo, Michigan. Thanks to

Tom Hawkins and Sylvia Carter for their continued moral support and to Steve Knoebber for digital magic.

Thanks to my friends, whose encouragement, intelligence, and high spirits sustain and inspire me every day, and in memory of one, Suzanne Quigley (1949–2012), who left the party too soon.

Finally, these acknowledgments would mean nothing if they didn't conclude with love and gratitude for Fritz Lentz, who put up with me during this long process and helped in countless ways. Writing a book can be hard but I doubt it's as difficult as living with someone who is. You made it easier (and so much more delicious). Thanks, F, for a thousand salads and a million laughs, and for your ideas and imagination, which make the world more interesting.